CALL KINLEY

Adventures of an Oil Well Firefighter

Myron M. Kinley, Firefighter

CALL KINLEY

Adventures of an Oil Well Firefighter

Jessie D. Kinley

Cock-A-hoop

PUBLISHING

TULSA, OKLAHOMA

CALL KINLEY
Adventures of an Oil Well Firefighter

by Jessie D. Kinley

Published by
Cock-A-Hoop Publishing, L.L.C.
P.O. Box 4358
Tulsa, OK 74159-0358
918/747-4777

Edited by E. Andra Whitworth
Designed by Carl E. Brune

99 98 97 96 95   5 4 3 2 1

Library of Congress Catalog Card Number: 94-69870
ISBN 0-9640706-1-8

The following publishers have generously given permission to reprint copyrighted articles in their entirety: *Reader's Digest*, "Old Firehorse Kinley—Man Without Fear," by Robert Hugh Rogers, May, 1953, © 1953 by Kiwanis International. *The Houston Post*, "Titled Texan," by Marie Moore, October 11, 1954, © 1954 by The Houston Post. *Oklahoma Today*, "The Monster's Tale," by Bill Burchardt, © by Oklahoma Today. *The Saturday Evening Post*, "He Fights the Wildest Fires," by Stanley Frank, May 2, 1959, © 1959 by The Curtis Publishing Company. *The Fort Worth Star-Telegram*, "Oil Well Fires Bring Flame and Fortune," by Cindy Rugeley, © byThe Fort Worth Star-Telegram.

Appendix D of the present work appeared in chapters 7 and 8 of *The History of Petroleum Engineering*, New York: American Petroleum Institute, 1961, © 1961 by American Petroleum Institute. Permission to reprint granted by American Petroleum Institute.

For the grandchildren:

Laura Kinley, Karl Kinley, Dan Kinley Jr.,
Karen Bruno, David Kinley, Vicki Reynolds;
and in memory of Lucie Knoble.

*The story of your grandfather
written with love,*

JESSIE

TABLE OF CONTENTS

Foreword by Coots Matthews   viii
Preface—Arkansas Boy's Notes   x

PART ONE

The Call Kinley Story Begins

Karl and Rose   3
The Carefree Years   5
Runaway Boy   8
Life With the Wildman Family   12
The Taft Oil Fields   14
The "Shot Heard Around the Oil World"   16

PART TWO

From the Oil Fields to the Western Front
21

PART THREE

Life as a Firefighter

Back to Tulsa—The M. M. Kinley Company   33
The Cromwell Fields—The Rise of Explosives   35
Necessity Is the Mother of Invention—A Sideline Career   37
Disaster on the Sinclair Oil Fields—
The Stamper No. 3 and Cole No. 1   40
Romanian Battlefield—The Moreni No. 160   45
At the Drawing Board—The Caliper   48
Firefighting on Display—
The International Petroleum Exposition   51
Off-Shore Inferno—Lake Maracaibo, Venezuela   54
A Close Call—Accident at Bay City   56
Goodbye to a Brother and Partner—The Death of Floyd Kinley   59
Working on the Railroad—The Greta Fire, Texas   61
Working for Women—The No. 4 Rigney   66
A Burning Sensation—Accident in Venezuela   71
Westward Ho!—Going to California   74

Desert Demon—Naft Safid, Rig 20   80

Qum and Get It—Alborz No. 5, an Islamic Inferno   84

Chaos in the Cradle of Civilization—Fire on the Ahwaz No. 6   89

To Everything There Is a Season—Times of Joy and Sorrow   92

A Born Diplomat—Fire in Nagoka, Japan   95

Calling It Quits—A Legend Takes a Rest   97

PART FOUR

A Life in Print

"Southern Personalities" by Anna G. Wilson   103

"Old Firehorse Kinley—Man Without Fear" by Robert Hugh Rogers   110

"Titled Texan" by Marie Moore   114

"The Monster's Tale" by Bill Burchardt   119

"Fighting Oil Well Fires" by Gerald F. Benedict   124

"Firefighter" by George Goodlet   132

"The Figure in the Flames" by Ernst Behrendt   135

"Taming the Wild Ones"   142

"His Specialty: Taming Wild Wells"   147

"Oil Well Fires Bring Flame and Fortune" by Cindy Rugeley   152

"Kinley Fights Oil Well Fires" by Weldon Hill   154

"He Fights the Wildest Fires" by Stanley Frank   157

London Day 168

"Rig 20"   169

PART FIVE

Appendixes

Appendix A, Myron Kinley's World War I Diary   173

Appendix B, List of Important Fires   177

Appendix C, Excerpt from *The History of Petroleum Engineering*   179

Appendix D, "Caliper Well Logging," by William H. Farrand   181

Appendix E, Cole No. 1, Gladewater, Texas   191

Appendix F, Myron Kinley's Diary of Rig 20, Naft Safid   197

Appendix G, *Field News* Articles on Ahwaz No. 6   201

FOREWORD

Early in 1946, after a stint in World War II, I went to work for Halliburton Oil Well Cementing Company in Houston, Texas. At that time, Myron Kinley already had a national reputation as a firefighter, and was known to me in name, though not in person.

It was while working for Halliburton that I came to know Myron Kinley and his crew. Myron Kinley worked extensively with Halliburton, as Halliburton often delivered equipment to Myron and his crews as they fought well fires. During the ten years I worked with Halliburton, I made quite a few of the jobs in Southeast Texas, and was many times requested on the fires by the Kinley Company because I was willing to help them when needed. Here, I developed casual friendships with Myron's assistants, Red Adair and Boots Hansen, as well as the oil company personnel on the jobs. I looked forward to these trips, because they were exciting, dangerous, and the other workers respected you more. Besides, firefighting was the highest paying job in the oil patch, with lots of world traveling!

I guess you could say that money, pure and simple, was what drew me to firefighting. Fire crews were well paid and, after getting fired from Halliburton in 1957 for wrecking too many company cars (I never learned how to drive one while asleep), I packed up and headed out to see my friends at M. M. Kinley Company.

Red Adair led the firefighters at M. M. Kinley Company, and Mr. M. M. Kinley hired me to fight oilfield fires in 1957. My tenure with the Kinley Company was not long; it was little more than a year before Red and I quit to start the Red Adair Company. Boots Hansen stayed with Mr. Kinley for about six months before coming over to the Red Adair Company.

On December 6, 1977, Red fired me and Boots over some mis-understanding, so Boots and I started Boot & Coots, Inc. on January 1, 1978, and were quite successful. We sold our company on July 9, 1993, to four employees and Lamar B. Roemer. After the sale, the company was changed from a corporation to a limited partnership known as Boots & Coots, L.P. Boots and I agreed to stay with the company for five years as its consultants.

But the time I spent working for Myron Kinley was an intense training period that taught me the most important aspects of skilled and safe firefighting. Myron Kinley was a task master, and working for him was tough. He demanded long, hard hours of tiring and dangerous work, but he was a good boss. He cared for his workers, and put safety first. Sometimes he would give us a real good eating out, but we always deserved it.

The Kinley name still carries weight in oilfields across the country. To this day, I know of no other man in the petroleum industry who is respected as much as Myron Kinley. He is esteemed in the industry for his inventions and contributions to firefighting, his honesty and hard work, and his dedication to safety in the fields.

When Boots Hansen and I formed Boots and Coots, part of our success was due to the fact that we had trained under Myron. People knew when they hired Boots and Coots that they were getting hard workers who knew the business and would put the safety of the crew first.

Myron Kinley's contributions to the petroleum industry were tremendous, but I would have to say that his greatest contributions were in firefighting. In modern firefighting, we have upgraded the equipment we use and spray more water on the fires, but never have we improved upon his tactics or basic approach.

This was very clear to me in Kuwait, just after the Persian Gulf War, where government officials and oil executives all tried to get us to use their new techniques and strategy to put out the costly fires that were destroying the Kuwaiti countryside. They had it all mapped out on their computers how we were going to put out these fires. Well, I'm not afraid of job security—computers cannot put out oil well fires! After all their planning and scheming, we stuck with the basic approach.

It was under Myron's influence that I learned and cultivated the qualities that make a good firefighter: the willingness to work hard in extreme, difficult circumstances; and dedication to taking care of the other workers. It is a dangerous job, and the philosophy of "every man for himself," will simply not work without dire consequences. In the field, every man has to help his fellow worker, and there are few men who can direct a crew in such an atmosphere without getting them killed.

Myron Kinley was such a man. He taught us a lot.

COOTS MATTHEWS
September 1995

PREFACE

One time when Mr. Kinley stopped by my office at the Little Nick Oil Company on his way somewhere or other I asked him never to let anyone but me write the story of his life. He laughed and asked: "Why, Jessie, when would you ever have time to write a book?"

I said I didn't know, but I didn't want anyone else to do it. And so he promised. But he did not tell me that once upon a time, many years before, he had told someone else to write it. And thereby hangs a tale that is well nigh unbelievable but nevertheless true.

The tale I am going to tell you unfolded when, by the sheerest of accidents, a fragile collection of notes fell into my hands. It almost seems as though Providence had a hand in getting them there. The notes consisted of several pieces of paper so old they were in danger of disintegrating as I perused them for the first time. They were water-stained and scorched, and in some places the paper had worn too thin to read.

The notes were a type of diary kept by an unnamed young man consumed with the desire to be a writer. They record his journey from a small rural farm to an oil field in Arkansas where tragic circumstances led to a heart-warming acquaintance with Myron Kinley.

The notes are not lengthy and span only a brief period of time, perhaps no longer than three months. Their content reveals little specific information on either the author or his surroundings—he does not mention his name or destination. The only references to time are made when the author records its passage in number of days, and it is only by working with the notes—arranging and rearranging them over and over—that I have been able to put them in a reasonable and coherent sequence.

I have long treasured these notes as the most sincere illustration of the seemingly endless courage, generosity, and loving kindness that characterized Myron throughout his life. The rest of the story I will leave for you to read in the notes themselves. And when you are finished, I shall be surprised indeed if you do not find a compelling reason for loving this admirable man.

I can't believe I'm really going. It really has taken a long time to make up my mind, but if ever I am going to be a writer, I have to go back to school, and that takes money. I know Dad will never forgive me, and I may never forgive myself. . . .

Aunt Mae fixed me a lunch. . . . Aunt Mae has really been Mom to me. I wonder what would have happened if she hadn't come and got me and took me to school. Lord, thank You. You must have known how badly I wanted to learn to write. . . And I really mean write.

Aunt Mae told me about plenty of men who wrote, cause Dad always said that wasn't manlike. I remember when he found my papers. He called me in (and Aunt Mae came, too) and said I was to tear up all that paper. He never heard of anyone writing what he wanted to talk about. I guess it is strange, but I think it'll help me to really be a writer. I cried and Aunt Mae got some of my papers. Dad tore up a lot. Aunt Mae said to bring all my papers to her after that. . . . Well, Dad never said anymore —but Dad and I never talked. If he'd read my papers he'd of really known how much I loved him. I wanted to, but I didn't tell him. He didn't believe in wasting words on stuff like that. . . .

I can't wait to get there. I really don't know what I'm going to do. Work on an oil rig, whatever that means. . . . I plan to work one year then I'm going to school and I can get a part time job. . . . Boy, on paper this sounds good. Won't be long now and at last when we get off this train—then I'm gonna start.

Boy, I can't believe my eyes and ears. I couldn't do nothing but just look. I've never seen that many people—even at a funeral. Horses and cars and trucks—people everywhere no room to walk—to set down—my goodness, I've got to write and tell Aunt Mae about some of these ladies. They're wearing some of the most pretty clothes—hats—fancy shoes—and colors on their lips and eyes. It's really dazzling. . . .

Mr. Anderson told me to get me some pants and things. I hope I have enough. . . . I went into the store to see the boots, and one of the men who works with Mr. Anderson was there. I asked the man about boots for the oil field and he asked me who I was going to work for. When I told him Mr. Anderson got me the job, and I hadn't even got to the rig yet, guess what this man was selling there. He just come right over and patted me on the back and said: "Son, I'm a friend of Mr. Anderson. I'm gonna set you up." Well, I just couldn't believe it. The shoe man told me how much those boots were, and I couldn't believe that either. Well, I said I'd have to wait a spell till I got some more money. Boy, I didn't have enough to buy one boot. . . . Could you believe that the man said? "Son, you can't work on that rig without some tall boots. And here you go. And soon as you get your first pay, come in and pay for them." Well, I tell you I was so happy I could cry, but I'm sure these men would think that sissy. I've always cried a little when I'm happy. Aunt Mae said I had soul.

Today I saw my first rig. It looks sort of like my old windmill. Really, I think my windmill was in better shape. . . . I know very little about this job, but I'm gonna learn. This is the rig floor, and I'm standing on it with my new boots. I've met John, the Driller, I'll have to work on all the men's names. They showed me what to do. It's so noisy and dirty. It's great! Isn't this wonderful? . . . I'm sure I'll never forget this day . . . . It's strange and I already love all of it.

I'm living in a bunkhouse with 4 other men. It's not far from the rig . . . that never stops. There's some men that live in town. If something goes wrong they roust everyone around out. So, you might get in bed. And out you go!

I really don't like this old bunk house. It looked good when I got here but since I don't drink and go around—the guys tease me. That's OK cause I'm saving. I seem to have a struggle cause I need clothes and things, and I want to send Aunt Mae some money. She won't want it, but I'd sure like for her to have some nice things.

I know one thing I've learned, it's dangerous—Someone gets hurt nearly every day. The men are great teasers. They say I'm tight, well, I guess I am. But as fast as things are happening, I'm sure that will change too. I'm trying to write and read but I sure don't have much time. I want to learn so much I would do any job and do it good.

I'm going in town with the men tonight. I guess I'm going to move in with the Driller's family. They have a room and it'll be nice. . . . I'm glad. . . .

I'm learning that a lot of schooling can go on here. . . . So here goes another day in "school." John, my Driller, said the bunkhouse was always noisy. He's really right there. I never knew there was so many cuss words. Boy, some of the men can't say two words without cussing. Some of the men gripe. John said they'd gripe if you hung them with a new rope. I've really been amazed how many of them cannot write. I do a lot of letter writing at least when I have time.

I really do look forward to John's house. His wife cooks so good. I've been in town several times. The people sure are funny when you tell them that you work out at the well. It's really not a good feeling. It's like you was not as good as they are. Sort of like people treat dirt farmers at home. Well, I guess that's part of my education.

Seems like a long time since I left the farm, but it's only been 8 days. I think I've started to grow up. I'm really thinking about lots of things. It was like the men talking about their women. I don't know if I'm ever gonna know. Who am I gonna ask? Who tells you what to do? I know about goats, cows, and pigs, that makes you really think a lot. . . .

All I've done for days is eat, drink, and sleep the well. That oil well is all there is in our world.

I moved in to John's today. It's sort of like a rooming house and its great! John's wife mothers all of us who live there and her 4 kids and John and anyone else who gets anywhere near. She said to bring all my rags in to her. Maybe she could sew them together and make one garment.

She cut my hair and told me I needed to learn to shave. I've never had a beard. It was more like peach fuzz. She said: "Never mind, shave and soon it would be a beard." So now I'm gonna shave.

She's a fine woman. It's so strange—the men talk about how they feel about women in town. They talk so much about those women in town I wonder if they are pulling my leg. Maybe someday I can talk to John. I have my own room with a door, a real bed, and a real you-know-what. I just want to stay here.

John just came in and said trouble was sure going to happen at the rig. It could be fire. He said all hell was going to break loose! I'm so scare I can't even write.—SCARED—I never say anything like this. . . . I don't know when I've been so tired.

John said: "Wee writer, you got something to write about now! Go do it!"

Boy, a man can go till he drops—they just put another one in your place, but this thing never stops. I go in and lay down with my boots on and sometimes get up, go back, and I've never taken them off. . . .

Well, I thought I'd sleep from now on, but you know I just can't seem to stay down. Oh, if I could do something! The men say the men who are coming tomorrow will be able to put it out. Sometimes it blows . . . . They say that's the danger. . . . I wish I knew more about all of this. I want to learn why and how all this happens and what can be done. . . . I'm going to get up and go wash and get something to eat and get ready for tomorrow. . . .

About 2 this morning John got us all up. Boy that old well was really roaring and fire was a hazard, John said. I know I don't have any idea what is going to happen—there is no way I'm going to be ready for all this. When the men talk, it sounds like a story. . . . Well, I'll have to write later. . . .

We've been at it for about 16 hours. I'm so tired I can't go to sleep yet I can hardly see my writing. I've dug ditches and we've been getting ready if the well does catch fire—I guess I don't really have any idea what I'm doing. . . . I have no idea how many hours we have worked. I cannot believe what is happening. My beautiful rig is on fire. It's so awful. Back home a forest fire was that bad. I hope it's a nightmare and I'll wake up.

I guess I'm going to have to go back. John said they are supposed to have some real firefighting men out here in the morning or soon . . . . Well, here goes some more work.

Dear God, I can't explain any of this. That fire is so hot and so mean. The guys get smoked. . . . Well, better go to sleep. I'm black. All my clothes are sand caked—but sleep is more important than cleaning up. . . .

Hi—It's hard to realize it has been 9 weeks since I was burned. If I write funny it's because my hands were so hurt. It hurts to write, but I'm going to do it. And I never really wrote with one of these pens. They are sure nice. I don't even know what day it is. It's taken me two days just to write this.

I can't believe all this has happened. I remember going on the floor, the Fire Fighters were there and they was telling everyone to move away—So much happened then. I really don't know what happened. The nurse and John's wife told me. Pressure blowed in and I don't know where I went or how. They said I was knocked out and stuff was blowing everywhere. They said the Fire Fighting man ran into all that and dragged me out just before things really went. He was sitting by the bed—only I didn't know him—when I woke up. He patted me and said: "Now rest, kid." That's what I'm gonna do. He's coming back when he can.

I'm up today. It seems infection has set in on my face—boy, my hands look spotted where the old skin is gone and new grows on. They won't let me look in the mirror. I was ugly anyway.

Boy, I had pain I can't believe. Constant. Then they gave me a shot and I'd never had one of those and I could have gone right on without!

Oh, Lord—I'll be so glad to get out. The men are so good to me. I was lucky. 2 of our men died, and 3 or 4 hurt. John got singed (I don't know spelling). Boy, I'm using and writing words I never heard of.

Nurse says she's gonna take this beautiful pen. I was supposed to write for 10 minutes. I told her I had to think about things longer than that. It was the most beautiful thing in the world—that rig.   Boy, it was really powerful.

Pain has become my world. I just can't move—but I'm writing—writing—and my hands are working. Brain may not be.

Today is special. Mr. McKinley is coming. I think his first name is Myron. But I'm not sure how to spell it or his last name at all. He's brought me some nice books and my own pen. He said to tell him if I needed anything. I wonder if I should tell him I would like some real paper. . . .

Myron McKinley was here. I can't believe how wonderful he is. Today we talked about the accident. I told him how scared I was and did that make me not a good man? . . . He told me a good smart man who had sense enough to be scared was the best man. He told me crying was the best way to help your pain—It was OK! . . . I told him the fire was really terrible. He laughed and said there was other things as bad but right now he couldn't think of anything. He looked at my hands and told me a doctor friend of his could fix them. Wouldn't that be great? And my face, too. I told him it was OK— cause I could write and the good Lord let me write. But he said as I grew older, I would have more trouble. I told him I could never thank him enough. He said: "Son, just get well and write the story of my life, it'll be a best seller."

He told me about his life and why he fights fires and he knows some day he'll come up with something to help the terrible fires. He talked about my Dad and my Aunt Mae and about my wanting to write. He said: "Son, anyone who has tried so hard to be a writer sure ought to have a chance."

We talked about Dad and why Dad feels like he does. I think I understand about his love for that land and why he felt like I should help him and why he felt like he did when I didn't stay there.

We talked about Aunt Mae and can you believe we talked about women! He laughed and said there were books written on the subject and they still didn't really explain—or maybe he just didn't understand. He said it was something that would come around at the right time. He said, "Now if you want to learn something not so serious like learning to walk on a high wire—well, he could tell me about that."

The nurse came in and said I was going to get to go to John's in a few days. I don't really know what I'm going to do. I can't work for a while. For a long while.

(At the bottom of that scorched and water stained sheet of paper, Myron had printed his name—KINLEY, MYRON M.—for the boy.)

O God, Pain—I just got my hands to working when they pulled off the burned skin. I guess it could be worse. I could have lost my hands—they say that someday an operation can help where the skin growed together. It melted—they say.

There were brief handwritten notes with the boy's notes. The writer is not known, but they are copied for you here:

The young man was badly burned—entire body. One of the men hired to put out the fire saved the young man's life. The boy was 19 or 20—farm boy who had never been off the farm.

Possibly from Arkansas. He was very poor—carried his shoes around town, saving them.

The man who saved him went farther than the company. He saw to it the boy was taken to a rehab (or something of that sort) and had surgery. The man who saved him paid for it himself. The man saw to it this boy had a job.

The young man was staying with the driller's family. It seems the driller kept records for the Company and must have put the young man's papers in the file.

The young man lived about 4½ years after that fire. Two men died in the fire—3 died later, including the young man.

It seems the man who saved him really was great—made his life bearable. The man who saved the boy later was famous. A movie was made either of his life or how he fought rig fires! He lived in or around Chickasha.

When Myron and I began to talk in specifics related to a book about his life, it was immediately apparent that the thing he was most interested in was leaving a record of his work as a firefighter so that future generations—including his own grandchildren—might have the opportunity to know and understand as much as the written word can convey of the dangerous and exciting aspect of the oil business known as firefighting.

I have been trying to write this book about Myron for many years, and although I have wanted terribly to write it, something has held me back. I think it must have to do with the awe in which I held him over a long period of years and, subconsciously at least, may still hold him in the sense that I am not sure I can do his story justice.

As you read this book, any sense of awe you may already feel about the work this very special man did for almost forty years will not only be undiminished. It will be overwhelming. He killed wild wells in almost every country where oil is found and produced on this planet. His adventures took him to fiery wells from as far away as Africa, Alaska, Canada, France, Great Britain, Italy, New Guinea, Pakistan, Venezuela, Columbia, California, Louisiana, Oklahoma, and Texas as well as at sea and north of the Arctic Circle.

You see, Myron Kinley was a most remarkable man, and the things there are to tell about him are uniquely wonderful. Many things have been written about him. There is something about a fire that fascinates the human race, and to read and know of men who dare to challenge oil and gas well fires is to share to some extent at least, the vicarious pleasure of conquering such monsters. But in working with reams of copy that made their way into newspapers and magazines, and glancing over scores of photographs of terrifying yet breathtaking beauty, I have come to know many things about this quiet, keenly intelligent man, and they must be told. So I must write the book.

JESSIE KINLEY
Chickasha, Oklahoma

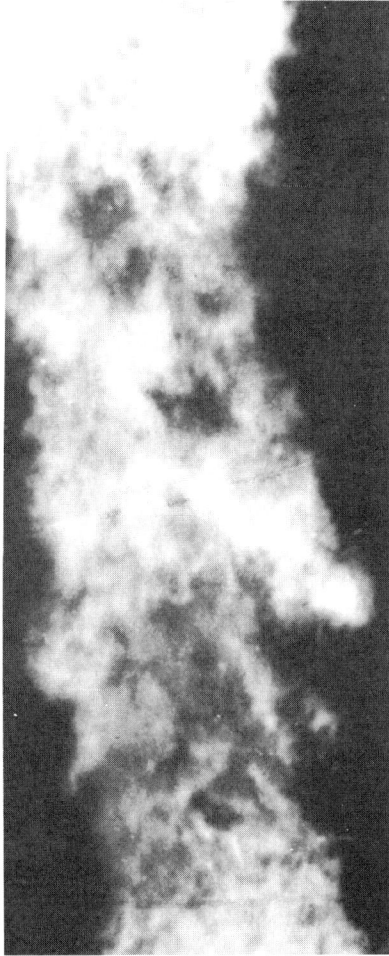

THE CALL KINLEY STORY BEGINS

KARL AND ROSE

So the Kinley story begins with the marriage of Karl T. Kinley and Katherine Rose Scholl in Pasadena, California, on July 4, 1896. At the time they met, Rose was working as head housekeeper in a large hotel in Pasadena and Karl was employed in a butcher shop. Little is actually known about the courtship, but their daughter Lucille thinks it likely that their work brought them together, as Karl probably delivered meat to the hotel where Rose worked.

The surviving relic of their wedding is a charming, aged photograph of the wedding supper—most likely taken in the Pasadena Hotel. If the high spirits and the laughter which the picture portrays were in any way indicative of the kind of marriage Rose and Karl shared, they were a lucky pair. Myron often spoke of the laughter in the young Kinley household, and his memories of the brief time they had together as a family before the death of his mother were, without exception, happy ones.

Sometime between their wedding in 1896 and Myron's birth in November, 1898, Karl and Rose left their jobs in Pasadena and relocated to Gaviota, California. No one seems to know exactly when or why they decided to make this move, but it seems likely that the lure of steady work drew them to Gaviota, where Karl was immediately employed in the asphalt mines.

Perhaps the mines paid better than housekeeping and butchering, but it was hard and dirty work. Karl spent his days in the dark mines digging for asphalt, which the workers cut into huge blocks and used to build roads.

Life could not have been easy for Rose either, as conditions in the mining town were primitive. As an early mining town, Gaviota had not been built for long-term, or even comfortable, residence. Other than local boarding houses, there were few places to live as most "homes" were really only poorly constructed temporary structures, lacking the domestic comforts of indoor plumbing and running water. In Gaviota they were also

Myron Macy Kinley.
Bakersfield, California, ca. 1899.

forced to endure high crime rates typical of mining settlements. Life for Rose was not only hard, but was undoubtedly lonely, as she was the only woman to accompany her husband to the township.

But the loneliness did not go on forever. In early 1898 Rose became pregnant with her first child. She left Gaviota during the late stages of her pregnancy, when she traveled to Santa Barbara to give birth. On the second day of November, 1898, the Karl T. Kinleys became the proud parents of an eight-pound baby boy. They named him Myron Macy.

THE CAREFREE YEARS

The Kinleys picked up their young son, and as soon as Rose and Myron were able to travel, gathered what few possessions they had and made their way to a small frame house on a road called Chinee Grade on the outskirts of Bakersfield. Although the specific reasons for the move are unknown, it was doubtless due in some part to the difficulties in caring for a new baby in the primitive conditions of turn-of-the-century Gaviota.

It was a gladsome day, no doubt, when they left the asphalt pits behind and took up their new life on the outskirts of Bakersfield, and it was during these brief years in Bakersfield that the little family enjoyed the only carefree years it would ever know.

During the early years on Chinee Grade, there seems to have been nothing to detract from the joy in Karl and Rose's marriage, or in their love for their young family. It was in the house on Chinee Grade where Lucille was born in the year 1902, and it was there that young Myron wept in bitter disappointment one Christmas Day, when he did not receive a gift he had set his heart on. Moved by the child's tears, Karl Kinley embarked on a long Christmas walk to and from Bakersfield to retrieve the missing gift. In later life, Myron remembered this incident with mixed emotions—amusement that he cared so much about a Christmas gift, yet embarrassment for sending his father on such an errand on Christmas Day.

The Kinleys later moved from their comfortable home on Chinee Grade to a house on Bundrage Lane, also on the outskirts of Bakersfield where, in addition to their house, they had a small piece of acreage and a billy goat. They were living on Bundrage when Floyd, the youngest Kinley, was born on November 28, 1904. Myron often recalled the years on Bundrage as years filled with laughter, as indeed, the household must have been a lively one with a new baby, a two-year-old girl, and a small boy of six who knew, even at that early age, exactly what he wanted and more often than not, exactly how to get it.

When Floyd was born in 1904, Karl Kinley supported the family by managing the steam plant that furnished heat for the

Myron, Floyd, and Lucille Kinley, ca. 1905.

hotels in Bakersfield. Rose Kinley stayed busy at home with a house to keep and three small children to tend, and doubtless had little time for herself. But with Karl steadily employed, Rose was able to make annual family visits, and early in the summer of 1905, she and her children set off for Illinois on a trip that would leave a lasting impression on her oldest son.

Rose's brother, Will, was an Illinois farmer, and on Will's Illinois farm young Myron discovered a brand new world. Being the curious little boy he was, he left no stone unturned acquainting himself with as many aspects of American farm life as the visit would permit.

Family accounts of this trip tell of an episode in which Myron was particularly eager to copy the adult activities of his Uncle Will. It seems that the women were planning to cook some fryer chickens for supper one night, and had sent Will to gather and kill some of the chickens from the hen house. Myron watched his uncle carefully as Will proceeded to kill the chickens one at a time by wringing their necks, and present them to the ladies for cooking.

The very next day found young Myron in emulation of his uncle. That afternoon he caught and killed five of Will's highly prized baby ducks. Not only did he wring their necks but, in a display of prowess, he fastened all five of the ducks to a board which he presented to the grown-ups. The women were horrified. His uncle almost had apoplexy. The boy himself never quite understood what all the commotion was about—nobody had objected when Will killed the fryers.

Home again from Illinois, time found Myron a little older, but no wiser, concerning the consequences of boyish behavior, and instances of that became more evident as time passed.

According to his sister, Lucille, Myron showed his enterprising spirit early. She claims that as young as ten years old, Myron began nurturing his entrepreneurial skills by sending off for cheap jewelry to sell. Unfortunately for him, this did not generally gain him favor with his parents, as they usually ended up paying for the merchandise out of Karl's wages.

But Myron was not alone in his childhood exploits. He and mischievous friends more than once troubled Bakersfield residents with their boyish pranks. One of their unsuspecting victims was a Chinese laundryman employed in a Bakersfield hotel. The traditional short braid he wore at the back of his head was irresistible to young Myron and his friends and, although the laundryman was a quiet man who minded his own business, the boys were often guilty of sneaking up behind him, grabbing the braid, and trying to cut it off. There is no record that the boys ever succeeded in taking his braid, but it's true they gave the man no peace until someone—very likely Karl Kinley himself—put a stop to the harrassment.

Stealing watermelons was another favorite pastime of Bakersfield youth, and it was while stealing melons one summer night that Myron and his young partners in crime got a hard-learned lesson that nearly scared them to death.

It seems that a Bakersfield farmer had been forewarned that a group of local boys would raid his watermelon patch. The farmer, in preparation for the impending theft, got his gun, hid near the spot where he knew the boys would come for their loot, and waited for them to make their stealthy approach. Finally they arrived, and while they pilfered melons, the farmer patiently waited for them to finish pulling their quota—one melon per boy, no less. As the boys began to leave the field, all hell broke loose. The farmer fired his gun into the air and the boys fled, dropping watermelons as they ran.

Later the farmer confessed to the culprits that he was not mad at them but was simply playing a joke. He invited them to come back and eat all the melon they could hold. The vandals' appetites were a long time being satisfied, but Myron always expressed regret that they had not been able to eat the stolen melons, for he was sure no other could have tasted as good.

RUNAWAY BOY

As it turned out those adventures were child's play for a youngster whose imagination and ingenuity demanded more exciting worlds to conquer. The old adage which says that coming events cast their shadows before them was proven true in the case of one small boy on April 29, 1909.

He was not quite 10½ years old when he made the front page of a Los Angeles daily newspaper with headlines and a photograph that would have turned a seasoned publicity seeker pale with envy. Facing the camera stood Myron Kinley, dressed in a cowboy uniform and wearing a broad-brimmed hat that framed a face so innocent of guile that it would have melted a heart of stone.

He stole (his own word for it) five dollars from an unknown, and unknowing, benefactor and invested part of it in a cowboy suit and a "pneumonia gun" so that when he reached his destination—Los Angeles, no less—he would be properly outfitted to hunt wild game. He also expected to find the city overrun by wild Indians. That it was not was a great source of disappointment to him.

In addition to a front-page story, the Los Angeles daily ran a second story on page two. These newspaper accounts have always held a special fascination for me because the discrepancies in them are so typical of the ones that dogged his footsteps as a firefighter for half a century. In this instance the paper lists both his name and age incorrectly. The article gives his name as "Byron" and states he was 12 years old when in reality, he was not quite 10½.

One day not long before we were married I asked him how old he was. I had read several newspaper and magazine stories which mentioned his age, but rarely did any two of them use the same figure. He answered the question by claiming that he didn't really know how old he was. He had lied about his age so many times in connection with his early work in the oil fields that he had long since forgotten. "But," he said, "you can ask Sis. She will know!" To him it was of no consequence.

BYRON KINLEY, WHO CAME TO LOS ANGELES TO FIGHT INDIANS

Runaway Boy, Armed, Comes to Los Angeles to Hunt Wild Game

Thursday, April 29, 1909

BYRON KINLEY, WHO CAME TO LOS ANGELES TO FIGHT INDIANS

Runaway Boy, Armed, Comes to Los Angeles To Hunt Wild Game

Throws Away "Pneumonia" Gun and Gets $1 Worth of Sympathy from Chief

Having pictured Los Angeles as a typical border town, where Indians and wild game abounded and waited to be converted into targets for his ammonia—he called it "pneumonia"— revolver, 12-year-old Myron Kinley, son of Karl Kinley, a Bakersfield machinist, purchased a "Wild West" outfit, and ran away from home.

He arrived in Los Angeles early yesterday morning and, finding the city down to date and very, very much different from that which his boyish dream had pictured, he threw aside his glass and rubber revolver, and appealed to Patrolman Bonar for aid in locating a cousin, who, he said lived on "G" street."

At the city jail building and in Chief of Police Dishman's private office, he told a story between nervous sobs that created sympathy, and not only won belief in his tale, but coaxed a silver dollar from the pocket of the police chief. His story that he had arranged to meet his parents here, on their way from Kansas City, was unshaken. It was not until nearly 5 o'clock in the afternoon that the chief of police and his subordinates were undeceived. A long distance message from his anxious father conveyed the information to the police that the boy was a runaway.

In the meantime he was taken to a restaurant, where he gave a generous order. Half way through the meal, the boy leaned back and murmured: "I'm all stopped up, but I'll get away with the rest or bust a-trying."

Afterward the runaway lad was taken to a detention home to await the arrival of his father, who will be here today.

Thursday, April 29, 1909

CUTE LITTLE ANANIAS
Boy Sadly in Need of Spanking,
Works On Feelings of the Chief of Police

Myron Kinley, 12 years old, with the make-up of a rough rider and the imagination of Ananias, reached Los Angeles yesterday morning and proceeded to rope in the police department for a day's outing about the city.

The boy invented a sick father on a trip to Kansas City, an imaginary family with whom he had lived during his father's absence, and wound up his tale by stating that he had come to Los Angeles from Bakersfield in order that he might welcome his father upon his return from the East. He was such a cute little chap, and told such a straight story, and wept such lovely, sobby, baby-like tears that Chief Dishman opened his heart to him.

The boy was picked up by Patrolman Bonar on Broadway yesterday morning. He said he didn't want to be arrested, and that he was crying simply through nervousness.

He told the Chief that his father had been taken ill and had gone to Kansas City to recuperate. The father had written a letter to the boy to meet him in Los Angeles, and young Kinley purchased a train ticket, made the trip in the chair car, and landed in Los Angeles. He then proceeded to go first class. He bought a Wild-West outfit, a khaki hat, a small ammonia gun—trappings. He was a cute little man.

The Chief of Police sent little Kinley out to see the city under charge of an officer, and gave him $1 to buy a big breakfast and dinner. Kinley enjoyed himself to the fullest until his wiles were exposed.

The Chief telephoned to Bakersfield, and the irate elder Kinley came to the phone. He denied ever having been in Kansas, said the boy ran away from home, and that he will get a paddling as soon as he gets back.

Myron used to laugh about the story. The part he loved the best was the "eat or bust" bit, and I never saw him tackle a chunk of fresh strawberry shortcake without being reminded of that long ago incident. His account of the episode always ended with the remark that, "If it had not been for my mother, my father probably would have left me in Los Angeles."

Many years later he was reading a book about the early days of Los Angeles, given to him by his friend, Trevally Dalton. Reading was Myron's happiest pastime, and this particular evening he had taken the new book to bed with him. Suddenly, out of a long silence, he fairly shouted: "Hey! That's the chief of police who bought me the strawberry shortcake!"

I hope the chief's life was long enough that he came to know what a remarkable man his little manipulator had turned out to be.

LIFE WITH THE WILDMAN FAMILY

It was in the spring-summer of 1909, shortly after Myron ran away to Los Angeles, that Rose Kinley was taken seriously ill. At this time, Karl had found steady work in the Taft Oil Fields of Bakersfield, and was doubtless busy supporting his family and helping Rose with the children. But as Rose's illness progressed, Karl became unable to nurse her himself, and arranged for his wife and children to move into the Wildman home, where Rose could be properly nursed by Mrs. Wildman and the Kinley children could be tended by the other members of the Wildman family.

Despite Mrs. Wildman's ministrations, Rose finally succumbed to her illness and died in September of 1909, leaving a husband and three children aged eleven, seven, and five years old. The newly widowed Karl found himself unable to both work and properly care for three small children, and it was therefore decided that Myron, Lucille, and Floyd should remain with the Wildman family. The three continued living under Mrs. Wildman's supervision with little incident until one fateful day that would break up the children and place Myron back in Karl's care and near the oil fields.

It seems that Mrs. Wildman, as matriarch of the household, had a rocking chair that she had designated her special sitting spot. It was in this rocker that Mrs. Wildman busily worked on many of her routine tasks, and in which she regularly reposed at the conclusion of the day; and it was in this chair that Mrs. Wildman was working one day only a few months following Rose Kinley's death.

During the course of her activities Mrs. Wildman was called from her comfortable seat, from which she dutifully rose to see to the matter at hand. It appears that the sight of the empty rocker was a mighty temptation for little Myron, a mischievous and daring boy by nature, for he took immediate advantage of her absence to move the chair from its customary location. Upon her return to the beloved rocker, Mrs. Wildman habitually went to the spot where her chair had been only moments before, and sat down without realizing that it was not in its previous place. To say she was surprised to find herself sitting on the floor is an understatement, and in her fury she chased the youngster round and round the table scolding him in her native German tongue until he finally ran out of the house and into the streets of Bakersfield.

Late that night Myron paid a final visit to the Wildman home to collect his few belongings and say goodbye to his younger sister and brother. Using a ladder from the Wildman's windmill, he stealthily climbed to the window where Lucille and Floyd were sleeping, and managed to waken his sister by throwing gravel against the window pane. Lucille opened the window and, after a hurried and whispered conference, fetched her brother's clothing and dropped them down to him, then watched him back down the ladder with his arms full of clothes, and disappear into the streets.

How long and how far he walked that night searching for his father, I do not know; but the incident had a happy ending for it brought the boy one step closer to his destiny as a firefighter. Ultimately, the road from the Wildman home led the adventurous youngster to the Taft oil fields where, under the supervision of Karl Kinley, he began his life-long love affair with the oil patch.

THE TAFT OIL FIELDS

Throughout Myron's early youth Karl Kinley had determined that the boy would receive the formal education that he, himself, had missed, and sternly demanded that Myron continue his schooling rather than join him for work in the oil fields. But the California wells held a powerful fascination for the younger Kinley, and his ardent desire to be with the oil men consistently drove him from the classroom and to the derricks, where he witnessed first-hand the excitement and challenges of oil field work.

It was not long before Karl was informed by school authorities that his young son was playing hooky, day after day taking a sneaky leave from the stuffy classrooms to learn the hard-taught lessons of the oil field. Myron's father, with higher goals for his bright son, was not pleased, and was forced to punish Myron for these unexcused vacations from school. But apparently no amount of punishment could effectively diminish the appeal and allure of the oil patch and, despite the punishments, Myron only persisted in skipping school.

Until one day when father and son had a most unexpected meeting on the Taft streets, when Karl had assumed that Myron was in class. Myron's bright blue eyes used to dance when he told how the irate elder Kinley grabbed him by the collar and threw him in an iron building where, armed with a horse-whip, the past whip-master ferociously cracked the whip on either side of him, sending the disobedient child scrambling towards the walls for escape. When finally the whip was still, both father and son realized that they had reached a turning point in their relationship.

Fortunately for Myron, his repeated resistance to formal education finally persuaded the elder Kinley to let him out of the classroom and into the world of the oil business. Myron ended his formal education in 1912, when he left school to pursue his dream of a career in the oil patch. At thirteen years old, Myron was employed for wages in the Taft oil fields, where he labored alongside his father, learning every aspect of Karl's important work.

When Myron left school in eighth grade, he was no longer a child and was ready for man's work. From his first day in the oil patch until 1917, when he enlisted in the Army during World War I, he was constantly surrounded by the sights and sounds of the oil fields, and he surely felt a keen satisfaction with that life. He was working in the great outdoors. He was working with men, and if the work he learned embraced extraordinary danger, that was all the more reason for him to love it wholeheartedly.

During those early years, the wells in the Taft fields were at the perfect stage in their development for a young man to learn first-hand the mechanics of finding and producing oil. The early stages of the Taft fields allowed Myron a unique opportunity for thorough involvement in virtually every aspect of the oil business, and Myron's exposure to oil work began with finding a drilling location for a new well, continued through the entire drilling process, and ended only when the well was either completed as an oil or gas well or abandoned as a dry hole.

In 1912 the Taft fields were enormous, and their highly productive wells surely presented virtually every possible problem inherent in the production of oil and gas. But the production problems of the Taft fields were not problems for young Myron, as they captured his imagination and inspired him to dedicate his professional career to finding the myriad solutions to those difficulties.

Although Myron's work in the early Taft oil fields exposed him to all phases of oil production, he never actually worked as a part of a drilling crew. Rather, he was involved mainly with production problems in wells after drilling was completed and casing had been set.

Perhaps the most common production problems of the time, and the ones most immediately evident after drilling, were those of restricted oil or gas flow, generally occurring when the pay sand was not porous enough to yield oil or gas in commercial quantities. During the early oil days, "well shooters" were called on these jobs to loosen the sand formations and thereby increase the rates of flow for the oil and gas wells.

When Karl Kinley first went to work in the oil patch sometime in 1908, he was trained as a well shooter, and it was that trade that he taught his young son. An eager learner, Myron accompanied his father on every well shooting job he could, taking keen interest in the dangerous and exciting work of the shooters, and learning every aspect of that challenging job.

It's no wonder that early well shooting captured Myron's active imagination, as it was undoubtedly an extraordinarily high-risk job that was absolutely vital to the commercial production of oil and gas. On these early jobs with his father, Myron watched in fascination as daring men dropped explosives into a producing well, felt the thrill of the blast as the explosives shattered tight sand formations, sat in anticipation of the success or failure of the shoot, and exulted in triumph when blasted wells began producing oil and gas at much greater rates.

As he observed the many production problems imaginable (and even more that were unimaginable), he learned the valuable lesson that no two problems are exactly alike, and furthermore, he discovered that ingenuity, creativity, and the ability to improvise are the best problem solving tools for any oil worker. It was this simple fact which encouraged him to develop his inventive skills and laid the groundwork for his amazing ability to build oil field tools, many of which involved the use of explosives. And indeed, his genius for invention would serve him well, for he soon gained an international reputation for his inventions, and his skill for creating tools according to his particular need was the basis for his worldwide success as a firefighter.

THE SHOT HEARD AROUND THE OIL WORLD

Although Myron's early lessons in the oil patch centered on well shooting, there were wild and burning wells in those early California oil field days, and it is certain that Karl Kinley worked to bring some of those fiery wells under control, for he was then employed in the well shooting business by a Taft man named Ford Alexander, who later gained considerable fame as an early oil well firefighter.

It was during his days as a well shooter that Karl Kinley developed a grand theory for extinguishing oil well fires using

The shot heard around the oil world. Bakersfield, California, April 29, 1913. Myron (sitting, middle) and Karl Kinley (standing, far right), made history when Karl snuffed the Taft fire with nitroglycerin. Karl's right hand rests on the box of explosives he used to put out the fire.

explosives. Karl described his fledgling theory in later years, "I was a well shooter when I conceived the idea of shooting out the flame with an explosive that would separate it from the fuel and thus put it out. The idea is just like that of blowing out a candle or an oil lamp. The force of the breath blows the blaze from the fuel. I figured that if I could get a strong enough 'breath,' I could do it."

Karl was fascinated by the fact that gas and oil fires differed. In gas wells there was a space between the mouth of the well and the bottom of the fire. He called this the mixing chamber, the space where gas and air mixed, and he believed that an explosion set off close enough to the mixing chamber would break the flow of gas, causing the fire to die. In oil fires the flame started at the mouth of the well so there was no mixing chamber visible.

And so it happens that Karl Kinley, with young Myron in tow, was on a well shooting job in the Taft field when his theory was finally put to the test on April 29, 1913. Perched atop Signal Hill was K.T.O No. 2, a wild well that caught fire and had been burning uncontrollably for several months. The Signal Hill fire was initially treated in the traditional manner, moving batteries of steam boilers to the well where steam and mud were generated to extinguish the flame. However, the steam and mud tactic proved to be a tedious and inefficient firefighting method, as it demanded tremendous resources with little effect. In the meantime, the owners were growing desperate to kill the fire and control the troublesome well, for it threatened neighboring wells nearing completion in the drilling phase, and was poised to cause catastrophic losses.

Karl Kinley knew that his time had come. He carefully presented his theory to the owners who, in their desperation, granted him leave to test his method, and he promptly set about his new task.

That his proposed solution to the oil well fire was previously unproven was no deterrent for a man with vision, and by carefully packing a heavy charge of nitroglycerin into a crude bomb, Karl constructed the first explosive to be used in oil well firefighting, a tool that would soon make the cumbersome and inefficient steam boilers obsolete.

Crafting the bomb was only the first of Karl's many challenges, however. Karl had calculated that an explosion detonated within three to fifteen feet of the mixing chamber would provide a strong enough blast to separate the flame from the fuel, thereby killing the flame; his only problem being how he might battle extreme temperatures to place the explosives at the chamber, and how he might detonate the explosives in safety from shrapnel and other fallout. Karl turned to the only solution he knew. He picked up the bomb and carefully carried it as close to the well head as he possibly could. Then, in a decisive moment, he threw the bomb towards the mixing chamber and ran like hell away from there.

The shot of nitroglycerin landed right on top of the well head and exploded, exactly as planned. After months of battling the Signal Hill fire with steam and mud, the fire was out within minutes. Karl's experiment with nitroglycerin was a success, and the young Myron, a witness to his father's victory, got his first exciting glimpse of the world of firefighting using explosives.

According to Myron, this was not the first time a fire had been blown out using explosives, but it was the first that resulted in well shooters using the method thereafter to deliberately put out fires in burning wells.

After the Kinley men became professional firefighters they always used explosives to put out well fires. Their success as firefighters was in large part due to an intimate understanding of explosives. The Kinley men respected the awesome power of explosives, using them only with extreme caution. And it was also that profound respect that enabled the Kinleys to use explosives fearlessly—a necessity in becoming the great firefighters they were.

Before joining the Army in 1917, Myron took a temporary break from the field work he had so actively pursued since the eighth grade, and assumed work as a forger in a blacksmith shop that crafted machinery and heavy equipment for the nearby Taft oil fields. Although his tenure in the smith shop was brief, it undoubtedly left an indelible mark on his naturally creative mind. Here Myron was engaged daily in crafting tools for oil work, and it was here that he learned how to build customized tools to solve highly specific production problems. This first hand knowledge undoubtedly enabled him in later life to invent tools spontaneously, and eventually led to his reknown as a pioneer in the development of modern petroleum engineering technology, with several patents in his name and numerous other inventions to his credit.

Myron often spoke of his smithing experience with relish, as he readily admitted to enjoying the work immensely and taking pleasure in the company of his fellow workers. At the smith shop Myron was surrounded by strong young men, all of whom worked hard at their manual labor from morning till night. He fondly recalled the voracious appetites that he and his companions worked up and the noon meals they took at a local boarding house; remembering how they hungrily devoured hearty meals topped off with entire pies, then scrambled outside for lively wrestling matches before the end of the noon hour break.

And thus passed the first nineteen years of Myron's life—undoubtedly filled with fun, adventure, and learning, they kindled his passion for oil work, nurtured his talent for firefighting,

encouraged him to actively search for solutions to complex production problems, and thereby laid a solid foundation for his
future career in the oil business. But it is also easy to see that for
Myron, a keen observer, a creative thinker, and an enterprising
businessman, the Taft oil fields were only the first stop along the
road to a whole new world of adventure. For a young man with
the world before him, a strong sense of duty coupled with the lure
of excitement moved him to enlist in the Army, when he was
transported across the seas to the Western Front during World
War I.

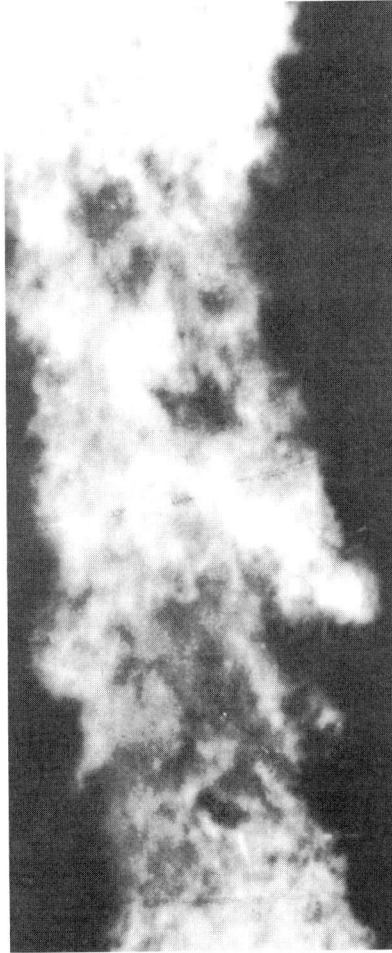

**FROM THE OIL FIELDS
TO THE WESTERN FRONT**

Myron was but a sixteen-year-old boy when Archduke Francis Ferdinand, heir to the throne of Austria-Hungary, and his wife Sophie were assasinated in Sarajevo on June 28, 1914, precipitating the declaration of war made on July 28 between the Allied powers of France, Great Britain, Russia, Belgium, and Serbia and the Central powers of Germany, Austria-Hungary, and the Ottoman Empire. But President Wilson's formal declaration of war against Germany on April 6, 1917, found Myron a nineteen-year-old man ready for adventure. Without hesitation he enlisted in the American Expeditionary Forces to serve the Allied cause in the First World War, the ramifications of which would be seen as he commanded wars against wild and fiery wells for years to come.

ABOVE: *Doughboys, 1918. Myron (far right) joined the American Expeditionary Forces to fight in World War I.*

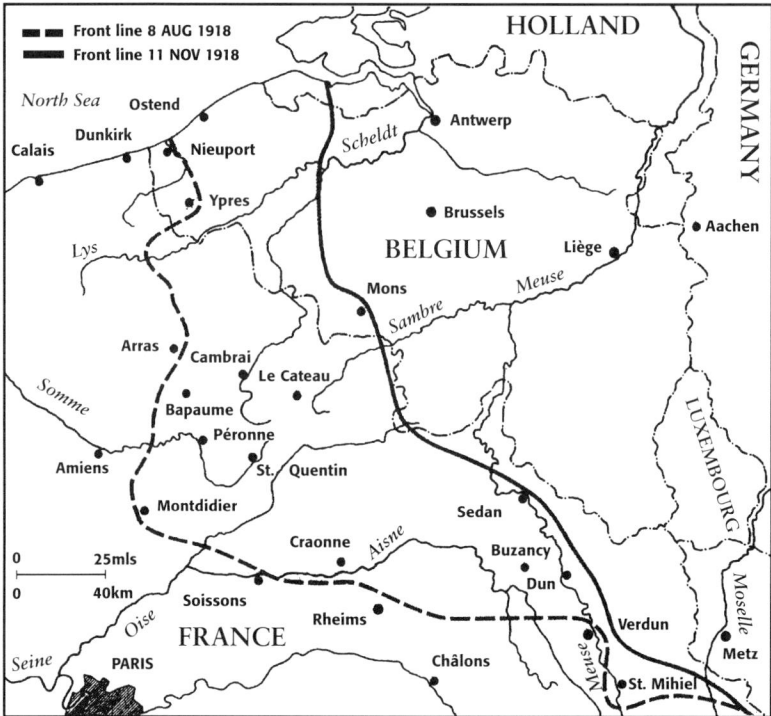

The Western Front, 1918. The 59th Coast Artillery Corps assumed positions at St. Mihiel, then moved north to fight in the Argonne Woods.

Because of the relative inexperience of the American troops, only select units were immediately sent overseas, while the bulk of American enlisted men were retained in the United States as General John Pershing negotiated for permission to command the American Expeditionary Forces as an independent military force on the Western Front, a line of battle stretching over six hundred miles from the English Channel to the border of Switzerland. After months of negotiations with French and British commanders, Pershing was granted his own sector along the southern end of the line, and given orders to establish troops at St. Mihiel, where German offensive forces had been entrenched since 1915. The negotiations paved the way for the first independent American operations of the war, and demanded mass transport of American doughboys from the home front to the Western Front in France.

Summer of 1918 saw the wholesale deployment of American troops under the American Expeditionary Forces and their transport to France. It was this mass deployment that called Myron Kinley from the Taft blacksmith shop and loaded him with thousands of untried American soldiers at New York Harbor, where they set sail for Europe in June of 1918 in preparation for the upcoming American offensive on battle-weary German forces in September.

The mass landing of doughboys on the European front in July marked their induction into the Great War, a conflict that revolutionized modern warfare. Here American troops met with weaponry and battle strategy never before encountered in war. During World War I, young Myron and his fellow soldiers witnessed the first use of airplanes in bombing raids. Artillery technology also gave rise to new and powerful weapons, pitting Allied troops against such formidable wartime innovations as the German machine gun and "Big Bertha," the first long-range gun, capable of firing on targets from a distance of over seventy-five miles.

The newly developed machine gun effectively destroyed all possibilities of forward movement, forcing armies on both sides of the battle line into trenches, with the area between the frontline trenches of the opposing forces known as "no man's land," land unclaimed by either side, but marking certain death for those soldiers forced into it during offensive attacks.

The stalemate resulting from trench warfare forced troops to adapt the trenches into permanent living quarters, which they developed into highly complex structures suitable for food and equipment transportation and shelter from the European cold. Living conditions in the trenches proved a bitter test for Myron and the other doughboys. Infested with gigantic rats, sometimes as large as cats and small dogs, the squalid trenches were bitterly cold and damp, and were often flooded by heavy seasonal rains and snowfall.

Frustrated by the continuing deadlock along the Western Front, the Allies determined to develop and implement their own wartime invention to penetrate the German line and turn the tide of the war. The first military tank was conceived in a desperate effort to free Allied forces from the trenches and to proceed with

Myron Kinley, 1918. Military service nurtured Myron's skill for strategic planning, increased his knowledge of explosives, and encouraged him to develop his talents for invention, adaptation, and improvisation.

final offensive maneuvers of the war. The tank debuted in late 1918, shortly before the arrival of the American Expeditionary Forces in Europe, and proved to be a huge success in combatting the German machine gun. The manufacture of more tanks, combined with the imminent arrival of American troops on the Western Front breathed new life into the Allied forces, giving leaders the hope that American assistance would provide them with the resources needed to crumble the German army in a final offensive push.

The American forces began landing in France in July, 1918, and promptly despatched to positions near St. Mihiel at the southern end of the line. The young Kinley noted his arrival at an unnamed port on July 10, where the soldiers were loaded onto trains bound for LaHarve, and then LaContini, where he arrived on July 17 and remained until August 13.

Myron records that he was placed in the 59th Coast Artillery Corps on July 19, 1918. As a member of artillery, Myron's daily routine consisted of the cleaning and caring for heavy machinery

and large guns, moving the artillery to the front lines, coordinat-
ing the firing and use of the artillery, positioning equipment for
battle, and providing for the safe and timely transport of the
weaponry to the next area of battle. These responsibilities doubtless shaped his future career as an inventor and oil well firefighter,
as they added to his knowledge of machinery and explosives, and
provided him with a unique opportunity to develop his innate talent for strategy that was so apparent as he waged battle against
fiery wells around the world.

Myron records that the 59th Coast Artillery Corps then proceeded to Village Sue Marne, where they conducted clean-up
operations for the French, and during which they resided in abandoned country barns. He records that his unit arrived at St.
Mihiel's Pwinelle Woods on August 31, where American units
consolidated with more experienced American units, relieved
weary French troops, and equipped themselves for the upcoming
advance on the Germans.

General Pershing ordered the American attack on St. Mihiel
on September 12, at five a.m., following four hours of bombard-
ment on the retreating German defense by Allied artillery. Myron
records in his diary that the barrage began at one o'clock the
morning of September 12, and continued until nine a.m. of
September 13. His diary also gives witness to the dwindling
resources of the German forces as he recounts seeing the German
prisoners of war, whom he describes as "mostly old men, a few
boys." Although the battle at St. Mihiel, waged against under-
manned and ill-prepared German troops was, from the outset,
regarded as a sure American victory, it was nonetheless a crucial
battle for the Allies, as triumph there revived flagging French spirits and protected strongholds in Verdun.

The success of the American Expeditionary Forces was made
complete by September 16, 1918, and having attained the goal of
St. Mihiel, General Pershing agreed to transfer his forces to the
densely wooded area between the Argonne woods and the Meuse
River to participate alongside French and British forces in the
final offensive of World War I. Americans began their tranport as
early as September 16, when they loaded artillery and moved
north to the Argonne, where they replaced French soldiers along
a ninety mile stretch through the forest. The transfer of the entire

American Expeditionary Forces took fourteen days and involved the movement of more than 600,000 troops, 93,000 horses, and supporting equipment for a distance of over sixty miles. Myron noted that his regiment was despatched to the Argonne on September 17 and arrived on September 20, when they immediately positioned artillery for the ensuing operations. He also recorded that his regiment was billeted in old trenches at Camp Dubeville near Florent and personally testified to the horrors of trench life, as he and his companions lived in burrows flooded with rancid water and breeding "rats as big as cats."

With men and artillery in place and ready for action, General Pershing launched a surprise attack against the Germans. Myron recorded the beginning of the battle at Argonne on the morning of September 26 with open fire on Varinnin. Although American forces outnumbered German troops by four to eight times, victory did not come as easily for the Allies here as at St. Mihiel. The haste of the offensive caused confusion for American troops, the heavily wooded terrain greatly inhibited forward movement, and American casualties began to mount.

Allied armies were not deterred, however, and continued to push through the Argonne, forcing German leaders to seriously consider peace negotiations, and by November 6, 1918, the first peace delegation was sent to discuss an end to the war. But with the prospects of peace came some of the most fervent fighting, and Myron dutifully made note of the increased intensity of battle and the resultant American casualties occuring between November 6 and Armistice on November 11.

In later years, Myron would remember the war for its tremendous physical demands, often recalling how he fought to exhaustion, just as he did while waging war against unruly wells in the oil fields. He remembered one night in the Argonne when battle was at its fiercest level, and his company was exposed for several days to continuous overhead artillery fire. Battle weary from weeks of sleepless nights, some of the soldiers dug caves in the side of a rising hill in an effort to dull the sound of the guns and get some much needed sleep. Myron also later claimed that, one night when the barrage was at its worst, he was so completely exhausted he slept the whole night through without hearing the overhead artillery at all.

Myron duly notes Armistice on November 11, 1918, eleven a.m., the signing of a peace agreement and the end of hostilities between the Allied and Central powers. He then indicates an immediate withdrawal of his regiment from the area to Dubeville, where they were ordered through a series of moves as part of the American evacuation from war-torn France. He reports travels through Vignory, Vassy, and Dijon before boarding ship in Brest in December for final transport home.

Myron often spoke of his journey home from France, and his unit's hearty welcome at New York Harbor in January, 1919. Upon arrival in Brest in December, Myron went to get his mustering out papers for his transport home and ultimate release from military service—but he was ill. The soldier issuing the papers told him to take the forms and board ship as quickly as possible, but not to tell anyone he was sick until after he was safely on board. He was told that the soldiers in France were dying like flies from a raging influenza, and only after his passage home was secured should he ask to be sent to sick bay.

After making a full recovery from the flu, Myron helped the ship's nurses with their chores in sick bay. He later claimed he became an expert at making beds and scrubbing floors, and it seems that his services did not go unnoticed. With a shipload of sick soldiers on their hands, the ship nurses were grateful for the towhead's help, and repaid him with extra food from the kitchen.

He fondly recalled his unit's reception as they came to port in New York Harbor, and loved to talk about the girls that met the boats, waving enthusiastically at the heros as they washed up to shore. He often raved about their beauty, claiming they were just as beautiful, if not more so, than the women who had waved good-bye to them just months earlier when they set sail for France.

Throughout the remainder of his life, Myron remained reticent concerning his war experiences, though I recall his accounts of the many friendships he made with French families. He used to tell of one family—just a man and his wife—whose three sons had all been killed in the war and the immense gratitude and generosity they showed the American soldiers. Myron would tell of the many privations endured by this couple—how wartime conditions had reduced them to poverty and hunger—yet he marvelled at the kindnesses they continually showered on the Americans, as the couple repeatedly offered to feed them when they barely had food enough for themselves.

Likewise, he occasionally described the forays into the surrounding French countryside made by soldiers looking for souvenirs and other war booty, an activity that would become a lifetime hobby. He remembered it as a popular pastime for overseas soldiers, occasionally mixed with horror when he and his companions would discover dead bodies, some of them fellow American soldiers who had perished in their common cause. The interest in war and war memorabilia was a lifetime interest for Myron, as he counted scouting for war booty among his personal hobbies, and often stole moments while working on well fires to scavenge the area for shrapnel and other mementos.

And thus did these military adventures leave an indelible mark on the young and impressionable man, as they provided him with strategic planning skills and encouraged him to nurture his talents for adaptability, invention, and improvisation according to immediate need. It might be said that Myron was a natural soldier and certainly his illustrious firefighting career would attest to that. He was usually forced to work till the brink of exhaustion and, drawing upon his military experiences, often used some form of artillery to execute offensive and defensive strategies against the burning enemies he battled.

See Appendix A, Myron Kinley's World War I Diary

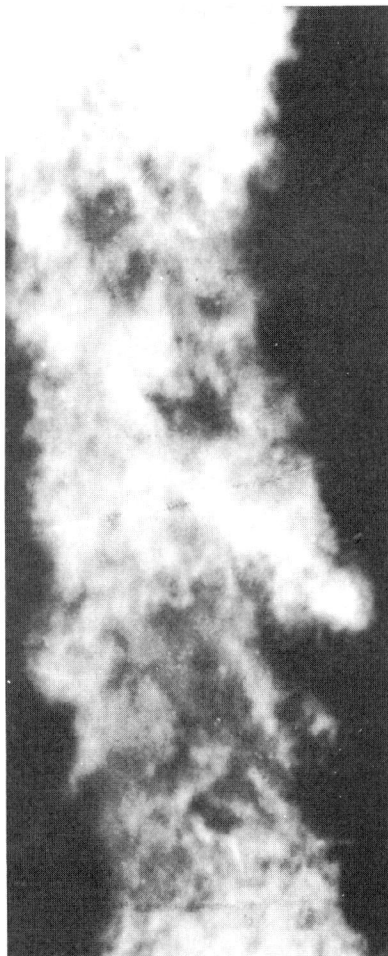

LIFE AS A FIREFIGHTER

BACK TO TULSA—THE M. M. KINLEY COMPANY

Home again from the battlefield, Myron returned to the California oil fields, where he and his coworkers eagerly listened to stories of the petroleum boom then taking place in the legendary oil lands of faraway Oklahoma. Telltale accounts of the amazingly productive wells were simply too much temptation for any self-respecting youngster with an entrepreneurial spirit, and it was not long before he and fellow well shooter, John Percival, formed a partnership and headed for the "oil capital of the world," where they went straight to work shooting wells.

Eager to resume life in the oil patch, Myron and John formed the Western Torpedo Company in Tulsa, only to find themselves unemployed by the end of the year. Unable to pay its mounting debts, the fledgling company folded and was forced to distribute its capital and machinery to employees in lieu of back pay. For his services, Myron received an old pickup truck and the company's tools. Myron loaded the tools in the old truck and drove alone to the oil fields looking for work, and thus began the M.

ABOVE: *Karl Kinley and John Percival. Tulsa, Oklahoma, ca. 1919.*
Karl (left) found work shooting wells in oil-rich Oklahoma.

The old Dodge. Tulsa, Oklahoma, ca. 1922. The Western Torpedo Company truck, used for shooting wells in the Oklahoma oil fields.

M. Kinley Company, still in existence today as the J. C. Kinley Company of Houston which, despite its humble origins, is internationally recognized as a leader in the design and development of outstanding oil field tools and provision of expert oil field services.

The troubled wells to which Myron was initially called were usually shooting jobs, only occasionally offering the added attraction of a burning well. Unable to lead the battle against these fires, he nonetheless eagerly participated in the fights against them, preparing for the day when he would direct crews of men against such infernos.

The time was the early 1920s, and Oklahoma well owners were wary of using explosives in firefighting, preferring instead the steam and mud method—a tedious and grueling task at best. But it was these early experiences that taught him valuable lessons in firefighting, and he later noted the Elk Hill fire in 1920 and the Bald Hill and Deep Rock fires in 1923—extinguished primarily by steam and mud—as some of the most important fires of his early career.

See Appendix B, List of Important Fires

THE CROMWELL FIELDS AND THE RISE OF EXPLOSIVES

Myron continued in this vein until 1923, a year full of new experiences that enhanced his life with both the responsibilities and rewards of family. Myron met and married Rowena Percival shortly after his move to Oklahoma. The couple was married in Tulsa in 1923, when Myron took Rowena and her two young sons and assumed the roles of both husband and father, roles which he served faithfully and dutifully until Rowena's death in 1957.

The young couple added to their small family late in the spring of 1929, when they adopted an infant daughter, Joyce, whom they raised with Rowena's sons, Jack and Dan. Jack and Dan later paid ultimate tribute to Myron's devoted parenting when, in 1933, they asked him to initiate adoption procedures and allow them to take the Kinley name. Dan later remarked that, "Jack and I felt he was acting as our father and the relationship should be formalized if he also would like it that way. Myron was pleased. We changed our name to his and the relationship as a parental one continued to grow over the years."

But as his rewards in the home multiplied, so did those in the oil field. Myron's first big break as an independent oil well firefighter came shortly after his marriage when two wells on the same lease in an Oklahoma oil field caught fire simultaneously. These wells lay in the vast Cromwell fields of Oklahoma, and it was Myron's successful fight against them that finally convinced the oil world of the superior efficiency of explosives in combatting oil well fires.

When the fires broke in early 1924, H. F. Wilcox, owner of the Cromwell wells, responded in the traditional manner and immediately ordered a tedious steam and mud war on the burning wells. Hearing of the Cromwell disaster, Myron fled to the scene and watched as oil crews, armed only with twelve obsolete steam boilers, embarked upon a long and costly struggle. Crews finally extinguished the first of the two burning wells after twelve days of continuous battle, when they drudgingly began preparations for the ensuing fight against the second blaze that promised to be equally difficult to conquer.

Myron mustered the courage to approach Wilcox to present his method of explosives as a more effective strategy against the second fire. Wilcox received Myron's theory with great skepticism and claimed that the dangers of explosives were too great to risk trying them against his wells.

Determined to test his theory in the Cromwell fields, the entrepreneurial Myron Kinley presented Wilcox with a deal the owner could not refuse. Myron promised Wilcox that he would extinguish the fire in two days using explosives. If he failed in his objective, the Wilcox company would owe him nothing, but if he succeeded, he would be paid a five hundred-dollar fee. And so a deal was struck between the two men.

Taking his brother Floyd as his partner, Myron immediately began his plan of attack. Myron ordered the first stage of the firefighting operations, demanding the immediate removal of all machinery and equipment near the fire. He then hired an old World War I Jenny airplane and, slowly circling the burning well, calculated the strength of the fire and located the "mixing chamber" where he would soon drop a charge of explosives. Within twelve hours Myron was once again in the plane, confounding spectators by stringing hundreds of feet of strong cable down through the fire and into the mouth of the well. What was their surprise when he then sent a load of gelatin explosives sliding down the cable into the mixing chamber, which he exploded from the air. Witnesses remember the incredible blast that followed, and the immediate silence of the deafening blaze.

In defiance of all expectations, Myron and Floyd Kinley earned their five hundred dollars in exactly eighteen hours, and in the process forever changed the method of oil field firefighting. Myron was only twenty-six years old and Floyd a mere twenty, but it was in that year of 1924 that the brothers established themselves in lifetime careers as professional firefighters.

NECESSITY IS THE MOTHER OF INVENTION—
A SIDELINE CAREER

The late twenties proved to be formative years for Myron. The M. M. Kinley Company enjoyed tremendous success, and the young Kinley family was blessed with many fond memories.

It was during the years between his marriage and 1930 that the M. M. Kinley Company developed a firm footing providing oil field services, as Myron continued to solicit well shooting jobs, tame wild wells, and work on burning oil field fires at every opportunity. Not only did these years provide Myron and his business with national exposure in practical oil field services; but they also encouraged him to invent, develop, and manufacture tools for use in well surveying and the correction of drilling and production problems.

And thus was Myron's second great talent—his incredible gift for invention and improvisation—given birth, and he embarked upon a sideline career as a mechanical engineer and inventor, leaving an indelible mark in the history of petroleum engineering by virtue of his tool inventions alone.

In his day-to-day field work, Myron continually encountered new production and drilling problems, many of them requiring unique solutions. However, as Myron gained exposure to such problems, he began to see similarities among them and to search for common solutions by developing specialized tools.

He spent the next years developing and perfecting equipment for use in production problems and began applying for patents as early as 1926.

And so Myron, with only an eighth grade education, developed national fame for an uncanny ability to visualize, predict, and correct problematic conditions hidden thousands of feet down a well hole. His abilities for invention and correction were tremendous and were recognized as such by many professional mechanical engineers, as he was often called upon to lecture to the Association of Petroleum Engineers and various professional geologic and petroleum societies throughout the nation.

These were definitely busy years for Myron and not a

moment was wasted. On the rare occasions when Myron was not in the fields, he was generally testing and refining his firefighting techniques and educating oil well owners and field crews alike in the use of explosives in oil field work.

Before his thirtieth birthday Myron was a reknowned expert in the use of explosives. Explosives were certainly Myron's tool of choice, and it was clear to all that he was an artist with a thorough understanding of his medium.

Although the first fire in the Taft fields, extinguished by Karl Kinley in 1913, used a crude bomb which exploded on impact, the refined Kinley technique used solid nitroglycerin bombs in gelatin form, as they were less likely to detonate on impact and were therefore more predictable and controllable.

Eye witness accounts testify to one of Myron's remarkable explosive feats as he tested a new nitroglycerin bomb. Myron hired a friend to take him up in an airplane from which he dropped the gelatin bomb. Observers held their breaths as they watched the bomb fall hundreds of feet to the earth, and shook their heads in disbelief when the nitroglycerin did not explode! The aviators then landed and Myron, to further prove the stability of his bomb, detonated it with a blasting cap and shattered the morning quiet with the jolt of the powerful explosion. Myron had proven the superiority of his gelatin bombs with a vivid demonstration that no one in attendance was likely to forget.

But the tireless Myron did not let the hectic pace of his professional life interfere with his young family, and the hallmark of these years would certainly be the cherished time he lavished on his wife and children during numerous carefree outings and family vacations. The bonds of family ties often took the Kinley family on the road, and a favorite person for visitation was always the notorious grandfather, Karl. It was during this time that Karl Kinley, who jokingly called himself "The Sire" in proud reference to his sons, retired from active employment in the oil fields, permanently settling in his native California. Myron and Karl relished their time together and Myron frequently took time from his busy schedule for family vacations to California to visit "The Sire." The two obviously enjoyed a very informal relationship, and were able to openly express their feelings and frustrations with each other, oftentimes resulting in humorous situations.

Dan Kinley later recounted a special memory of his father and Karl on one such California vacation in 1927. He fondly recalled a family outing to a movie in Hollywood, shortly after the debut of sound pictures. The movie shown was a new comedy, and Dan remembered Karl's unforgettable response to the film as he laughed uproariously throughout the show. Slightly annoyed by his father's loud laughter, Myron gently tried to quiet his father with a "shush," only to be silenced himself when Karl returned in a loud voice, "What the hell! I came here to laugh, didn't I?"

Jack Kinley also recalled funny family experiences from some of the long road trips they often made together. Jack's many fond stories reveal that, although family relations were unquestionably amiable and loving, there was absolutely no doubt as to who was the boss.

One of Jack's most vivid childhood memories was of a family car trip, taken when he was very young, not many years following Myron and Rowena's marriage. Jack remembers embarking on vacation with his mother and father, brother Dan, and a family friend, with the family's luggage strapped and tied to the top of the car. He remembers that, at some point in the day's travel, the friend's suitcase fell off the roof, requiring the Kinleys to backtrack for several miles along the highway in search of the missing bag.

In the meantime, Jack and Dan began to argue in the back seat, and Myron issued an authoritative "Be quiet!" from the front.

In obedience to his father's stern order, Jack settled in his seat and looked out the window for the duration of the day, from which vantage point he managed to spot the delinquent suitcase lying in the grass beside the road. In the back seat he struggled with the choice of whether or not to tell Myron of his find. But he had been told to be quiet and, knowing that his father meant what he said, elected to say nothing of his discovery.

Jack later recalled visiting Myron in Bel-Air upon his return from Guadalcanal in World War II, some twenty years after the incident, when the missing suitcase of that long-ago trip crept into the conversation. Jack chose that minute to tell Myron about having seen it as the family drove along desperately looking for it. He remembered Myron's easy nature and contagious laughter, and how they had a good and hearty laugh thinking about that trip.

Although Myron was able to schedule time out for his family, the unpredictable and demanding nature of his work made it difficult to spend individual time with his children on a day-to-day basis. But for Myron fatherhood was not a passive word, it was an active verb, and when he was unable to spend time alone with his family, he often took the boys with him on job-related excursions. Indeed, some of Jack and Dan's favorite memories are of their first airplane rides, cherishing the thrill of the wind as they soared, hundreds of feet above the ground, with their father in open biplanes as he circled and studied burning wells raging in the troubled fields below.

DISASATER ON THE SINCLAIR OIL FIELDS— THE STAMPER NO. 3 AND COLE NO. 1

Although Myron certainly pursued a variety of interests, he by no means forgot his main love—taming wild wells and fighting fires—and his reputation as an ace firefighter only grew as the decade neared its end. Panicked requests for his expertise poured into the Kinley Company office from across the country; among them the Sinclair fires, two of Myron's more famous battles.

The first of the fires blew out in October of 1929 in the Sinclair fields on the outskirts of Oklahoma City, when the Stamper No. 3 well struck gas unexpectedly and ignited in a deafening explosion. The vicious fire quickly grew into a raging blaze which could be seen from as far away as Texas, and seriously threatened the multibillion dollar Oklahoma City oil field.

The Sinclair Oil Company quickly realized the dangers of the fire and, desperately hoping to prevent its spread to nearby wells, paged Myron and Floyd Kinley to help with its demise. The fire on the Stamper No. 3 was by no means easy to extinguish, but true to form, the Kinley brothers were successful in their pursuit.

Upon arrival, Myron was granted full authority and responsibility for all field maneuvers against the burning well, and quickly prepared a strategy to direct his crew against the flames. Dressed in asbestos suits and protected by an iron shield, Myron and Floyd deftly moved towards the fire to remove all machinery and debris from the vicinity, while field crews sprayed them with a continual stream of water. The brothers then prepared a thirty-quart load of gelled nitroglycerin and, with the help of an improvised boom, placed it at the mouth of the well. After reaching cover they detonated the charge, killing the brutal fire within seconds.

At the Stamper No. 3, Myron and his partner, Floyd, amazed the Sinclair Company executives with incredible feats of cunning and daring. And, on April 29, 1931, when even bigger trouble blew in on the Sinclair Oil fields, the wizened executives knew exactly who to call.

The Cole No. 1 in Gladewater, Texas, made national headlines when ". . . a spark caused by tool friction suddenly turned a plenteous natural blessing into a howling inferno. Some of the workers managed to dodge out of the flames, two jumped for safety into the slush pit where they were boiled alive. The rest were quickly roasted. Fatalities, originally estimated at twelve, then nine, were finally put at seven, with two other men perhaps fatally burned (*Time*, May 11, 1931)."

The Kinley brothers were at the scene within hours, working at the toughest fire yet encountered in their careers. By their arrival on the first of May, the flames and smoke pouring from the burning well loomed threateningly over more than twenty miles of countryside.

Procedures at the Cole No. 1 began as normal, and oil crews were sent toward the blistering heat of the blaze to move surrounding equipment. In the meantime, structural problems in the casing delayed further action on the well. Myron and Floyd were faced with two loose kelly joints that blocked the well head, and thereby prevented them from ending the fire with a blast. They quickly went to work to dislodge these joints so that a load of nitro could be exploded over the well head, the fire killed, and the well tamed. These maneuvers were costly to the crews, as they tired the men and left them blistered and burned from the intense heat.

The Cole No. 1. Gladewater, Texas, 1931. ". . . a spark caused by tool friction suddenly truned the well into a howling inferno."

The task ahead of the crews was daunting, and several workers were severely injured. Myron himself suffered his first serious injury during the preliminary work at Gladewater when an iron beam fell on him, pinning him to the ground where he was almost burned to death by nearby flames. Myron was, however, saved from the flames by his brother Floyd, who heroically pulled him from under the beam and across the field to safety.

But even injury did not deter Myron from his duties on the field. With his foot in a temporary cast, Myron hobbled to the frontline on crutches, shouting orders and giving encouragement and comfort to the tired crews. When the crutches proved too slow and cumbersome, the charismatic war horse led the battle like a cavalry general, riding horseback to the front line to direct his fighting men. Only after the fire was out did Myron have his broken ankle properly treated, suffering for almost two weeks before going to a hospital where doctors rebroke and reset his leg.

Finally Myron was ready to end the battle with a final shot of nitro-glycerin. There was a problem in lowering the nitro into the well head, as the crews could not safely get close enough to place the explosives. Admittedly a problem for most people, this challenge was merely another opportunity for Myron to exercise his inventive genius, and he quickly commandeered the creation of his first hook, a tool that he would use on fires throughout the rest of his career.

The hook was crafted from discarded oil field pipe, and was designed to remove debris from the fire area and to place explosives at the mouths of burning wells. Myron's hooks were water-cooled to keep them from melting and to protect the charges of nitroglycerin that they transported, thereby making them especially useful in firefighting.

Using an early version of this hook, crews cleared the area of debris and lowered four fifty-quart barrels of nitroglycerin through the blaze and into the well head.

Gladewater, Texas, 1931. Myron, on crutches, directed crews in the fight against the Gladewater fire.

The crew. Gladewater, Texas, 1931. Left to right: Myron, Jobe, Punk, Pingalli. Man standing in background is unidentified.

When all was in place, Myron exploded the barrels with a blast that killed the great Gladewater fire, a fire that burned for over two hundred hours, consumed over three hundred thousand barrels of oil, and killed seven men.

See Appendix E, Cole No. 1, Gladewater, Texas

ROMANIAN BATTLEFIELD—THE MORENI NO. 160

The Sinclair fires were valuable testing grounds for Myron's great talent, but only whetted his insatiable appetite for excitement. Aways on the lookout for a challenging blaze, a well blew wild in the spring of 1929 that made headlines around the world and beckoned him across the sea to test his wits against its unquenchable flames. For the remainder of the year, Myron studied the burning Romagno-Americano Well No. 160, the Moreni well in Romania, through numerous newspaper and professional articles that seemed to never tire of the untamable blaze. The stubborn fire captured Myron's active imagination, and he soon determined that he would be the one to kill it.

Myron was fascinated with the frequent accounts of the devastation and strength of the Moreni inferno and yearned to help fight the mighty fire. Finally, after the fire had raged for over a

ABOVE: *The Moreni No. 160 as it looked when it first ignited. Romania, 1929.*

year, Myron packed his bags and made his first trip to Romania to study it first hand and to get himself hired for the job.

Upon his arrival, Myron met face-to-face with a fantastic and powerful blaze that lit the skies for seventy miles and was visible from as far away as Bucharest. Certainly a formidable task, he felt sure that he could conquer the hazardous blaze, as it was not altogether different from many of the fires he had fought in American oil fields.

The Romanian government proved kind to Myron but distrustful of his radical firefighting method, and balked at the very thought of using nitroglycerin against the uncontrollable well. Government representatives met with Myron, claiming too many lives and too much money had been lost to justify the dangers of using explosives. Myron persistently defended his approach, but the answer to his plea was always no. Seeing that he had little alternative, Myron returned home. But out of sight was not out of mind for Myron and he faithfully kept the Romanian well in his thoughts, always with the idea that he would return to snuff it out.

He spent the next year in the United States, rushing from job to job, putting out fires and taming wells. By the beginning of 1931 Myron had put out at least fifty well fires, and was the leading name in firefighting. He was quickly gaining international fame and his exploits in the oil field were the subject of a short motion picture.

In the meantime, the fire on the Moreni No. 160 still raged, daily becoming more dangerous and costly. The well had defied all attempts to kill it, and it only continued to worsen with no sign of burning out naturally. Still confident that he could help the Romanian situation, Myron decided once again to approach oil and government officials about working on the fire.

When he arrived in Romania, Myron knew that his time had come. The fire was wreaking havoc. In the two years since Myron's first visit the well had claimed more than fourteen lives and cratered like a volcano, leaving a gaping hole over two hundred feet across and almost seventy feet deep, with scores of smaller fires dotting the landscape.

Standard Oil executives and the Romanian government were desperate, and this time the persistent firefighter found the two

The Moreni crew. Romania, 1931. Myron furnished his own men to fight the Romanian blaze. Left to right: American Grady Chupp, Myron, and Romanian Costeca Luper.

parties ready and willing to do business. It was not long before a deal was struck. Under the terms of agreement, Myron had to successfully put out the fire and cap the well, or he would be paid nothing.

However, Romanian officials did not make Myron's job easy for him. He was allowed only two partners, and was charged with the added responsibility of capping the wild well. Nor was financial remuneration guaranteed, as it was completely contingent upon his triumph over the billowing well whose acrid smoke rose and lingered over the countryside like a spectre.

This time Myron was up against a monster. Never had a fire burned so long and hard as the Moreni No. 160, and Myron immediately knew that its strength and fervor demanded an approach unlike any other he had used. His first step was to attack the small fires surrounding the flaming crater one by one, until he had cleared the periphery and could approach the main blaze, pulling scrap metal and debris from the disaster area as he went. Myron then proceeded to fill the crater with liquid concrete kept cool by a constant spray of water and directed that two loads of nitroglycerin be prepared—one to be placed at the well head and the other in a tunnel that intersected the well.

With these loads Myron blasted the well and, on November 4, 1931—three hard months after his arrival—he forever silenced the deafening roar of flames that had burned continuously for nearly three years. Myron Kinley had stunned the world; he had done the impossible. The Moreni No. 160 was out. The mettlesome Kinley had proven that he, too, was a mighty force to contend with; that he was truly a "man without fear."

AT THE DRAWING BOARD—THE CALIPER

Myron capped the Romanian well in January, 1932, and returned home to life as usual with the family and the daily operations of the ever-growing M. M. Kinley Company. Naturally, he and his brother were busier than ever working on oil fires and wild wells; nevertheless, Myron still found plenty of time to dedicate to invention, and the next few years gave birth to his greatest mechanical contributions to the petroleum industry.

Despite a lifetime of developing tools, it was the invention of 1935 that established his lasting reputation as a mechanical engineer and earned him an article in the History of Petroleum Engineering.

Years in the oil field had given Myron ample opportunity to completely familiarize himself with literally hundreds of problems that either prevented him from successfully completing his work or resulted from it. As he had focused his career on firefighting, well shooting, and well surveying, his inventions centered primarily on solutions to problems often encountered in these activities.

From his earliest days in the Taft oil fields, Myron realized that well shooting, although absolutely necessary to increase or enable well production, altered the original measurements of the well hole. This oftentimes caused additional difficulties, as there was no reliable method to correctly remeasure the width of the shot hole or to accurately calculate the amount of cement needed to fill it.

Always a man to see a need and meet it, Myron settled down at the drawing board to remedy the problem. His goal—to develop an apparatus that would correctly measure the diameter of a shot well hole and enable engineers to determine the amount of cement necessary to properly and safely plug it.

After toying with the idea for years, it was 1935 when Myron emerged with his first model of the oil well caliper. This model was designed to measure the diameter of a blasted well hole, but was successful only in measuring dry holes and was useless in holes filled with oil, water, or mud. Despite its faults, the original caliper received much attention and, with some refinements, promised to be highly beneficial in well shooting and drilling.

The caliper. Tulsa, Oklahoma, 1938. Myron's caliper was displayed at the International Petroleum Exposition.

But Myron was not satisfied. In 1935 he packed up his family and moved the Kinley headquarters to Houston where he went right back to the drawing board to improve upon his first model. After some months of hard work, Myron proudly unveiled a surprise for the oil world—the oil well caliper redesigned to operate in fluid.

The new caliper met with success and received acclaim from the petroleum engineering world. The caliper was granted exhibition space at the International Petroleum Exposition of 1938 and was soon in use across the nation as a control mechanism and a tool to increase the efficiency of well shooting.

The usefulness of the caliper became more apparent as time went on, and soon was regularly employed to gather information about holes and constrictions in an oil well that was valuable in several production operations.

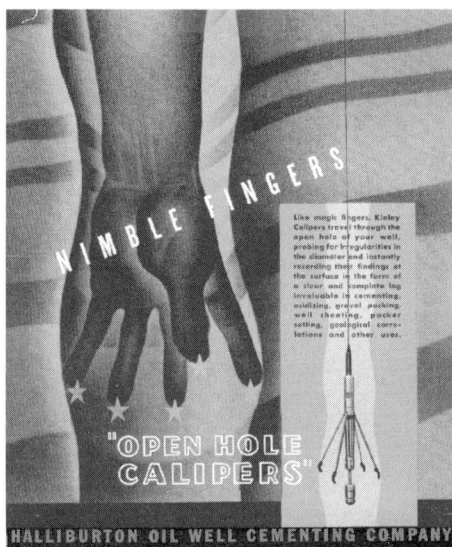

Like magic fingers, Kinley Calipers travel through the open hole of your well, probing for irregularities in the diameter and instantly recording their findings at the surface in the form of a clear and complete log invaluable in cementing, acidizing, gravel packing, well shooting, packer setting, geological correlations and other uses.

"OPEN HOLE CALIPERS"

HALLIBURTON OIL WELL CEMENTING COMPANY

The oil well caliper was in demand and sales of the product mounted. Myron, his hands in many pies, found himself increasingly unable to effectively manage the sales and marketing of his product. In 1940, Myron made additional revisions to the caliper, then entered into a sales agreement with Halliburton Oil Company on August 1. The terms of this agreement stipulated that Halliburton would sell and manage the caliper, paying the M. M. Kinley Company on a royalty basis. Finally, on January 1, 1947, the M. M. Kinley Company sold the caliper patents outright to the Halliburton Oil Company who then commercially offered the caliper service to the oil industry.

Despite their ages, Myron's inventions have proven to be somewhat timeless devices. Certainly the caliper was a landmark invention of the early oil industry, serving as a model for many measurement devices that would follow and as a testament to the creative genius of the inventor. But his devotion to improving and creating tools was only symptomatic of his lifetime dedication to oil field work in all of its facets—drilling, production, trouble shooting, and firefighting—which earned him international fame and an undying reputation for expertise in the petroleum industry.

See Appendix C, Excerpt from *The History of Petroleum Engineering* and Appendix D, "Caliper Well Logging" by William H. Farrand

FIREFIGHTING ON DISPLAY—THE INTERNATIONAL PETROLEUM EXPOSITION

The 1930s were nothing if not busy years for the Kinley brothers and their firefighting enterprise. The successful battle against the Romanian well in 1931 had brought Myron immediate international fame as an ace firefighter and the curious public was hungry to see the legendary Kinleys in action.

On invitation from the International Petroleum Exposition, Myron and Floyd were recruited to give a demonstration of their firefighting skills before thousands of curious onlookers. The Kinleys accepted the invitation and, in May of 1934, provided the high point of the eighth exposition with a fantastic display of their techniques for extinguishing oil fires.

For the demonstration, the Kinleys built a simulated derrick equipped with the usual drilling supplies and tools, and then had gas under high pressure piped to its floor. The derrick was ignited with a sudden whoosh, sending a tower of flames thundering

skyward which consumed the rig and deafened the crowd as it rose nearly one hundred feet into the air.

Myron and Floyd then donned their asbestos suits as they waited for the derrick to cave in. When the derrick collapsed to a pile of hot rubble, the brothers used grappling hooks to remove the burning debris. Myron then laid a charge of gelatinous nitroglycerin near the fire, and immediately extinguished the blaze by choking off its oxygen supply.

The spectators were thrilled. Never before had audiences witnessed such daring, and the demonstration was so well received that the International Petroleum Exposition invited the Kinley brothers for repeat performances throughout the rest of the decade, when the enormous crowds attracted to the popular display finally grew beyond control and the demonstrations had to be discontinued.

The Kinleys' first encore performance at the International Petroleum Exposition came in 1936. It is recorded as one of the most memorable events of the Expo and enjoyed tremendous attention from the local media. IPE histories later recorded the event, claiming that the pavilion was filled to capacity with excited onlookers who, at the end of the show, ". . . applauded the Kinleys thunderously after sitting for a moment in stunned silence (Walker, *The International Petroleum Exposition*, 1984)."

Back by popular demand, Myron Kinley returned once again to the oil show in 1938 ready to give eager onlookers the best show yet.

The *Tulsa World* referred to this event as "perhaps the most spectacular thing we've ever seen. . . . Tulsans who haven't seen it will be foolish to miss the second demonstration. . . . It's a hot sure-fire drama filled with high pressure entertainment."

Yearbooks of the International Petroleum Exposition written decades later proclaim the 1938 performance as one of the most

"spectacular events" of the 1938 Expo fair. True to expectations, Myron delivered an unparalleled performance of his incredible firefighting skills, dazzling a record-breaking audience whose "tumultuous applause . . . almost equalled the thunderous clap of the nitroglycerin."

However, the huge crowds attracted to the demonstrations soon became problematic. The firefighting show proved so popular that ". . . spectators crowded into the viewing stands in numbers greater than they could bear. During the evening performance of May 16, a section of the overburdened grandstand collapsed, tumbling spectators in every direction but causing only minor injuries (Walker, *The International Petroleum Exposition*, 1984)."

OFF-SHORE INFERNO—LAKE MARACAIBO, VENEZUELA

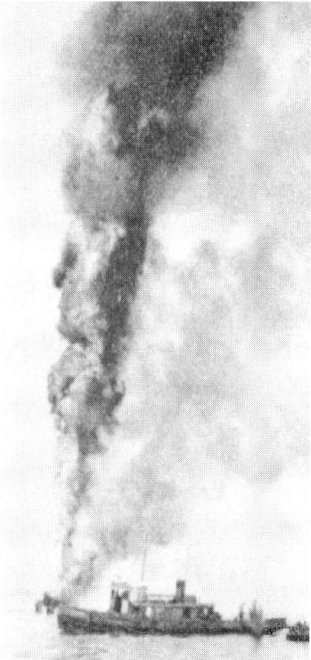

Fire on water. Lake Maracaibo, Venezuela, 1936.

etween inventions and firefighting demonstrations, Myron continued full speed ahead with his firefighting career. Now operating out of Houston, the M. M. Kinley Company was virtually flooded with desperate calls for help fighting deadly and vicious fires around the world.

The Kinleys were soon summoned in early 1936 to set another precedent in the history of oil well firefighting. After receiving an urgent cry for help from Largo Petroleum Corporation in Venezuela, the Kinley brothers set off to conquer the first off-shore fire of their careers and arrived to find onsite experts baffled by the ferocious blaze. The roaring fire in Lake Maracaibo placed entirely new obstacles in the paths of the crews working to control it, and it was soon obvious that traditional techniques of firefighting would not be adequate to kill this vibrant burner.

The battle waged on Lake Maracaibo was fought on untried territory, as it was one of the first wells to be extinguished and capped on the water. From the time the fire broke, it was clear that only Myron Kinley possessed the ingenuity to tread this ground, and he soon proposed a solution so unique it dazzled and amazed oil experts around the world.

The well owned by Largo Petroleum Corporation in Lake Maracaibo, Venezuela, caught fire three miles off shore in early 1936. The fire ignited and immediately grew beyond control, sending a two hundred-foot tower of flames rising above the water. Even the resourceful Myron was stumped when he arrived at the blazing lake, and was forced to let the fire burn while he and his partner, Floyd, contrived a strategy for war. After hours

Myron and Floyd Kinley moved a 25,000-pound oil derrick in one piece. Lake Maracaibo, Venezuela, 1936.

of consultation and tedious planning, Myron emerged with a startling and unprecedented scheme for his skirmish against the savage well.

For the first time in history, the Kinley brothers directed the transportation of a twenty-five thousand pound oil derrick in a single piece to a spot within six hundred feet of the flames. Never before had this been attempted, but the fire's precarious off shore position made it impossible to dissemble the derrick, move it in pieces, and reassemble it on site. With the new derrick in place, the Kinleys drilled a second well that cut into the base of the blaze, from which they pumped mud and water to the base of the fiery well and shut off the flow of oil. With its supply of fuel cut, the troublesome fire eventually died on the water, leaving welcome silence in place of the deafening roar of the blazing inferno and oil experts in disbelief of the daring feats accomplished by the Kinley brothers.

A CLOSE CALL—ACCIDENT AT BAY CITY

The Venezuelan victory only added to Myron's fame and prompted even more calls from vexed well owners. With little thought for his personal safety, Myron was quick to help with as many of these crises as he possibly could and, although he had not yet suffered serious injury, he realized that he risked death with each job he took. Indeed it was not long after the historic feats in Venezuela that Myron, by his own admission, came closest to death during the fray against the Bay City fire in Matagorda County, Texas.

Myron was summoned to Bay City late in 1936, and promptly arrived at the towering blaze ready to do battle. It was a fire much like any other, and operations against it were standard. By the time he appeared on the scene, the derrick had collapsed in a burning heap, strewing discarded pipe and equipment across the fields.

Men were immediately despatched to remove debris from the area. As with many fires, Myron and his seasoned crew encountered bits of stubborn scrap metal or stuck pipe which could not be moved with grappling hooks. The Bay City well was no exception, as there was a large drill pipe stuck over the well head that prevented the fire from being extinguished and, as he had done so many times before, Myron prepared a charge of explosives to remove the bothersome pipe.

Myron had just straightened up from his bent-over position when the shot he had prepared exploded unexpectedly, crushing his right leg and filling his entire right side with shrapnel. The brutal accident killed the man standing beside him, and left Myron so seriously injured that he spent an entire year and a half in recovery.

The unfortunate event had many repercussions—Myron's right leg was severely crippled and nearly paralyzed for the remainder of his life and was eventually the cause of later injuries, as his lame leg prevented his escape from danger. The injuries caused additional problems in his everyday life. He found himself unable to use his right leg for many mundane activities, and even had to have his cars specially rigged for left leg driving.

Myron was also left with a permanent limp that served as a constant reminder of the 1936 mishap.

Despite his obvious affinity for perilous situations, Myron did not consider himself exceptionally brave. Fighting fires was his way of life, and he enjoyed it to the fullest. He always managed to pull through these life-threatening experiences undaunted, stoically accepting the injuries without question and faithfully marching right back to his life's love—firefighting and capping wild wells. But the wounds Myron suffered did not leave him unchanged. With each affliction he was made acutely aware, not only of the danger and pain of his own job, but of suffering in its many forms. Indeed, it might be that Myron's exceptionally dangerous lifestyle helped to make him the sensitive man that he was—a man sincerely sympathetic to others' pain and dedicated to the alleviation of discomfort wherever he found it.

Myron always kept his wonderful humor despite conditions, and family stories tell of his hearty laughter and nearly unslakable appetite which shone through even in this dark hour. Immediately following the accident at Bay City, the inert Myron was sent to the Methodist Hospital in Houston for medical treatment, where he was immobilized with his right leg in a cast. Myron spent several months confined in the Methodist Hospital, but as his condition progressed, was eventually granted permission to spend a day at home with his family.

From his days in the Taft blacksmith shop and World War I, the blue-eyed blaze battler loved to eat good food, and was mighty displeased with the fare at the Methodist Hospital. After many weary months of hospital food, Myron rejoiced at a gourmet meal that Rowena fixed especially for him on his one day home. Doubtless, every bite of that dinner was delicious, but he never recovered from his surprise and delight that she had fixed him buttered artichokes, and he often recalled that meal at home as one of his most memorable and savory dinners.

Myron was finally discharged from Methodist Hospital and returned home where, with his leg in a cast, he was once again confined to his bed. By this time he was accustomed to being bedfast and the discomforts of his leg. However, the irritation of his right leg eventually surpassed normal aches and pains, and nearly drove him to distraction.

It was summer and the Houston weather was sultry. That alone was probably enough to make him miserable, but the leg in the cast began to itch, and the itching got worse and worse without letting up. Finally, it got so bad that he could no longer stand it without some sort of relief. So he called his nurse, Marvin, who dutifully cut a hole in the cast near Myron's ankle to see what the trouble was. Instantly, tiny red ants poured out of the cast, scurrying as fast as they could towards the daylight.

In astonishment Marvin said, "Why Mr. Kinley, there are ants in your cast."

"Ants?" exclaimed Myron.

And with his usual response to an undeniable need—whether ants or oil field equipment—he figured out a way to get rid of the little red devils. He asked for his cane and used it to tap on the cast from the top down to his ankle, and it was not long before the itchy pests were gone. He often told the story in later years, always with an unrestrained laugh as he remembered how the ants fled as he tapped on the cast.

However, times of injury were times of stress for the entire family, and Myron never ceased to show his tender emotions during these periods of trial. His daughter, Joyce Knoble, remembers that his accidents and hospitalizations took an exacting toll on everyone.

She further recalls Myron's vivid display of love for his family in these times of tension, as his care and concern for them caused him to shed tears before them all.

Undoubtedly, Myron's life as a firefighter constantly threatened his life and undermined his health. But it was all in a day's work for the old war horse. He accepted the challenges and risks of his job as a necessary evil and, despite his injuries, his zeal for and faith in firefighting never flagged. The Bay City accident was a tragedy but, thankful for his life, Myron continued to pursue his calling.

Brothers and partners. Edinburgh, Texas, February, 23, 1938. Myron and Floyd laid plans to shoot and cap the Davenport Well in the La Blanca Fields. It was the last job they completed together.

GOODBYE TO A BROTHER AND PARTNER—
THE DEATH OF FLOYD KINLEY

True, Myron had almost been killed at Bay City and suffered crippling wounds from the accident, but no one could deny that the Kinley brothers had been blessed with tremendous good fortune for the eighteen years they had been in business. But in March of 1938, the Kinleys met with more than an accident—they suffered a family tragedy when Floyd was mortally wounded while fighting a fire in Goliad, Texas.

The Dreir No. 1 blew wild during the first week of March, catching fire soon after. Windward Oil
Company, the owners of the well,
put in an urgent call to Floyd at his
Tulsa office, asking for his expertise
to extinguish and cap the wild well.
Floyd arrived with Myron at the
Goliad oil field within hours, where
they quickly noticed that the Dreir
No. 1 was a fairly standard blaze,
much like dozens of other fires they
had snuffed out over the years.

Together the brothers decided to
begin preliminary work on the well.
As Myron had not yet fully recovered from his injuries at Bay City,
Floyd assumed control over the field
work and, with a crew of three men,
began to clear the field of discarded
metal and pipe.

*Floyd and Marguerite Kinley,
ca. mid-1930s.*

Floyd was busy clearing the derrick floor when a sudden gust
of pressure drove a forty-five-foot kelly joint loose, blowing it out
of the well. When the white-hot debris fell it landed directly on
Floyd, crushing his skull and burning his body.

Myron witnessed the horrible event and, despite his crippled
leg, hurried into the flame to help with the rescue. The rescue
team miraculously managed to drag Floyd out of the fire while he
was still alive, and immediately rushed him to the nearest hospital
in Victoria. But his wounds were mortal, and doctors were helpless to reverse his condition. Distraught by the tragic event,
Myron kept vigil at his brother's bedside, where he remained until
Floyd's death on March 12.

The disaster at Goliad caused Myron much personal grief.
Throughout their lives Myron and Floyd had been companions
and trusted confidants. For the final three years of their adventures together they were separated by distance—Myron lived in
Houston while Floyd resided in Sperry, Oklahoma—but they had
shared their lives and work, growing closer as they labored

together as brothers and partners. And, it seemed, in one quick, terrifying instant Myron had lost it all.

Myron had loved his brother dearly and the memory of Floyd's death never left him, but neither did it cause him to even consider leaving the firefighting business. Rather, he pursued his career with whole-hearted dedication, almost in tribute to the work he and his younger brother had undertaken together.

Like no other event, the Goliad tragedy left him with a true and complete understanding of his own mortality and the dangers of his job. But he bravely accepted those risks and, with an undying faith in the importance of his work, continued without question.

WORKING ON THE RAILROAD—THE GRETA FIRE, TEXAS

T rue to the Kinley legacy, Myron was quick to get back to work in the oil fields and, within a year of Floyd's death, was called to handle a blowout he later claimed was his longest and toughest job.

A well near Refugio, Texas, went wild on June 19, 1936, and, three years later when Myron was finally hired for the job, had erupted into a crater and destroyed a nearby highway and a right-of-way on the Missouri-Pacific Railroad. The burning well, widely known as the Greta Crater, had become a gaping hole in the ground whose violent and costly leaks daily threatened the owners with bankruptcy.

Hired by the Missouri-Pacific Railroad in a last-ditch effort to temper the indomitable well, Myron arrived in Greta on February 25, 1939, to a gaping gorge over six hundred feet in diameter and more than seventy feet deep, completely filled with water. Myron's crews made four attempts to pump the water out, only to have the well ignite from escaping gas with each effort.

Experts on the scene reasoned that there was a "doodle-bug hole" at the bottom of the well, where hidden debris was causing sparks that relit the fire whenever the water level neared bottom. With deft maneuvering, crews eventually cleaned all excess mate-

The crater. Greta, Texas, 1939. The well erupted into a crater, more than 600 feet wide and filled with muddy salt water. The eruption destroyed a nearby highway and railroad right-of-way.

Pumping the water. Greta, Texas, 1939. Water was pumped from the crater into ditches running for two miles on both sides of the Missour-Pacific right-of-way.

Measuring the water. Greta, Texas, 1939. Workers entered the crater to measure the depth of water. The remains of the Missouri-Pacific railroad track, destroyed 2½ years earlier, can be seen in the background.

The well reignites. Greta, Texas, 1939. A "doodle-bug hole" in the crater hid debris that caused sparks and relit the well whenever the water level neared bottom.

Preparing the blast. Greta, Texas, 1939. The crew sprayed a steady stream of water on themselves and the equipment, as the man on the right (with hood) readied the explosives and carried the blast to the fire.

The explosion. Greta, Texas, 1939. Crews shot the well, but the load of nitro was not enough to snuff the stubborn blaze.

The night sky. Greta, Texas, 1939. The Greta fire lit the night skies for more than three years before its flames were finally extinguished in November 1939.

rials from the doodle-bug hole, and once again pumped the water from the crater into ditches running for two miles on both sides of the Missouri-Pacific right-of-way.

But the water level and repeated ignitions were only two of the obstacles thrown in Myron's way. On September 18, after seven months of grueling labor on this stubborn well, the crew hit an underground spring that flowed water directly into the hole, and prevented the tired workers from capping the well. Myron built a cofferdam to reinforce that side of the hole and keep the unwanted moisture out of the well. With that grand gesture he was able to finish the job some nine months after he started, when he capped the well late in 1939.

His perseverance paid off for all involved. Admittedly not his most glamorous job, the Greta fire made Myron Kinley a millionaire and saved the fledgling owners from bankruptcy. With his conquest he was paid twenty-five thousand dollars in cash from the Missouri-Pacific. As additional payment, Myron was given a lease on twenty acres in the oil field which he later sold to a drilling syndicate for a 25 percent interest in the royalties. The lease proved to be a lucrative move for Myron, as the drillers later struck oil with a well that produced for over twenty years.

The fame of the Greta fire served yet another purpose—it made insurance companies realize the tremendous financial losses resulting from oil well fires and the necessity of hiring professional firefighters to minimize those losses. It was in large part due to the Greta fire that insurance companies began to offer packages much like the pioneer deal offered by Metropolitan Salvage Corporation, whose policies automatically entitled holders to the firefighting services of the M. M. Kinley Company in the event of an oilfield fire.

WORKING FOR WOMEN—THE NO. 4 RIGNEY

The date was July 17, 1944, when two frantic women rang the M. M. Kinley Company office needing immediate help with a wild well. Mr. Kinley returned their call within an hour, promising to arrive at the blowout within a day. True to his word, Myron arrived the next morning at the well in Oklahoma's Cement fields near Chickasha.

But it was not Myron's first trip to Chickasha to help these ladies, as he had dropped by once before in 1941 for a quick job on a lease held by Little Nick Oil Company.

It was then, on a sunny afternoon late in the autumn of 1941 that I got my first glimpse of Myron Kinley. At that time I was working as office manager of the Little Nick Oil Company and was onsite at the troublesome well when Mr. Kinley arrived.

Now most people in the oil business in the year 1941 knew the Kinley name, but until he was called in to work on that shallow gas well, I had never heard of him. I had been told only that a wild well expert had come to help with the well, and then I was told some stories of his great adventures that made me curious indeed to see him.

When I arrived at the scene, John Nichlos, owner of the Little Nick Oil Company, pointed out the legendary well tamer. He directed my eyes to the derrick floor, where three men stood with their backs turned to me, diligently guiding casing pipe into the well hole. I was surprised to learn that one of the men was in fact the notorious expert, but later discovered that he was well-known for his willingness to work right alongside the crews, never asking an employee to do work that he would not do himself.

As it turned out, our little gasser was not much of a wild well, as wild wells go. Myron quickly sealed the gas leak and took off for his next job, but that first brief encounter with the world-famous well tamer was not to be the last.

In September of 1942, a year after Myron's visit to Chickasha, the Little Nick Oil Company suffered a tragic blow when John Nichlos died unexpectedly. Overnight, and without warning, Marjorie Nichlos and I assumed ownership and control of the small business. Almost immediately we were faced with a pivotal decision—either to drill a new well or risk losing a valu-able lease. We had confidence in the potential productivity of the lease, and decided to drill a new hole.

We named the new well the No. 4 Rigney and began drilling in mid-May of 1944. After several days of drilling we decided to abandon the well as a dry hole if we did not strike oil by 5,500 feet. Suddenly, at 5,492 feet, the well blew wild, spewing gas sky-ward. On that first day, we watched the well in fear as the white column of gas, wavering candle-like above the well, turned black against the night sky.

Although Mrs. Nichlos and I surely didn't know what to do, we did know who to call, and we promptly put in a message to the M. M. Kinley Company, requesting Myron's expertise in this matter.

The second time I saw Myron Kinley was on July 18, 1944, when he came, a knight in shining armor, to the aid of the two damsels in distress. The power of his presence on the crews was indescribable. From the moment he arrived we were trans-formed. His self-assured calm completely converted us from panic-stricken amateurs into a cohesive team, confident that the well could and would be brought under control.

We all drove to the lease together, where Myron walked to the screaming well and sized up the situation. He returned some time later to present a solution to our problems. We then went to the car to discuss the well and as we did so, he smiled and, his lively blue eyes atwinkle, confided that this job marked a personal first for him—he had never before worked on a well for a "couple of women."

We soon discovered that the drill pipe had been damaged in the blowout, spitting a mixture of mud and gas over the rig and upwards into the sky. The sight of mud spewing into the sky abrubtly ended all hopes of controlling the well with traditional well taming techniques, and our disheartened group listened in a mixture of fear and excitement as the renowned expert before us proposed a daring and risky solution to our malady. He advised us to drill a directional well named the No. 4-A, a well that would intersect the No. 4 Rigney and through which we could pump mud into the Rigney to stop the flow of gas.

Directional well drilling in 1944 was an uncommon and cost-

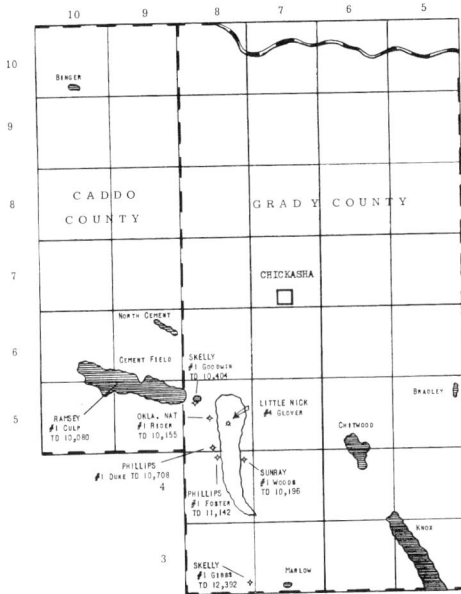

ly tactic in controlling wells and was used only as a last resort. In fact, the No. 4-A was to be the first such well drilled in Oklahoma, and promised to present our crew—novices in such matters—with a whole new world of drilling problems. Were it not for Myron's steely resolve and unshakable faith in the venture, we could not have mustered the courage to embark on this journey into the unknown.

Our fledgling group at the Little Nick felt over-whelmed by the task, but with little alternative, placed our entire trust in Myron's expertise and immediately undertook to move the derrick and drilling equipment from the No. 4 Rigney to the new site, taking every precaution not to ignite a fire above the gassing well.

However, once the equipment was transported, the gas blowing wild above the No. 4 Rigney posed great risks to the new well. So, ironically enough, on the advice of the great firefighter himself, we decided to ignite the No. 4 Rigney and let it burn while we drilled the directional well.

Now Myron had left Chickasha some weeks before to help another desperate well owner with a wild one, and we were on our own. True, he had told us to light the well, but he had neglected to propose a method of igniting the gas from a safe distance. Needless to say, we were dumbfounded as to how we could set fire to the No. 4 Rigney, so we pooled our brilliant minds to birth our first (and we thought clever) strategy to set the rig afire with a thunderous boom that would reverberate for miles across the Oklahoma countryside.

During the brain-storming, someone suggested we shoot Roman candles into the well, and the sparks from the fireworks would turn the column of gas into a tower of smoke and flames.

The more we thought about the plan, the more we liked it. It was August, and fireworks left over from the Fourth of July could still be found in town, so we quickly sent a man to buy a supply of roman candles. However, the man we assigned to the important errand was apparently so confused in all of the excitement that he mistakenly bought skyrockets instead of the desired Roman candles. When we fired the skyrockets, they went every direction except towards the well, and left us back at square one.

Other ploys were discussed, though none as humorous as the Roman candles. Finally, we decided to procure a fuzee—an obscure tool used on railroads and looking somewhat like a candle. The drilling superintendent got the much desired tool, lit it, took it towards the gas flow and threw it into the well, running to safety like the devil himself was at his heels. And finally, with a thundering roar and an earth-shaking jolt, the gas yielded to the fire.

After drilling on the No. 4-A began, it was soon evident that we were not going to be successful in opening a channel to pump mud into the wild well. We did the only thing we knew to do—we put in a call to Myron's office and asked for his help once again.

This time Myron arrived at the Cement fields greeted by a flaming well, but was encouraged by the progress of the last few months. Myron reasoned that the No. 4 Rigney could now be tamed through the original hole and, using a mere thirty quarts of gelled nitroglycerin, amazed us all as he blasted the well, pinching back the gas flow until it made only dry gas. Then, exactly as he had guessed, the well accumulated fluid and ultimately drowned itself out. And that is how the illustrious Myron Kinley so nobly helped two ladies save a well which, despite a discouraging beginning, eventually struck oil and became a lucrative and productive hole after all.

On May 26, 1944, the spectre of billowing smoke, hovering over the Cement oil fields and haunting the countryside for miles, was snuffed out for good. We lived with that blaze for ten months, during which time I grew to love the fire, even if I didn't understand it. As the well continued to burn, it became for me a thing of beauty, and was no longer a dreaded enemy. As it illumined the skies it served as a beacon for airplanes flying by night, and was a constant source of interest, conversation, and speculation by all who watched the towers of smoke waft over the countryside.

The fire was a source of indescribable beauty. The colors of the flames changed constantly as atmospheric conditions changed, and I could watch it smolder endlessly without tiring. The colors I remember most were the vibrant and living golds, the lilacs, and the pale, pale greens, much like a sunset I saw many years later while standing on Waikiki Beach.

Nor was I the only living creature that loved the fire. Several times at night, deer would come, two and three at a time and stand gazing in fascination at the fire before them. One evening I drove to the lease to watch the fire, only to find six owls perched on the wire fence leading to the well. They were not at all alarmed by my presence—they were too busy blinking at the brilliant and mysterious light. They sat motionless on that fence, except for their blinking eyes, and it was at that moment that I felt the intense power, excitement, and majesty of an oil well fire, and understood the passion that drove Myron to a fire wherever it might be.

The end of a story of another Successful Crater Job

LITTLE NICK OIL COMPANY No. 4 RIGNEY
CEMENT, OKLAHOMA, FIELD

M. M. KINLEY COMPANY
PHONES: DAY OR NIGHT K 3-1221   RESIDENCE K 3-3649
P. O. BOX 6177, HOUSTON 1, TEXAS

A BURNING SENSATION—ACCIDENT IN VENEZUELA

Although a trying experience for the Little Nick Oil Company, the No. 4 Rigney was just another day's work for Myron Kinley. Those were indeed busy days for Myron and no sooner had he put our fire out than he escaped to his next assignment where, undoubtedly, some frantic well owner eagerly awaited his arrival.

The phones at the M. M. Kinley office rang constantly, and it was obvious to Myron that he needed some additional help servicing and marketing his products. His son Dan, just home from Harvard Business School, was drafted for the job in 1943 and established the D. D. Kinley Company in Corpus Christi, Texas. Under the terms of his agreement with Myron, Dan was to service the tools in the South Texas area and, when Myron was working on a blowout, he would call Dan to help with field work.

They continued working in this way with great success until 1945. It was in that year that Dan noted Myron's increasing hesitance to call him out on those dangerous jobs. Although firefighting was a fine life, strong paternal instincts urged Myron to protect Dan and his young family from the very real dangers of the business.

Then one fateful day in 1945, an urgent plea for help came over the wire from Venezuela. A well had gone wild and owners were in desperate need of Myron's assistance. Myron accepted the assignment unquestioningly but, almost in premonition of the tragedy to follow, called Dan, telling his son that he would not be helping with this blowout. Myron also made out a will before leaving and left instructions for legal proceedings in the event of an accident.

Myron arrived at the wild well and, dragging his lame leg behind him, directed proceedings to clear the area and stop the escaping gas. Despite every precaution, fire erupted on the well while moving equipment from the vicinity and, without warning, the site was immediately engulfed in red-hot flames.

Since his injury at Bay City, Myron had always known that it was only a matter of time until his bad leg would be tested in a real emergency. Dan recalled Myron's remark that he always wondered if he would be able to run from danger if he really had to and, in 1945, he got the unfortunate opportunity to find out.

With the mighty roar of ignited gas, the crew scattered, leaving Myron alone in the field. He tried to run from the searing flames, but could not. Held back by his crippled limb and his heavy wet clothing, the heat of the blaze almost steamed him to death. But Myron never lost his senses, and he quickly spotted a tractor that he could use as shelter from the spreading fire. As he desperately walked to the tractor, his backside caught fire, leaving him severely burned, his back a mass of burn scar tissue.

Lucky to be alive, Myron spent the next six weeks lying on his stomach in a Venezuelan hospital until finally he was released and flown to Houston, where he was again hospitalized for a full recovery. Family and well wishers flocked to the Houston hospital to visit him. Dan recalled his first visit with Myron after the accident and his loving father's words of greeting: "Well, Dan, I don't want to take you on any more of these jobs." Dan remembers this moment as a demonstration of love, as Myron fired him from their work together and prophetically encouraged him to sell his business in Corpus Christi. Dan obediently listened to his father's wise counsel and returned to Harvard Business School, permanently ending his career in the oil business. Dan later appreciated Myron's advice even more, as the man who bought the D. D. Kinley Company died less than a year later when he blew himself up while preparing a charge of nitroglycerin.

Despite his injuries, Myron never lost his vitality. His amazing love of life actually turned the tragedy into a time of thanksgiving; and some of the fondest family memories are of Myron's slow recovery from his burns. His children still remember this period as a rare respite from the demands of business, during which time he took full advantage of every opportunity to lavish his attention on his family. Although immobilized by a body cast and confined to bed, Myron relished every chance to play with his grandchildren and hold his newborn granddaughter, Karen, whom, as his recovery progressed, he often babysat.

But as time dragged on, Myron made more assertive efforts to seek out what activity he could find. Definitely a restless sort, Myron always liked to be where the action was. It happened that one summer evening, there was a gathering downstairs that grew rather loud and the merry sounds of laughter and conversation floated up to him in the upstairs bedroom where he was imprisoned. Unable to stand it any longer, Myron deftly managed to pull some nearby clothes over his body cast and wriggle out of bed and onto the carpeted stairs. His gift for improvisation shone in its full glory as he proceeded to convert his cast into a sled, slip-sliding down the stairs smack into the midst of the evening festivities on the ground floor. Myron was certainly received as the honored (and unexpected) guest of the evening, and he revelled with his friends until the end of the party when willing and able helpers were recruited to carry him back to his sick bed.

But his good humor and natural optimism were not enough to shake the lingering effects on his physical and emotional well-being. Months of intensive hospital care could not repair the mass of burn tissue that covered his torso. For years afterward, Myron was self-conscious and somewhat embarrassed of his appearance. He was hesitant to bare his scarred back until one day when swimming with the young son of a close family friend. Expecting the child to be appalled by the burn tissue, Myron was surprised and delighted that the youngster actually envied his battle-worn body, seeing his scars as physical proof of courage and heroism. From that day forth, he no longer viewed his wounds with shame.

Despite the happy ending, the accident was undoubtedly a humbling ordeal for the brave firefighter and a constant reminder of his mortality. But if he was afraid he did not show it and, as soon as the Venezuelan burns were healed, he took off on more adventures, fighting flames and taming wells as he went.

WESTWARD HO!—GOING TO CALIFORNIA

T he years following the Venezuelan accident were years of change for Myron and, after more than ten years in Houston, he and his wife prepared to move West where they might possibly find some spare time to enjoy together. In 1946, Myron took preliminary steps to slow his frantic pace when he hired his son, Jack, to manage sales, patents, tool development, and marketing for the M. M. Kinley Company. Also in that year Myron took a formal assistant, a young firefighter by the name of Paul "Red" Adair. Red worked for Myron for the next dozen years, during which time he learned the firefighting and well taming business.

With Jack and Red Adair to help operate his Houston-based businesses, Myron decided in 1949 to return to his native

ABOVE: *Myron Kinley (right) and Red Adair, ca. 1950s.*

*Myron and grand-
daughter, Lucie Knoble.
Bel Air, California,
March 1955.*

California. During the course of his career, family time had grown less frequent and he now made time for a long over-due outing with his wife and daughter. Myron packed up Rowena and Joyce, loaded them onto an excursion boat, and whisked them away to Catalina Island where they took a brief vacation before house hunting in Bel Air.

As an adult, Joyce recalled this trip as one of her most cherished memories of her father. She remembered the wonderful time she had with him, staying at the famous old hotel and strolling leisurely through the town. He was a gallant and gentle man, and showered his daughter with his undivided attention and companionship as they went horseback riding in the hills and ate in the local seafood restaurants.

The Kinley family located a house and, in 1950, Myron settled back to enjoy his hiatus from the business world from his luxurious new home on Bel Air Road. Perhaps this extended break was simply too much rest and relaxation for an energetic man so used to being on the go. Needless to say, his initial respite at age fifty-two was short-lived and with the casual comment, "I guess I'll quit when they take me out in a box," he returned to his beloved business with renewed fervor.

Though field fires were on the wane, the blowout business boomed as oil companies began to use deeper drilling technologies that resulted in tremendous gas pressures and, more often than not, wild wells in need of a taming hand. Eventually, the

Myron Kinley, June 3, 1951.

marked increase in physically demanding blowout jobs took its
toll on the aging entrepreneur, leaving him bankrupt of both ener-
gy and time to devote to the other endeavors of the M. M. Kinley
Company. Finally, in 1951, an agreement was consolidated
between Myron and Jack, a graduate of Cal-Tech, Harvard
Business School, and Massachusetts Institute of Technology. Jack
Kinley bought the M. M. Kinley Company from Myron and
reestablished it as the J. C. Kinley Company, while Myron
retained his blowout and firefighting business. Under this agreement, the J. C. Kinley Company gained control of and responsibility for the patents held by the M. M. Kinley Company,
supervised tool development, production, and servicing, and
directed the sales and marketing of these products and services.

For the remainder of his career, however, Myron remained an
integral authority in the J. C. Kinley Company, and participated
in tool development and patenting as much as he was able.

Finally, with the responsibilities of patents and tools placed in
trusted hands, Myron was free to pursue his own adventures to
his heart's content. And so he did, as the exciting jobs of the next

few years sent him to nearly every continent. He regularly made headlines around the world, and reports on his magnificent work literally took over the files. Fascinated and adoring audiences from across the globe read articles about this daring man with intrigue. As stacks of fan mail rose skyward like the towering flames he conquered, it was clear that Myron had truly become an international celebrity.

EDITION NUMBER FOUR

My Weekly Reader

Vol. XXXV   Week of October 5-9, 1955   No. 4

Fire Fighters on Land and Sea

A "little squirt" is a good fire fighter on a ship.

Airport fire fighters try out a new "crash truck."

FIRE FIGHTERS on ships are as important as fire fighters in towns. The *America* is one of our biggest ships. It has 38 fire fighters on every trip.

The ship fire fighters are on duty night and day. Some of them stay on the ship when it is in harbor. The ship is guarded against fire at all times.

Some ships carry their own fire trucks. Aircraft carriers have fire-fighting jeeps. The sailors call them "little squirts."

A fire-fighting jeep on a carrier can pump water or "bean soup." This soup is a sticky foam. It has millions of tiny bubbles in every gallon. It makes a thick blanket over anything on fire—even burning gasoline and oil. This

—— MY WEEKLY READER Diagnostic Sli

Meet Some People in the News

A fireproof suit is a help in fighting oil fires.

Mr. Kinley Blows Out Fires

Myron Kinley has put out 300 of the world's most dangerous fires. They were burning oil wells. Mr. Kinley has put out oil well fires in all parts of the United States and in ten other lands.

Fire-fighter Kinley put out the world's worst oil well fire. It was in Romania, a land of eastern Europe.

This well had been burning for almost three years when Mr. Kinley was called. Ten men had been killed trying to put out the fire.

Even Mr. Kinley had trouble with this fire. He set off a powerful explosive near the fire. The explosive blew out the fire as you would blow out a candle. The trouble was that the fire would not stay out. Mr. Kinley kept trying. He worked for three months. Finally he put out the fire and kept it out.

Mr. Kinley invented most of his fire-fighting "tools." One is a water-cooled "arm"

to put explosives close to a fire. This arm is made of pipes. It is fastened to a tractor. The arm is as long as three automobiles.

The explosive is put at the end of the arm. The tractor pushes it into the fire. When everything is ready, the tractor backs away, leaving the explosive. Everybody near by runs. There is a roar and a puff and the fire is out.

School Goes to the Desert

Mimi, Bent, and Astrid Schmidt-Nielsen will soon be in the Sahara Desert, in Africa. They will spend a year there with their parents. Their mother and father are going to find out how camels live in the desert.

Bent and his sisters will be out of school for a year. They will not have a year's vacation. Schoolbooks are going with the children. Teachers will help them by mail.

When the children come back, they will know this year's lessons. They may know even more. They may know some camel secrets!

Mimi, Bent, Astrid, and their mother pack books.

*New Guinea,
n.d.*

LA COLONNA DI FUOCO

*Il pozzo metanifero n. 2 di Bordolano è, si
dice, il più potente d'Europa; ma ha co-
minciato dispettosamente, incendiandosi.*

*Po Valley, Italy, ca.
1950. Myron made
headlines in Italy
when he arrived to
fight the Po Valley
fire.*

Lacq, France, ca. 1950s. Myron made French news when called to extinguish a fire in the Pyrénées Mountains.

MYRON KINLEY, l'homme qui a su maîtriser LE PUITS 3 DE LACQ

LEFT: *Pakistani fire, n.d.* BELOW: *Eastern Pakistan, n.d. Triumphant over the Pakistani blaze, Myron (in the fore) supervised cleanup operations.*

DESERT DEMON—NAFT SAFID, RIG 20

No sooner had Myron resurfaced from his trial retirement than he was called to one of the most brutal and tedious battles of his long career, this time fought under the burning sun of the Persian deserts. Never before in that country's fifty-year history of drilling had a well caught fire, and when the Rig 20 ignited, officials of the Anglo-Iranian Oil Company knew they faced a monster. Helpless to act on the fire, they knew who to call, and hastily summoned the world-renowned expert, Myron Kinley.

The phones were busy on Wednesday, May 2, 1951, but when Myron received the emergency call from overseas, he dropped everything and boarded the first flight that would lead him from his comfortable Bel Air home more than eight thousand miles away to distant and mysterious Abadan. After four days in the air, Myron arrived in Abadan and was whisked away to the rich

ABOVE: *The Desert Demon. Iran, 1951.*

A **BP** *film*

Edited and Produced by
VERITY FILMS Ltd.

for the Anglo-Iranian Oil Company, Limited

Photographed by
MARTYN WILSON

oil fields of Naft Safid, deep in the Persian hill country, where he would match wits against the demon of the Iranian desert and his work would be immortalized in the film, Rig 20, winner of the Venice Film Festival of 1952.

As crewmen worked to routinely remove a stuck drill pipe from the well hole, the well suddenly ignited, sending a flame shooting more than a quarter mile into the sky. Eighty hours later, Myron arrived to find a raging inferno with ground temperatures of over 250° F, completely unapproachable by standard means.

Myron immediately knew that the Rig 20 was no ordinary fire, and quickly set about designing special tools and equipment to protect the men from the flames and intense heat. Myron's first step was to devise a mobile shelter, behind which the men would hide as they approached the blazing derrick. After preparing the shelter, he directed work to build his hallmark tool, the water-cooled hook, designed to remove equipment from the area.

Extended booms removed debris from the fire area. Iran, 1951.

Firefighters took cover behind the moveable shield as they approached the blaze. Iran, 1951.

But merely having the tools did not mean Myron and his men could begin work on the well. The intense and suffocating heat of the Naft Safid desert made any approach towards Rig 20 impossible without a steady and sure supply of water to cool equipment and protect crews. Myron and the crews he commanded were forced to locate the nearest sufficient water supply and quickly develop a piping system to deliver water to the fire.

They soon located a dam site in the nearest river, and began preparations to pipe water a distance of twenty-two miles to the front line at Rig 20. Having secured a constant and reliable water supply, crews were ready to begin work on the intimidating tower of flames.

Unable to work during the heat of the day, crews emerged under cover of the cool desert nights. Hidden behind the moveable shield and cooled with steady streams of water, disciplined workers slowly crept toward the fire, methodically removing debris as they went.

But the fire proved too tough for the work of mere men, even those protected by the aegis of the moveable shield. Although a clever device, the equipment actually threatened the men's lives as it deflected the white-hot flames and sent them shooting unpredictably towards other workers, and was ultimately an unsuccessful tool for clearing the well head. Fortunately, however, the master strategist had prepared for such obstacles and had the solution ready at his disposal. Using the ever-adaptable water-cooled hook, Myron placed a charge of gelled nitroglycerin near the hole and blasted over a half mile of stuck drill pipe from the leaking well.

The removal of the drill pipe marked the completion of preliminary measures, and paved the way to the death of Rig 20. Myron now had only to snuff the flames and cap the wild well. Using several fifty-pound loads of nitro, Myron rocked the desert with a blast that announced to the world that the dreaded Rig 20 had breathed its last. The fire was finally out and, as the documentary film, Rig 20, poetically noted,

> *The screaming roar became a whine;*
> *The whine became a whisper;*
> *The whisper became silence.*
> *For the first time in many weeks,*
> *men could speak and hear where*
> *once had been Naft Safid, Rig 20.*

From there out was child's play—albeit expensive child's play. Myron had the Anglo-Iranian Oil Company fly in two special valves—one from the United States and one from Great Britain—to be used to cap the well and forever halt the costly and dangerous escape of gas. The valves were duly flown in and skillfully placed on the well, putting a final end to a devastating fire.

See Appendix F, Myron Kinley's Diary of Rig 20, Naft Safid, 1951

QUM AND GET IT—ALBORZ NO. 5,
AN ISLAMIC INFERNO

Myron's victory at Rig 20 only increased his growing fame and the firefighting and well taming business seemed to boom. Especially did his reputation for fearlessness and genius flourish in the oil-rich Middle East. As the oil economies of the Middle East matured, blowouts became a frequent source of frustration, and always a source of fear. Should they ever be pitted against a wild well, Middle Eastern well owners knew the man they wanted fighting on their side— Myron Kinley.

Eventually the unthinkable happened, and before anyone could shout, "Call Kinley!" the phone rang madly in Bel Air, sounding the plight of the Iranian Oil Company. Myron was briefed on the tumultuous conditions of the accident by phone. Knowing before hand that the job ahead of him would be long and hard, Myron prepared yet again to journey over eight thousand miles away from the comforts of home to the front-lines of a formidable battle.

ABOVE: *Men in turbans help fight the Alborz No. 5. Qum, Iran, 1956.*

84

The blowout occurred on the morning of August 26, 1956, on the Alborz No. 5 in the Iranian oil fields near the city of Qum. Myron arrived on August 29 with his assistant, Boots Hansen, at a disaster scene that had already claimed one life.

As it erupted, the rig vigorously spat billows of gas into the air and literally saturated the surrounding countryside with oil. To make matters worse, the Alborz No. 5 was not secluded from the public, but lay immediately to the side of the busiest highway and a mile from the busiest railroad in Iran. Although the sheen of oil that coated the landscape forced officials to close the highway and Gulf Port Railroad, crews lived with the constant risk of curious onlookers setting fire to the escaping gas as they approached the fields by automobile.

But tactical conditions of the blowout were not the only problems that Myron would have to take into special consideration as he worked on this well. Because Qum is one of the great Muslim holy cities,

The wild well saturated the countryside with oil. Qum, Iran, 1956.

Leakage from the well created petroleum lakes as oil spilled into the valley. Qum, Iran, 1956.

local religious officials were very much opposed to petroleum drilling in the area. They demanded an immediate end to the blowout, but required a conservative approach that would not damage the surrounding culture or environment.

Therefore, Myron's first objective at the Alborz No. 5 was to prevent environmental damage to the surrounding valleys and villages. The damaged well was spilling approximately a hundred thousand barrels of oil per day, most of which was leaking into a dry creek bed that channelled the oil into the rich valley below. It was clear that this first battle would demand all hands, and every man was sent with shovels to build an earthen dam. Eventually, heavy equipment was moved into the area which was immediately used to build more dams. Small lakes formed as the oil accumulated behind the dams, and soon the valley was transformed into a series of small petroleum lakes, from which the Iranian Oil Company later pumped out two million barrels of oil.

Placing the valve. Qum, Iran, 1956. Crews faced oil bubbling at 240° F as they attempted to shut down the wild gasser.

Once the safety of the countryside was secured as far as possible, work on the screaming well could finally commence. At this point, Myron directed the usual preliminary work—to clear debris from the area and to remove from the well or derrick any equipment hindering his attempts to control the flow of gas. After removing several devices from the derrick, Myron ordered a special valve to be placed and closed over the well hole—a crucial step in finally shutting down the wild gasser.

Ardle Hill, family friend and attendant at the Alborz No. 5, later told of a humorous barrier to the proceedings that was placed in Myron's way at exactly this juncture, demanding the antsy and restless firefighter to muster all of his diplomatic skills and patience. It seems that just as preparations had been completed to close the valve, "work was suspended while the principals went to a noonday 'banquet,' really a 'rice pilau,' given by the commanding Iranian general in a huge tent, prepared and served by army cooks and waiters, complete with speeches and response. The lunch was good, but Myron was squirming to get back and close in that well blowing straight up hundreds of feet into the air." Undoubtedly eager to end the job as soon as possible, Myron fled the banquet at the first opportunity and returned to the field to close the valve.

But the cap would not hold. Hundreds of feet below the earth lay hundreds of thousands of barrels of crude oil, trapped under tremendous pressure, and it was soon evident that a different approach would need to be taken to relieve the situation. Crews faced bubbling oil boiling at 240° F and an uncontrollable thrust of gas gusting upwards from the well-head, as they industriously diverted the gas and oil outwards from the well and into a nearby hill. The gas was then ignited and, with a thunderous roar that echoed for miles, flames from the terrifying Alborz No. 5 shot into the air and hungrily devoured the escaping gas and oil from the well.

The blaze on the Alborz No. 5 burned bright in the Iranian skies for two months while Myron and his men worked day after day to contain the well pressure. The national oil company of Iran appealed to petroleum companies throughout the world for emergency equipment. Using this machinery, Myron was able to alleviate the tremendous pressure in the well by drilling a diagonal hole to intersect the Alborz No. 5. Finally, on November 16, 1956, well pressure began to drop. Within forty hours it fell to zero and oil flow ceased. Acting quickly, crews pumped mud into the hole to seal the gas flow. Battle on the Alborz No. 5 was over.

CHAOS IN THE CRADLE OF CIVILIZATION—
FIRE ON THE AHWAZ NO. 6

ut triumph on the Alborz No. 5 was not to be the last Persian victory for the intrepid Myron Kinley, and on the afternoon of April 19, 1958, less than two years after slaying the monster at Qum, the celebrated firefighter was urgently summoned from a leisurely lunch for a third emergency trip to the blistering Iranian desert.   True to nature, the ace well-tamer left the Houston restaraunt without finishing his meal and drove to the airport where he caught the first flight in a grueling but familiar eight thousand mile journey to Iran.

The terrifying desert blaze known as the Ahwaz No. 6, nestled in the arid lands between the Persian Gulf and the Zagros mountains, erupted on a quiet April morning with a shake, rattle,

ABOVE: *The Ahwaz No. 6. Iran, 1958.*

and roll that instantly catapulted the countryside into chaos. Bright flames leapt, roaring into the sky in constant, deafening explosions. Panicked Kashgai tribesmen watched in terror and awestruck Anglo-Iranian drilling crews rushed to prayer as the firmament shone a brilliant red-orange.

But news of the explosion did not frighten the seemingly imperturbable Myron Kinley. By this time, the seasoned expert well knew the major challenge of any desert battle. Acting with full authority from overseas, Myron calmly but resolutely requisitioned crewmen at the disaster to secure the nearest water supplies and channel them directly to the well. By his arrival on April 24, crews had already built a twenty-two mile pipeline to the Karun River and reopened a nearby well that had struck salt water nearly six years earlier, thus providing over a million gallons of water a day to the front lines of the battle against the ferocious Ahwaz No. 6.

Yet again, Myron and the his men were pitted against a fire-breathing monster, a tempest-pot of blazes boiling steadily at 260° F and compounded by the smoldering desert sun. Using the water-cooled hook, and advancing only under cover of the night, the unflappable warrior doggedly led his crew into phase two of the battle—to strip and remove the burning rig that was now only so much charred and melted debris.

Finally, on May 18, after the fire had raged without pause for an entire month, Myron ordered 450 pounds of explosives to the front lines. The old pro then packed the charge into an iron bomb which he detonated to clear the site of trace materials and refuse. Oil officials, crewmen, and Myron alike all exulted when the explosion unexpectedly extinguished the flame, silencing the burner that had roared thunderously for thirty days.

But the mind of a well fire is a fickle thing, and Myron knew that the fate and course of any blaze is as likely to change as the blowing wind. The Ahwaz No. 6 was no exception, and the stubborn inferno relit itself after a mere fifty-one-minute respite, sending the crew scrambling into phase three of the battle to extinguish the baffling flame.

The perservering crew continued its offensive charge against the willful blaze, sending first a 350-pound bomb, followed by a 600-pound bomb, followed, in turn, by another 800 pounds of nitroglycerine hurling against the tower of flames. But the vehement fire remained unchecked in its brutality and, by May 27, was costing the Anglo-Iranian Oil Company over one million dollars a day.

Utterly perplexed by the fire's tenacity, a tired but resolved Myron Kinley designed a special bomb, shaped like a horseshoe to surround the well-head and placed it at the mouth of the well. On June 4, the blaze on Ahwaz No. 6 was snuffed with a deafening boom and a bone-shaking jolt.

But the dirty job was not over and battle-weary workers drudgingly prepared for the final, but most dangerous, phase of conflict—capping the wild well. High and mighty desert winds whipped the escaping gas into deadly clouds which hung over the disaster site and contaminated local villages. Work on the rig was temporarily suspended as workers instead evacuated two nearby villages and sheltered themselves from the noxious fumes coming from the blowing well.

When eventually the winds changed, crewmen reemerged on the scene, removing damaged pipe and casing until gas spewed upward in a single column, rising into the air like a candle. Next, they brilliantly rigged waterlines to a cement truck. "Then, in an incredible emptiness of sound with the wild well silenced, there was only the chugging of the truck as it pumped cement into the well (Burchardt, "The Monster's Tale," *Oklahoma Today*)."

And that is how the desert was won.

See Appendix G, *Field News* articles on the Ahwaz No. 6

TO EVERYTHING THERE IS A SEASON—
TIMES OF JOY AND SORROW

It seemed that the unbeatable Myron Kinley had known nothing but victory throughout his brilliant career. However, the tide was soon to change when he suffered tremendous loss on the homefront with the death of his wife of thirty-three years on January 19, 1957. Perhaps his saving grace was his lifelong passion for firefighting, and after Rowena's death he thrust himself into the business with renewed vigor. As long as there were fires to fight and wells to tame, he would always love life and never be lonely.

Though he felt the pains of loss acutely, they only deepened his love for his family. He spent the following years nurturing his relationship with his children and, in his devotion and caring for them, seemed to lessen his sorrow.

During the years that followed Rowena's death, Myron found time to mix business with pleasure. His son Dan remembers a trip

ABOVE: *Myron and Jessie Kinley at home. Chickasha, Oklahoma, 1962.*

Myron made to New York City in 1958, where Myron was held over on his way to the Ahwaz fire. Myron and Dan met in the city and, like a couple of kids, decided to while away their afternoon together riding the rides at Coney Island.

As they explored Coney Island they soon discovered a new ride—the parachute drop. They stood below the parachutes and watched frightened faces as they fell straight down in open seats from hundreds of feet high until finally, the parachute opened and the rider was gently lowered to the ground. Dan remembers that they looked at one another and, neither of them wanting to appear "chicken," each silently dared the other onto the ride.

Together, the adventurers boarded the parachute drop and were lifted up, up, and up, all the while wondering aloud why in the world they ever got on the ride in the first place. Anxiety mounted with each second, as they never knew exactly when their chairs would be released and send them plummeting towards the ground. Finally, the ride ended and the father and son were gently wafted to the ground where they got out of their seats as soon as possible, leaving the parachute ride never to return.

Myron was also remembered by his children for the kindness and fatherly support he showed them throughout his life, and which was particularly evident to Dan at the death of his own wife, Kathleen, in 1958. At this moment of crisis, Dan recognized Myron's constant willingness to go out of his way to be of support, and described Myron's relationship with his children as a constant support and comfort.

Granted, the years after Rowena's death were difficult, but they were not all sad, and Myron learned that every bit of loss is an opportunity to gain. Myron and I had become acquainted when Mrs. Nichlos and I had hired him to work on the No. 4 Rigney in 1944, and I think he must have always been a little bit fascinated by the thought of two women running an oil company, for whenever he was in Chickasha he would stop by to ask after the Little Nick. These were happy occasions, and Mrs. Nichlos and I always enjoyed a chance to hear about his recent adventures or his inventions in progress.

Myron was a busy man in those days and his visits were never long, as he was always in a rush getting somewhere or other for a job. But apparently one beautiful day in early 1958, work wasn't

Miss Jessie Irene Dearing

and

Mr. Myron Macy Kinley

announce their marriage

Sunday, the second of November

One thousand nine hundred and fifty-eight

Chickasha, Oklahoma

the only thing on his mind, for this time when he stopped he proposed marriage. I was simply amazed, but honored, that such a great man would ask me to marry him, and I happily said yes to his offer. So in between his firefighting adventures we made time for a wedding, and were married on November 2, 1958, Myron's sixtieth birthday.

As I said, he was a busy man. The demands of his profession required him to make tremendous sacrifices, and our honeymoon turned into a working vacation in Freer, Louisiana, when Myron received an emergency firefighting call. But it was not all work and was even some fun; and as long as I was with my husband on my honeymoon, it was no sacrifice at all.

The honeymoon emergency proved an omen of our first two years of marriage, during which time we were separated for lengthy periods while he attended fiercely burning fires from as far away as the Arctic Circle and Argentina. The Argentinian fire was infamous for separating us, as customs officials would not allow me to travel with him because I had put in my passport application too late.

But I didn't have to live with these disruptions long, and in summer of 1960, Myron was called to the final international fire of his long and illustrious career.

*Myron Kinley was conferred a member of the Fifth Class of the Order of the Rising Sun. Tokyo, Japan, June, 1960. ***

A BORN DIPLOMAT—
FIRE IN NAGOKA, JAPAN

The fire that erupted in the Teikoku Oil Company fields in Nagoka, Japan, on June 17, 1960, truly had Japanese oil experts stumped. But in that day and age, there was a ready answer for any company that might find itself in such a costly predicament—get Kinley.

Japanese media called Myron "superhuman" as they watched him kill in a single day the fire that had stupefied their experts for over a week. But for the thoroughly-trained firefighter, it was not much of a job. He simply moved the drilling rig with a crane, then poured fifty tons of mud into the hole. Child's play for the man without fear.

His daring feats and display of courage garnered high praise from enthusiastic Japanese fans, and his acts were lauded in newspapers across Japan and in the United States. One article even called Myron an American diplomat, as relations with Japan had recently been strained when President Eisenhower cancelled a goodwill trip. Columnist Bill Clark credited Myron with healing the wounds between the countries: "Japanese-American relations were in serious danger for a few days. Then came Myron Kinley. . . . In what the press described as the most remarkable and daring accomplishment, Myron Kinley put out the great fire with relative ease."

Nor did the adoring praise showered on the American miracle worker end with print media. The sixty-four-year-old hero was transformed into an overnight television celebrity, appearing as a featured and honored guest on Japanese television.

Despite unparalleled attention from the news media, Myron had yet to reach the pinnacle of recognition from the adoring Japanese public. He finally reached that peak when he was conferred a member of the Fifth Class of the Order of the Rising Sun by the Emperor of Japan—status granted at the presentation of the prestigious Patent of Decoration awarded by the Prime Minister for acts of uncommon valor and expertise.

And thus did Japan celebrate the historic dousing of the Nagoka blaze. True, Nagoka had been an unremarkable fire, but it ended a brilliant career with all the fanfare befitting a hero.

* (Translation of Certificate) Patent of Decoration, Number 8781. The Fifth Class of the Order of the Rising Sun is hereby conferred upon Mr. Myron Macy Kinley, American Citizen, by His Majesty the Emperor of Japan. In witness thereof, the Seal of State has been affixed to these presents at Nasu this day, the twenty-third of the eighth month of the thirty-fifth year of Showa (1960).

Hayato Ikeda   *Takeo Yoshida*
Prime Minster   *Director of Decoration*

CALLING IT QUITS—A LEGEND TAKES A REST

With Nagoka as his swan song, Myron Kinley announced formal retirement. Still Myron found he could not make a permanent exit from the petroleum industry. For the next eighteen years he remained active in the petroleum business lecturing to professional associations and attending conferences and exhibitions. Myron especially enjoyed the petroleum conferences where he often met old acquaintances. Firefighter Coots Matthews recalls seeing Myron at the 1978 Off-shore Technical Conference in Houston, where Coots and his partner, Boots Hansen, had a pleasant visit with him shortly before his death.

But Boots' and Coots' association with Myron Kinley occasionally extended into the oil fields. Coots recalls an instance

ABOVE: *The grandfather of oil well firefighting. Greenwich, Connecticut, 1977. Picture taken while visiting his son and daughter-in-law, Dan and Margery Kinley.*

when he and Boots met up with Myron while on a job in West Texas. As Boots and Coots worked to put out the fire, Myron, from the spot where he was hunting quail, saw the smoke from the troubled well. True to his character, the inveterate flame fighter sped to the scene of the action, only to be halted at the gates by a young and inexperienced field worker. Despite introductions, the "grandfather of oil well firefighting" was not able to gain admission to the fire, as the gatekeeper, who had been instructed to keep the curious public out of the area, would not let him by.

Although his post-retirement ventures into the oil patch were infrequent, he took advantage of one last opportunity to try his hand against a fiery well burning wild in Canton, Oklahoma. The Canton well was surrounded by a flaming crater which Myron extinguished when he filled it with water. But it was not as easy as that, for the well reignited unexpectedly and catapulted red-hot rocks as far as one hundred yards. Myron was permanently scarred above his right eye when one of the rocks struck him in the face. Later, as he guest-lectured at conferences across the country, he made light fun of the dangers of his job, casually remarking that "a guy could lose an eye doing something like that."

But Myron gilded his golden years with more than professional obligations, and he gladly found time to indulge his mechanical and inventive interests to his heart's content. Always a handyman, Myron became a regular "Mr. Fixit," diligently making repairs or mechanical improvements in the machine shop he maintained behind our Chickasha home.

Myron had always shown a certain fondness for gadgets, and his retirement found him developing a few of his own or exploring some of the more exotic inventions of others. It was not long after his 1960 retirement that Myron invested in one of his more infamous and unsightly contraptions—the automatic pool cover—and with characteristic zeal immediately installed one on our private swimming pool while enthusiastically encouraging relatives and friends to follow suit. Unlike his other interests, the automatic pool cover never caught fire, so to speak, and eventually became an atrocious mess lording over the pool.

But I and his children will always remember Myron's

The Kinley family gathered to celebrate the marriage of
Vicki Kinley. Greenwich, Connecticut, 1977. Left to right:
Laura, Edith, Jack, Vicki, Myron, and Jessie Kinley; Joyce and
Robert Knoble.

retirement for the love he constantly showered upon us. Perhaps to compensate for the long hours he spent in the oil fields, family time became Myron's first priority, preferring to whisk one or more of us away on unforgettable cross-country adventures over America's back roads.

Certainly cars and travel were integral to Myron's retirement years, as they became the keys to his personal freedom. Having suffered extensive hearing loss from the deafening blazes he fought throughout his life, Myron regained his independence—if only temporarily—when in the car. In his car, Myron could steal away with a loved one for a faraway destination, all the while enjoying the pleasures of conversation and camaraderie of which, due to his deafness, he was deprived in other venues.

And so Myron renewed and nurtured the familial bonds he so cherished until failing health at last prevented the adventurer from taking to the open road. But as his health declined, his

The reunion. Chickasha, Oklahoma, 1978. Left to right: Joyce Knoble, Karen Bruno, Dan Kinley, Vicki Reynolds, Lucie Knoble, Myron Kinley, Laura Kinley, Jessie Kinley, Edith Kinley, Karl Kinley, Dan Kinley Jr.

family only continued to grow and before long was scattered throughout the country, making it impossible for him to see everyone in the few trips he was able to make.

So we decided to bring the family to him and, in the early spring of 1976, children, grandchildren, and great-grandchildren gathered in Chickasha for a family reunion in Myron's honor. Chronic heart problems had hospitalized Myron for several weeks immediately prior to the reunion. Although his strength was sapped, the proud patriarch delighted in the rare opportunity to visit with his entire family, and continually expressed his gratitude for the event.

In one fell swoop he was able to see his beloved family—the greatest product of his extraordinary life.

Described by colleagues as a "man's man," the seemingly unbeatable firefighter finally succumbed to the laws of nature. After more than 450 brutal fires and forty years in the most dangerous business going, the "Man Without Fear," died in Chickasha on May 12, 1978, happy and contented.

It was by all accounts a life well lived. Beginning with the "shot heard around the oil world" in 1913, through his illustrious career as a firefighter and inventor, Myron Kinley will always be remembered as the great innovator of oil well firefighting; the man who laid the foundations for modern firefighting method and technique. Although he made his exit from this world many years ago, the mark he left on the petroleum industry is an indelible piece of living history and its repercussions will be felt throughout the world for generations to come.

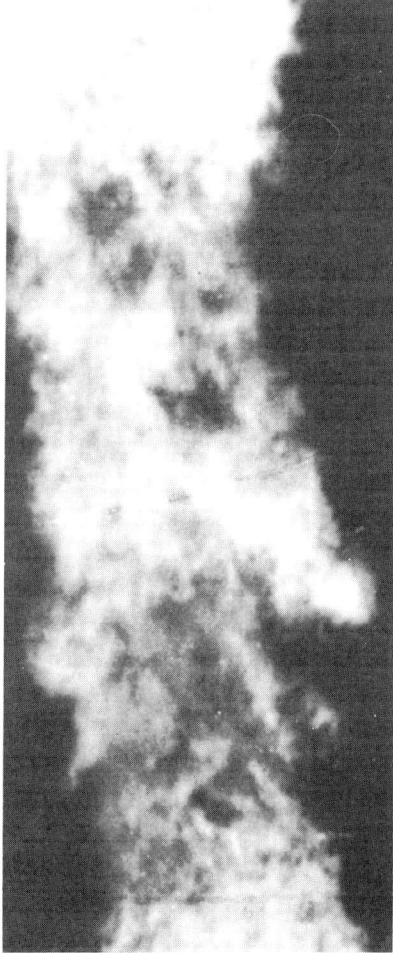

A LIFE IN PRINT

Holland's, the Magazine of the South, April 1934

"SOUTHERN PERSONALITIES"

Anna Gillian Wilson

Suppose your oil well catches fire! Perhaps it's in Russia or Romania or Venezuela or North America! Ask "Whom can I get to put it out?" The answer will be "the Kinleys." Go west, go east, go north, go south, and ask the question. The answer will be the same. For the Kinleys are the firefighting aces in the oil fields. No one else can extinguish an oil fire so quickly, so surely, so definitely as they.

Burning wells are no novelty in an oil field. Possibility of fire can never be prevented. Yet the successful oil well firefighters may be counted on the fingers of one hand. Three are from this family. The Kinleys—two brothers Myron and Floyd, and the father, who calls himself "The Sire"—have fought and conquered oil field fires all over the world.

Separately and together, they have extinguished more than fifty terrible fires. Myron has traveled to South America twice, once to Venezuela, and once to the Argentine for the purpose of extinguishing oil field fires. Two years ago, in Romania, he put under control a burning well which had destroyed the lives of 14 men and defied interference for more than two years.

A well on fire is a terrible thing. The roar can be heard for over a mile, and the light can sometimes be seen a hundred miles away. Those seen from such a distance are the gas wells, which burn with an upthrusting blue-white flame and look like huge candles as they glow steadily or flicker waveringly in the wind, against a night-black sky. Oil well fires are different. They lick the ground gyratingly for hundreds of feet, and throw an orange glow against a wide horizon.

Such a fire has all the beauty and destructive power of a storm. There is the sound of it, rising in sonorous harmonies; the sight of it, thrusting forth licking flames and rolling clouds of smoke; the strength of it, throwing men aside as the wind does a feather with its breath; the magnetism of it, sucking the night birds and eager insect life into its insatiable maw; the waste of it, destroying fortunes in a single day, digging into the bowels of the earth itself.

Oil well fires belong to the mystery class. They may ignite in a dozen different ways, all of which are known. Yet how a particular fire originates is seldom known. The drilling of oil wells has been reduced to a scientific and monotonous process. Machinery is set up, the well spudded in; the bit goes down; casing is set; the bit goes farther; more casing is set; the bit goes on—until, after a period of

months, the oil sand is reached. Then, if the gas pressure is sufficient, the oil comes up over the top; if the gas pressure is not sufficient, "well shooters," men efficient in the use of explosives, let
down their leashed forces and "blow it in." The well is then capped,
and the oil flows into the place provided for it.

Suppose, however, something should go wrong and the well "go
wild." Fire is then an immediate danger. If someone should drive an
automobile too close (a quarter of a mile is close enough) or light a
cigarette in the vicinity; or if a horse should strike a spark with his
shoe; or if a rock coming through the casing should hit the metal; or
if lightning be flashing somewhere near, all that inflammable matter—say 1,500 barrels of oil an hour—pouring out of the well, will
catch on fire and roar and burn like torrents from hell.

Oil and gas fires defy interference. Water, steam, ordinary chemicals make no impression upon them. Nitroglycerin, an explosive
which travels seven thousand feet a second, must be used to blow
them out. Just how powerful is this explosive? A tiny bit left on a
cork may explode and pop out an eye; a small amount dropped on
the floor may blow off an arm or leg; and that remaining on the side
of a can may send one into eternity before he knows what has happened. Handling nitroglycerin is all danger. "A glycerin man makes
but one mistake" is known to be immutable truth.

The explosive is not the only danger. To face the heat is to court
disaster. The temperature where the men work ranges from 200 to
800 degrees. Here the eyes and throat may be irremediably injured.
A man may fall and be burned to death in the few seconds before he
can be rescued. A sudden fitful wind may send a flame and make his
body a living torch. Holes of scalding water are ever present to
entrap his hurrying feet. Poisonous gases are always hovering near
to bring about his undoing.

How can men under such circumstances put nature, gone wild,
back under control? Ask the Kinleys!

"The first thing we do is to establish a water supply," Floyd
Kinley said, as we sat talking in his office on Admiral Boulevard in
Tulsa, Oklahoma. "When we are near a city reservoir, this is easy;
but when we're in the woods with only wells and creeks to draw
from, it is sometimes an awful job. You know, we have to have
water with pressure behind it around the burning well to cool things
off and protect us. We work under a steady stream of water all the
time."

"Why is that necessary when you wear asbestos suits?" I asked.

"We don't wear asbestos anymore. Asbestos gets awfully hot

after a time, and it's also very heavy. A suit will weigh a hundred pounds when it is water-logged. That's too much weight to carry in a place slippery with mud and oil when one is in a hurry," he smiled.

"Slippery mud, slimy oil, a hell-like fire! You have to watch your step, don't you?"

In spite of the fact that young Kinley has worked with oil men all his life, he is like few of them. He has none of the crudities of the roughnecks and roustabouts, none of the strut and swagger of the drillers or tower men, none of the hard-bitten dominant air of the successful executives. He is modest, well-poised, shy, reticent. One would never take him for a fighter of any kind, much less for an oil well firefighter. Slender, blond, of medium height, with a high forehead and deep blue eyes, he looks like an actor or painter. In fact, there may be something of the artist's temperament in his make-up, for when he was asked how he had become an expert at so extremely difficult a job, he replied, "I don't know. Something inside me must tells me I can do it, and I go ahead."

"Do you really like to put out a fire?" I asked in amazement. "Yes, it's fascinating," he said thoughtfully, "When I hear there is a burning well, I keep hoping we'll be called. In fact, I'm like an old war horse rearing to get into battle. Of course, after we've worked about forty-eight hours with little sleep, I'm not so eager."

Floyd Kinley is slightly deaf from working under the reverberations of burning wells. He has tried all measures for relieving the concussion without success. He even went up in an airplane, and asked the pilot to do all his stunts.

"Did it help any?" I asked.

"No, it didn't help my ears, and it nearly scared me to death. I don't mind dynamite, but I sure don't like airplanes turning flips."

"What do you do after the water supply is in?" I asked. The story had to be drawn from him by questions. He takes it all as a matter of course.

"The next step is to get out all inflammable material—trees, stumps, and bushes; everything that will hold a smoldering spark must be pulled up and carried away. In one field in Texas we pulled up and carried off twenty acres of timber. All red-hot metal, cables, casing—sometimes thousands of feet of it—machinery used in drilling, must also be got out of the way. Metal has to be cooled with the water faster than the fire can heat it; then someone must go in and hook a connection to each piece, so we can pull it out to a safe distance. If hot metal should be left, the fire would ignite again as soon as we blew it out."

"And then you shoot your explosive!" I said helpfully.

"No, it's not so easy as that," he laughed. "We have to get the fire in a straight-up column. Sometimes we have to devise apparatus to put over the well to throw the blaze up. Again, we have to remove a connection from the well which may be throwing the blaze on the ground. That's the hardest, because the red-hot connection must be broken loose. Throwing the blaze into the air sometimes takes days of thought and work. A gas well isn't so bad, but an oil well can have as many twists as a snake. Once we've got her up, we place the nitro, which has been packed in asbestos and then in steel drums—from ten to two hundred quarts, according to the size of the well—by the side of the flame."

He said it as if it were no more difficult than delivering a quart of milk. But in a temperature of 800 degrees, with slippery mud and oil, and flames that can burn a man to a crisp in a second—well, that is "not so easy."

"Wires which have been placed in the charge lead some distance away," he continued, "where either my brother or I shoot the spark into the torpedo with an electric hand detonator. One shot is usually enough, although we have had to shoot twice. If you miss the flame half a foot, you miss it altogether."

"Do you ever have any fan mail?" a bystander asked curiously.

"Yes, some," he replied. "Our letters are mostly from cranks.

My brother had one from a woman just before he went to Romania, saying if he would pay her, she would pray the fire out. These cranks are funny. They'll do anything to get their ideas to you. One man swam a deep, swift river where we were putting out a fire to offer us a grand idea of how to put a fire out. We said we'd listen, since he'd gone to so much trouble. But he wouldn't tell us unless we paid him."

"Do you ever have any proposals of marriage through the mails?" the curious one persisted.

"Well, some," Floyd laughed and blushed in embarrassment; "but as my brother and I are both married and have families—he has three children and I have one—we can't be bothered about proposals."

To know the Romanian story is to know blond, smiling Myron Kinley, for it illustrates his perseverance, his tenacity, his indomitable nerve. The well had been burning a year when he went to Europe to ask for the job of putting it out. It was a tremendous fire. The roar could be heard for miles, and the light was seen 70 miles away at Bucharest. Kinley says he knew as soon as he saw it that he could put it out. He had only to follow the same procedure he had used with dozens of other wells. But the money and lives had been sacrificed already, nothing could put the fire out, and they would not allow anyone else to try. Although they were very courteous and gave him many interviews, their answer was always the same. At last he saw that there was nothing for him to do but go home.

During the next year, a motion picture was made of the operations of the Kinleys in extinguishing a big oil well fire in Texas. Looking at it one day, Myron Kinley decided to go back to Romania and take the picture with him.

"Maybe when the Romanians see how we do it, they will let me put out that well," he said to his brother.

When he arrived he found the fire much worse than it had been the year before. The pressure of the gas had blown out the tubing and caused the sand around it to cave in, making a crater two hundred and fifty feet wide and sixty feet deep. From the bottom, volcanolike, shot a furious, torrential stream of fire over 300 feet high. Kinley still thought, however, he could put it out.

But again he was refused permission. The government officials said they were interested, almost amazed at the picture, but declared that their fire was different, that nothing could be done, that it would have to exhaust the field before it would stop burning. Again there seemed nothing to do but go home. Determined to leave nothing undone, however, Kinley went to the Standard Oil Company of Romania and asked them to look at this picture. The officials of this company were much impressed. "What are your terms?" they asked.

Kinley replied, "Extinguishing the fire and capping the well, or no pay."

Since the well had already burned about two million dollars worth of oil, they thought it extremely foolish, his terms being what they were, not to let him try. And it was finally through their influence that the government consented.

It was a task to tax all of Kinley's ingenuity. The contract specified that he was never to have more than two helpers and the neither should be Romanian. He was in a strange land where he could not speak the language. The tools and equipment were all different from those used in this country. Much of what he used, he had to invent and make.

First, he put in his water system right up to the mouth of the hole. Then he cooled all the machinery at the bottom of the gas-filled crater. This done, he went into the crater to hook cables onto the metal and drag it out. When the place was cleared, he lowered the nitro, shot it, missed the flame.

He lowered more nitro, shot it, put the fire out. It ignited again in five minutes. Conditions were not right for extinguishing the flame.

He began to devise ways and means to make them right. He made a funnel for the escaping gas. He cleaned out old tunnels and put in pipes and pumps; he built another funnel; he poured in concrete and mud; he built a gate valve; he poured in more concrete; he did this and that; he tried old ideas and new ideas, everything he could think of. For six months he worked, often 20 hours a day, going into the superheated crater hundreds of times, risking his life hourly, sidestepping cave-ins of earth many times, and being burned again and again.

"Wasn't your wife wild with anxiety?" I asked.

"No, I don't think so. You see, she has learned not to worry," he laughed. "I was a firefighter when she married me, and I've always come out of a fire all right. I've never had but one serious accident. That was when, in a big fire in Texas, an iron beam fell on me, broke my leg, and pinned me down. Fortunately, Floyd saw me immediately, and they carried me out before anything happened."

I learned when I saw the picture of the fire that the broken leg didn't stop him. The next day he was on crutches, holding his leg in its cast out in front of him, hopping about the fire to give orders. Later, finding that too slow, he rode a horse, sitting sideways and directing with arms and hands like an orchestra leader.

"I guess we Kinleys are pretty lucky," Myron said with a flashing smile. "My father is sixty-five. I'm thirty-six and Floyd is twenty-nine. We're hale and hearty. None of us have ever had a really serious accident."

"You're protected by insurance, of course," I commented.

"No, we can't get any," he said. "We take responsibility for our men also. Before we go on a job, we sign a paper releasing the oil company that owns the well from all responsibility. If any of our men should be hurt or killed, we'd have to pay the damages."

"The Sire" came in and sat on the table and swung his feet back and forth. He is round and fat and merry, like Old King Cole. His eyes twinkle, and he chuckles under his breath. But the intelligent precaution exercised by his sons in this dangerous work is of his teaching. He has been at the business of fighting oil-well fires for over 20 years. He has little academic education. He learned how to put out fires from experience. He was a well shooter, he said, when he conceived the idea of shooting out the flame with an explosive that would separate it from the fuel and thus put it out.

"The idea is just like that of blowing out a candle or an oil lamp. The force of the breath blows the blaze from the fuel. I figured at the time that if I could get a strong enough 'breath,' I could do it," he said.

There were pictures of burning wells all over the little office walls. "Five men were burned to death when that one exploded and caught on fire," he said, pointing to the photograph of a particularly virulent-looking fire. "Two men were entirely cremated, and the remains of three more I carried out in a bucket. What was left of each of them in no case weighed more than fourteen pounds."

He pointed to another photograph of a black-looking fire.

"I couldn't put that one out," he said, "I didn't even try. The owner wanted to superintend the job. One must have a free hand in work of this kind. And more than one boss is fatal to success. We always follow the practice of one boss on the job. In early days I had to be the boss, for the boys were too young. But now they do the bossing. On each job, before we go in, we decide who is to be the man in authority. Then we counsel and consult together. But when we go in to the fire, we obey the boss man, just as soldiers obey the commanding officer, without questions. I've always been a hard taskmaster, but we've never asked a man to do anything we would not do ourselves. We work right with the men. In fact, we do the most dangerous jobs ourselves. When we ask a man to do anything, we expect obedience with a smile. That is perfect cooperation. We must have it."

"Who was in charge, you or Floyd, when Myron was in Europe?"

"Floyd," he replied promptly.

"And you, the originator of this business, obeyed your youngest son, did what he said do? That is hard to believe."

"Certainly I did," he said. "There is no other way. Put the responsibility on a man, then follow him."

"Does anything funny, anything amusing, ever happen when you are trying to put out a well?"

"They are all funny when they are out, but never before," he said growing serious. "When you're on the job, handling explosives, it is always a ticklish business. There is a little while, two or three minutes, when a man feels he is living a whole lifetime. When that is over, and the fire is out, a man is so tired he wants to go home and just rest forever. The well is funny then, but not before."

"OLD FIREHORSE KINLEY—MAN WITHOUT FEAR"

Robert Hugh Rogers

In October, 1929, an Oklahoma religious sect, convinced that the end of the world had come, prayed for two days. They had seen apocalyptic signs: by day a pillar of smoke blacked out the sky, by night great tongues of flame set it afire. But it wasn't the end of the world; it was the worst fire in the history of Oklahoma's oil fields.

It began just outside Oklahoma City when Sinclair Oil's No. 3 Stamper well struck gas unexpectedly. The sudden pressure exploded a separator, and the uprushing gas blasted into an inferno that threatened the whole multibillion-dollar Oklahoma City field. The roar could be heard for miles; the glare could be seen as far away as Texas. As some 25,000 gathered to watch, its incredible heat melted the drilling derrick into hoops of twisted, white-hot steel. Oklahoma City firemen were helpless.

But the drillers knew what to do. They put in a call to 33-year-old Myron Kinley of Tulsa—a man utterly without fear, almost without nerves, who had already made a national reputation in the oil industry for putting out fires. At Sinclair's call, Myron and his younger brother, Floyd, rushed across state, gave the big fire a respectful but unterrified look and set to work. Wearing asbestos suits and using acetylene torches, they cut away the scorching steel debris, which could ignite the gas again even if they got the existing fire out. "Roughnecks" sprayed them continuously with streams of water to keep them from roasting alive.

Then Myron and his brother shucked off their cumbersome asbestos suits and crept into the flame, pushing an asbestos-lined shield, with only the spraying water for cover. They carried 30 quarts of jellied dynamite in an oil barrel wrapped in asbestos. Using a long, armlike boom, hastily improvised from oil field pipe, they pushed the barrel out over the flaming geyser. Then they ran back to a shelter and pushed a plunger. Came an earth-shaking roar, and silence. The great fire was gone, snuffed out like some giant candle.

The Kinleys, clothes in shreds, eyebrows singed off, collected their pay and departed. For them, it was all in the day's work.

In 1953, nearly a quarter century later, 56-year-old Myron Kinley stands as unrivaled world-champion fighter of oil fires. Fire is to him a personal devil bent on his destruction. It has already killed his brother; Floyd was fatally injured at Goliad, Texas, in 1937. It has crippled Myron himself; his right leg is permanently stiff, shattered by a well casing blown out by gas. His left arm and shoulder are a mass of scar tissue. In Venezuela, when a shifting wind whipped the fire onto him, he spent six months in the hospital on his stomach, able to move only his head. Yet as soon as he could leave he charged off to fight another fire.

Daredevil Kinley inherited his trade. In California, where he was born, his father, Karl, was one of the first oil well "shooters," setting off dynamite charges in newly drilled wells to help bring the oil out of close-packed formations. In 1913, when a well caught fire at Taft, California, the father was called to see if he could cave in the well. In the process he blew out the fire, thus discovering by accident the technique of "exploding" fires.

From boyhood young Myron handled dynamite as casually as other boys handled marbles. After a World War I hitch as an artilleryman overseas, he settled in Tulsa with his brother, Floyd. At first they had to tackle fires on a "pay if you win" basis. But soon their abilities were so well known that big oil companies paid handsomely to get them in a hurry. A $30,000 fee for a single job is cheap when fires can destroy $20,000 worth of oil or gas a day.

Kinley's biggest asset is experience, gained from fighting scores of fires. Kinley puts it, "I know what you can't get away with." As a boss he is stern as a drillmaster. He justifies his harshness by saying that a single mistake can cost a life. Roughnecks, instead of resenting his hardhanded ways, take confidence from his sureness. Panic, which accompanies any fire, vanishes when Myron arrives.

Like generals of old, Kinley always goes in ahead of his men; like them, he refuses to admit defeat. When his left leg was crushed among twisted debris, he got it set, came back on horseback to finish bossing the job. Two weeks later, with the job done, he took time to have the leg rebroken and reset.

Kinley shows his lifelong enemy the respect due a mighty antagonist. He has seen fire spring infinite ruses to defeat him, and for every one he masters it can always find a new one. "You make a move, the fire makes another," he says.

In 1929, when he read about an oil field fire which had raged for two years in Romania, he went over on his own hook, talked his way into a chance to put it out. The scene was like a Doré drawing of Dante's Inferno. The fire had collapsed the earth into a huge crater 300 feet across, and scores of smaller fires flickered up all over the surrounding area. In one effort to put it out the Romanians had drilled a 100-foot tunnel to intersect the well; the tunnel had collapsed, killing 14 men. After six months of work, during which he flooded the whole crater with liquid concrete cooled by sprays, Kinley put out the fire by setting off simultaneous blasts within the tunnel and at the well head. With that his fame became international.

Soon he was commuting all over the world. He kept his passport valid for every country open to him, prepared to go anywhere at a moment's notice. His only luggage was an overnight bag with khaki suit, razor and toothbrush; he improvised what tools he needed at the scene. He was once asked to go 7,500 miles to Arabia to extinguish a blaze on Bahrain Island. In 1950, while putting out a fire in Italy's Po Valley, he got a call from his headquarters, now in Houston, to tackle another one in Venezuela. Last year France summoned him to control a leaking well in its biggest oil field, at Lacq.

His toughest job came in Iran, where a blazing well was hemmed by a cuplike formation of hills which batted the heat back and forth until it cooked the very earth. Trying a thermometer on the periphery, he found the temperature was 260° F; with the possibility of the dynamite exploding in his hands, he kept it at a distance until needed. A pipeline had to be laid 22 miles to the nearest river to bring in water for his protective spray. Kinley directed the building of an asbestos-lined steel canopy atop a bulldozer, used it to place his dynamite when all was ready. When the fire was out, gas still belched skyward, and Kinley had to boss the delicate operation of capping the well with steel connections which could easily strike a spark to fire a new explosion. But he won again.

Kinley hates a fire on the water; this year he was called to fight one south of Morgan City, Louisiana, where a gas well being drilled by Pure Oil Company caught fire ten miles off-shore. He moved back and forth, now on a converted LST used as command post, now on a "spud barge," now on a speedboat. His stiff leg made it difficult for him to clamber from deck to deck, so when he changed ships the LST picked him up with its crane, swinging him above the choppy sea.

The battle raged like a small naval engagement for ten days. Kinley's main problem was to knock off the "Christmas tree" control valve from the well to permit the fire to rise upward so he could get dynamite under it. Under his command a four-man rifle team from Louisiana's Camp Polk blasted at the valve from noon to dusk, scored 32 direct hits, cracked it, but did not blow it off.

Kinley finally improvised a water-cooled boom, snaked it in to snap off the Christmas tree. By then the valve of a second well had cracked under the tremendous heat, leaking gas which had also caught fire. Kinley spent four more days jockeying to remove the second valve before risking his dynamite blast. On the tenth day the fire was finally snuffed out.

Between jobs Kinley gardens or loafs. His California home, a palatial one, is in fashionable Bel Air, near Hollywood. Oilmen estimate that he makes easily $100,000 a year, from his work and from returns on oil field tools he has invented. He could have retired years ago. But in spite of the scars, in spite of the fact that he is deaf for a week after some jobs, in spite of the fact that no underwriter will sell him life insurance, old Firehorse Kinley cannot resist a fire.

"I've stopped worrying," says his wife. "What's the use? I don't think he'll ever quit."

Kinley himself says: "I guess I'll quit when they carry me out in a box."

"TITLED TEXAN"

Marie Moore

Back in 1922, during the Cromwell Field boom in Oklahoma, a rickety World War I Jenny circled slowly over a burning oil well.

Inside the plane, along with the pilot, was a towheaded young fellow who peered intently down at the flame and black smoke.

"Durn fool," remarked a spectator on the ground, whose attention was divided by the double spectacle of a disastrous fire and a flying plane.

"Claims he can put this fire out in twenty-four hours, and he's just up there looking at it."

Less than 12 hours later the young fellow had strung a cable through the flames and sent a load of gelatin explosive sliding down it. A blast rocked the field and the flames disappeared.

Myron Kinley turned his back on the well and went to get his pay from the H. F. Wilcox Company. Like the spectator at the fire, the Wilcox firm thought young Kinley was a durn fool when he made a proposition that he would put out the fire in 24 hours or work for nothing.

Working close to a burning oil well was—and still is—hazardous business at best. And that idea of exploding a well to put out the fire, well, it sounded like a suicide trick.

Myron Kinley pocketed his $500 fee and hoped for another blowout.

"I used to be afraid a fire would go out before I could get to it," said the man whose Houston-headquarters business is known to oilmen all over the world.

"Now I get more midnight calls than a doctor, and I wish to heaven the fires would go out by themselves."

The telephone directory lists M. M. Kinley Company, Oil Well Fire Extinguishers, on Sage Road. At that site, in the Tanglewood vicinity, there is a little machine shop that looks out of place in the growing residential area.

It looks like a hip pocket operation, but if it is, Mr. Kinley has a mighty big hip pocket.

Since he first gained respect along with his $500 fee in Oklahoma, he has been called to fight fires and cap blown-out wells in the Middle East, South America, Canada and almost every oil-producing area of the United States.

He is reticent about the amount of money he makes to day, but other sources have said that the big oil companies pay him as much as $30,000 for a job. And he estimates that he has capped about 350 wild wells in his career.

"I've been out on sixteen jobs this year," he said, "Most of them were small ones. Last year I made every call we had, because my assistant got hurt and couldn't work.

His assistant, Paul Adair, has been fighting fires with Mr. Kinley for about eight years, and he considers it only a part-time job.

Contrary to the Oklahoma spectator's opinion, Kinley was not just trying a foolish experiment when he shot the Wilcox well to snuff out the flames.

His formal education had extended only to the eighth grade, and he probably could not, then, have discussed the physical principle involved. No one had told him that a big explosion would create a vacuum, and that flames could not survive without oxygen.

But he knew he could dump some nitroglycerin into a burning well and stop a fire, because he had seen his father do it.

Karl Kinley was an oil well shooter, and he reared his family under the California derricks around Bakersfield and Taft.

The shooting involved setting off dynamite charges, sometimes to remove the well casing and sometimes to bring out oil in close packed formations.

When Myron was about 14, he watched his father drop some dynamite into a burning well in the Taft field, trying to collapse the structure.

"Dad had been experimenting with several ways to put out oil fires," Mr. Kinley said. "The dynamite wasn't entirely successful on the Taft well, but it was good enough to convince my father that it could work, and it convinced me, too."

Mr. Kinley says his father was not the first man to shoot a fire, but both father and son were early practitioners of the technique.

Before Myron began making himself known in Oklahoma, the favored firefighting device was steam, pumped onto a flaming well from boilers rigged up at the site.

Mr. Kinley likes to act a little bit cynical about his work.

"It's just a job," he says. "I wouldn't go to work on a well if I was afraid."

His associates wonder what it would take to make Myron Kinley afraid. He saw his only brother, Floyd, die when he was blown off a drilling platform at Goliad. Myron got a broken ankle at Gladewater, and he walks with a limp from an accident at Bay City. He was badly burned on a job in Venezuela, and he is partially deaf from the concussion of all the explosive charges he has set off.

The Gladewater accident in 1929 was his first serious one, but it indirectly led to international prestige.

An iron beam fell across his ankle and while he was recovering from the fracture he read about a big fire in Romania, in a well owned by a Standard Oil Company subsidiary.

"I decided to go over to Romania, on my own, and try to get the job," he said. "But I didn't have any luck. The government was involved and they wouldn't give me a crack at it."

Almost two years later the fire was still burning and Mr. Kinley, then a Rotarian, decided to attend a Rotary International convention in Vienna.

While he was on the trip, he went back to Romania and found the oil people were ready to talk to him.

"The well had cratered, like a volcano," Mr. Kinley said. "The crater was about 200 feet across the top and sixty-five feet deep. They wanted me to put out the fire and cap the well, with the understanding that I would get paid only if I succeeded. I took them up."

Before Mr. Kinley took over the job, the oil company had tried to dig a 100-foot tunnel to intersect the well. The tunnel had collapsed, killing fourteen men.

Mr. Kinley flooded the whole crater with liquid concrete cooled by a constant water spray. Then he set off simultaneous blasts in the tunnel and at the well head. The fire went out and he capped the well. The job took six months and Kinley admits he got "several thousand dollars" for his work.

The Romania job was the first one that had included capping a well as well as controlling it. Now the capping is a standard part of his operation.

Mr. Kinley came closest to death at Bay City in 1936.

"A shot went off with me," he explained casually. "I had just straightened up, after leaning over the explosive when it went off. If I had still been leaning over I suppose it would have killed me. It did kill another man."

His right side was filled with shrapnel and his leg was almost crushed. He spent a year and a half recovering from the wounds.

The Venezuela accident—he says he doesn't remember exactly when it was—occurred while he was trying to control a wild well. There was no fire when he went to work, but flames shot up suddenly and caught him.

"If you knew where I was burned," he explained delicately, you would know I was running from the fire."

His longest job, and the one he considers hardest, was on a

blowout at Greta, near Refugio. It was not on fire, but the wild well was on the Missouri-Pacific railroad right-of-way, and it forced trains off the route.

"The M-P hired me," Mr. Kinley said, "and I worked on the thing eight months. It had cratered, like the well in Romania, and was shooting up a lot of mud and debris.

"I pumped out a lot of water, and finally we capped it and filled it up with cement."

Mr. Kinley's most publicized job was an offshore one for the Pure Oil Company near Morgan City, Louisiana, last year.

"It wasn't especially spectacular," Mr. Kinley said. "And I had worked on several offshore jobs before. But Pure Oil had a cluster of five wells off Louisiana, and two of them caught fire at a time when the tidelands were pretty much in the news."

Mr. Kinley employed an LST, a spud barge and a speedboat to get his tools in position for the Louisiana project.

Hampered in changing boats by his limp, he got a crane to lift him from one to another as he worked.

His main problem on both wells was to knock off the Christmas tree control valves so the fire could rise and he could get a dynamite charge under it.

A rifle squad from Camp Polk, Louisiana, fired volley after volley at the controls, but they stayed put. Finally, Mr. Kinley got a boom into position and used it to remove the valves. Then he set off the dynamite and completed the job, all within ten days.

Mr. Kinley learned early that he had to improve tools to fit each job as it came along.

Sometimes he could simply attach his explosive to a cable, and send it down to the well as he did on the early Oklahoma job. Often he has donned an asbestos suit and carried a load of dynamite up to the detonation spot, working under a fine water spray.

Once in Iran he built an asbestos-lined steel canopy for a bulldozer, which was used to place the dynamite.

Making his own tools for the well control jobs led Mr. Kinley into another career. During what he calls his spare time, when he is not working on or traveling to wild wells, he designs oilfield equipment. He holds several patents.

A son, Jack, is office manager of the M. M. Kinley Company and works with his father on business matters.

"But he isn't in the oil business," Mr. Kinley said firmly, "I've kept my family out of that."

Another son, Dan, is with Proctor and Gamble in Cincinnati. A daughter, Mrs. J. J. Knoble, lives in Los Angeles.

In 1950 Mr. Kinley was 50 years old, and he decided to retire. So he sold his River Oaks home and he and his wife moved to Bel Air, California, not far from Hollywood. The retirement lasted several weeks.

"I couldn't stay away from the business. It made me feel old," he said.

Mr. Kinley does not want to feel old. He won't let his four grandchildren call him grandpa.

He has gained a little weight since his leg injury slowed him down, and he has lost most of his hair. But his blue eyes are as piercing as ever. And he still keeps an overnight bag packed with a valid passport, a khaki shirt, a razor and a toothbrush so he can be ready to go when a wild well call comes in.

That is why his friends sometimes smile when Mr. Kinley says his firefighting is "just a job."

After he had finished the eighth grade in the Bakersfield, California, schools, Mr. Kinley decided he knew enough, and he went to work helping his father on a shooting wagon. Then he went to work for a firm that built galvanized oil tanks.

The only job he ever had that was not connected with the oil business was during his middle teens: He was employed in a blacksmith shop. But the shop was in the Midway Oil Field in California.

He served in the artillery during World War I and afterward joined his father and his brother, Floyd, in Tulsa, where his father had organized the Western Torpedo Company. The firm used gelatin instead of the more dangerous nitroglycerin formerly used to shoot wells in the Oklahoma fields.

"The Company went broke," Mr. Kinley said, "and they owed me so much money in back pay that I took it over and reorganized it as the M. M. Kinley Company" Mr. Kinley worked out of Tulsa until 1935, when he moved his headquarters to Houston.

His brother worked with him on fires until his death, but Floyd's main interest was in drilling and production.

A sister, who is not in the oil business, is Mrs. Gene Peddecord of Ventura, California.

Although he has spent all his life in the oil fields, Mr. Kinley has never owned a producing well. That side of the business has not interested him much until recently.

"I decided to drill a well last year," he said, "but it didn't increase my enthusiasm any. It was a dry hole."

Reprinted by permission of the *Houston Post*.

"THE MONSTER'S TALE"

Bill Burchardt

From the Persian Gulf to the wind-swept Zagros mountains of ancient Persia lies a hot, semi-desert land. It is the area drained by the Tigris, Euphrates, and Karum rivers—the very cradle of mankind.

Domain of Kashgai tribesmen, these nomadic, saddlebred descendants of the conquering hordes of Genghis Khan are proud, statuesque men. Aquiline faced, dark piercing eyed, horsemen without peer, their encampments of black and contrastingly bright hued persian carpeted tents are reminiscent of Marco Polo's travels.

During the spring of 1958 drilling was underway on Ahwaz Number 6—a wildcat well. On the morning of April 19th drilling was suspended to bring up a core sample. The mud got a little light in the hole. BLOWOUT! Within minutes, gas and condensate roaring from the wellhead at 3,200 p.s.i. flashed into fire.

There are no words to describe the sound of a burning well. It is a volume of unrelenting noise that stuns the senses. The monster cauldron of flame could be seen for twenty miles in the daytime.

The men of the Anglo-Iranian crew set about doing things they knew would need to be done—building a water pipeline to the Karun River twenty-two miles away—opening up the No. 5 Ahwaz wildcat which had struck salt water six years earlier. These sources delivered almost a million gallons of water a day to reservoirs the crew dug at the fire site. They began armoring bulldozers, track-mounted trucks and boom tractors with iron and asbestos fire shields. But they did not begin the actual attack on the fire itself. The sent for Myron Kinley.

Myron Kinley fought and extinguished his first oil well fire near Cromwell in 1924. Four years later he saw his brother killed as they worked together fighting a fire near Goliad, Texas.

In 1931, Kinley's leg was broken fighting a fire near Gladewater, Texas, where six men were killed. The same leg was almost paralyzed by shrapnel near Bay City, Texas, in a fire explosion that killed the man working beside him.

In 1945 he was twenty feet from a blowout in Venezuela which roared into flame. Unable to run with his crippled leg, Kinley walked, boiled in the scalding steam of his own water-soaked clothing, to shield himself behind a cathead. He spent the next six months in the hospital, able to move only his head. Most of his body is covered with scar tissue. He left the hospital to fight his next oilfield fire.

Kinley was at lunch in Houston when he was summoned to fight the fire in Iran. He flew 8,000 miles in 60 hours, arriving at Ahwaz on the fifth day of the fire. The inferno was a rampage of flame and black smoke raging out around the molten remains of the derrick, drilling platform, machinery, and an 8,000 foot tangle of red-hot drill stem.

All of this had to be removed before the fire could be fought. If not, the fire would reignite itself from the red-hot wreckage. Some of the Iranian crew had worked with Kinley on a fire seven years earlier at Naft Safid. They were courageous, competent men.

The next ten days were spent completing the rigging of tools, vehicles, and equipment. Then Kinley ordered the crew to rest until midnight. It would be impossible to approach the fire in daytime heat.

At midnight, clearing the debris began with a huge watercooled hook on the end of a boom. Kinley rode a bulldozer, driven backward, up to the fire. He stood on a platform at the edge of the cauldron, almost over the fire itself, peering out into the flames through a slit in the bulldozer's iron armor, directing the driver where to drop the wrecking hook. Fire hoses sprayed Kinley, the fire, the bulldozer, its driver, with constant sheets of water, keeping the heat barely within tolerance.

For eight nights they hooked and raked at the hot debris, dragging out tangles of drill stem, pieces of the derrick, and fused chunks of machinery often so heavy several tractors had to be rigged in tandem to heave out the obstinate loads.

An Iranian commentator called the endless, deafening noise in which they worked a "constant explosion." Perhaps that is as near as words can come. And the heat — a thermometer far back from the blazing turmoil registered 260°.

Anyone who has driven across the Arizona-California desert in 120° heat, or tried to work out in the sun during a 108° mid-summer heat wave, can perhaps speculate how it might be to attempt hard physical labor in heat more than twice that intense, and in a never-ending roar of noise that grinds at nerves like sandpaper on live bone.

On May 18th, 30 days after the fire's outbreak, Kinley decided to try to finish clearing the site with an explosion. An iron bomb was packed with 450 pounds of explosives and shoved up against the edge of the well cellar. The bomb was exploded, hoping to remove one of the blowout preventers that tools had been unable to budge. Unexpectedly, the explosion also blew out the fire.

From a distance, the crew watched in suspense. The huge jet of gas and condensate, spewing skyward under incredible pressure, did not reignite for 51 minutes, then it again burst into flames.

Kinley believes that some combination of the elements—water, oxygen, and gas—caused the reignition. Small puffs of smoke had appeared in the column several times as it tried to reignite.

Now, however, with all the wreckage dragged clear or blown away by the explosion, the fire was no longer a cauldron of flame. It was single tongue blazing skyward as though blown from the lungs of some mythical, medieval monster.

But this monster was not imaginary. Kinley prepared a 350 pound bomb and exploded it in the air beside the flame, trying to blow out the fire without damaging the well-head casing. This second explosion failed even to wound the monster.

He prepared a third charge, then had to wait three days for a fair wind that would blow the deadly gas away from the workmen should the fire be extinguished. This time the charge contained 600 pounds of explosive. The beast, angry in the earth, roared back in furious, unchecked defiance.

The fight went on, now thirty-one days old, in weariness, heat, ear-tearing noise, and constant danger. Again they had to wait for the wind to change. Then an 800-pound charge was exploded right against the wellhead. The fire was blown out.

It stayed out just ten minutes. By May 27th, the fire was costing nearly a million dollars a day. On that day Kinley tried another explosion against the wellhead. It failed. On May 28th he tried another.

The sight of that 60-year-old man, moving at the halting gait compelled by his crippled leg, day after weary day going up to confront the defiant fury of the fire, came to seem to the crew an incomparable example of intrepid courage.

By June 4th, Kinley had prepared a horseshoe-shaped bomb that would fit around the wellhead. Rails of slotted drill stem along which the bomb could be shoved into place, were moved up. Kinley's face, drained by fatigue, dulled by exhaustion, was without expression as he wired the charge into the hell box, but his fingers worked without faltering at the long familiar chore.

With the water-cooled boom the charge was shoved up to surround the wellhead casing on three sides. He exploded it. It blew the fire out.

Now the most dangerous job of all had to be done. The wild well had to be capped. Bulldozers and men dug for four days to expose a working length of the casing, which had been sheared off by the explosions until it was level with the earth in the bottom of the deep-blasted crater.

A change of wind direction blew the explosive gas and gasoline condensate in deadly clouds over the whole working crew. Kinley, holding a red flag before him, brought the crew up out of the pit. Two entire villages had to be evacuated.

In grim weariness, the crew took cover, watching, waiting. In the dim light of the coming dawn, the silhouette of a tall workman, in turban and work-stained coveralls, stood praying to Allah of the ancient Persians. His palms were reverently upturned in supplication, he made an ascetic gesture of contrition, and bowed his head.

When the wind changed, the men went back to work. In the gaseous drench and condensate they worked two days with hacksaws, sawing off the 18-inch casing to expose a collar of the 13-inch casing. They attached casing tongs on the collar, ran lines to it, and with a tractor and a crew of men to heave around on the lines, they unscrewed the collar. It flew rocketing skyward in the roaring jet of escaping gas.

Now with slips and guide ring they leveled and set a flange around the 13-inch casing. A new road was built and over it a winch truck backed, hauling the heavy valve assembly with which Kinley hoped to shut in the well.

A 3-inch steel pivot bolt was inserted to loosely connect the valve assembly to the flange on the casing. Teams of men handling the heaving lines drove the valve assembly, still suspended from the winch truck, around into the jet of escaping gas. The 3-inch steel pivot bolt bent like warm taffy in the powerful blast and the heavy valve assembly cocked over on its side, spraying gas and condensate everywhere.

The crew escaped to wash off the gasoline condensate under the stream of fire hoses. Then they returned to retrieve the off-center valve assembly, to remove and repair the flange, and to saw off the 13-inch casing.

Throughout all this a single spark—from a hacksaw—from a winch truck spark plug—from a bulldozer truck, or diesel motor— might set the towering column of gas afire and turn the crater in which Kinley and his small crew worked into a crematorium. No man could have escaped alive.

When the 13-inch casing had been removed the final source of their trouble became apparent. The explosions had flattened the end of the inner, 9-inch casing. Its jagged end now sprayed the gas into a gigantic fan. Using casing cutters remotely operated with heaving lines, they cut off the damaged casing end, and again the gas escaped in a straight, upward column.

The flange was once more set and leveled, the massive control valve again winched over it, set, and bolted down with high tensile steel bolts. Water lines were rigged to connect the valve assembly hydraulically with a cement truck.

On June 22nd, 65 days after the fire had begun, Myron Kinley opened a pressure test valve and a side jet, then gradually shut off the control valves hydraulically from the truck. Then, in an incredible emptiness of sound with the wild well silenced, there was only the chugging of the truck as it pumped cement into the well.

The Ahwaz fire brought Myron Kinley to the conclusion that it was about time for him to retire from actively fighting oil well fires. After Ahwaz, he tamed two burning wells in the Gulf of Mexico offshore from Louisiana, then another near the Arctic Circle in the Yukon Territory of Canada, in a sort of tapering off process. Now he has retired completely.

He lives quietly, at his home in Chickasha, but the tales of Myron Kinley's intrepid battles against the paramount fury of gas and oil well blowout fires will be told into immortality, for Kinley and his courage in the face of death is the very stuff of which legends are made.

"FIGHTING OIL WELL FIRES"

Gerald F. Benedict

Like a roaring cyclone, a 75,000, 000-cubic foot gas well three miles off shore in Lake Maracaibo, famous Venezuela oil region, prematurely blew in wild and caught fire, a huge weaving 200-foot torch blazing out of the water.

The raging fury offered a problem local engineers could not solve. Capping a wild gasser on land is difficult enough, but one out in the water had even the experts stumped. In the excitement someone thought of Myron M. Kinley, oil well firefighter of Houston, Texas.

"Get Kinley!" is the cry in the oil fields of the world when anything goes wrong and fire breaks out. Immediately the radio spluttered an SOS to Kinley, and a few hours later he and his brother, Floyd, of Tulsa, Oklahoma, were on their way by plane to tame the wild geyser, which belonged to the Largo Petroleum Company, a subsidiary of Standard Oil.

While the brothers were enroute, the big gasser unexpectedly turned into a 6,000-barrel oil well and, of course, blazing. This changed the problem.

When the Kinleys reached Maracaibo and saw what they had to tackle they decided that the only thing to do was to let the well burn while they devised a way to stop it. What they did amazed engineers and, when it was all over, even the Kinleys were surprised themselves at their success.

Picking up a huge 94-foot, 25,000-pound derrick in a single piece, they towed it intact on three barges to a spot 600 feet from the blazing well. Then they drilled an offset well, slanting to the base of the blaze. Tapping the oil sand at the bottom and pumping mud and water at the base of the fiery geyser, they automatically shut off the flow of oil.

Next the Kinleys placed a special cap, set in cement, at the mouth of the well to prevent oil from seeping into the lake when the well was reopened and placed on production. As the brothers frantically dug into the lake bottom to douse the geyser, there was always the threat that flaming oil would pour onto the surface of the lake, with staggering damage. It had happened once before in the case of another well, and the oil companies were swamped with lawsuits after the burning oil had traveled over the water to the city of Maracaibo, with a population of more than 100,000, and nearly wiped it out in addition to damaging a dozen other beach towns along the way.

Their unique firefighting feat accomplished, Floyd casually admitted that he guessed an entire steel derrick had not before been hauled to the scene by barge.

To this engineers agreed. The usual method of moving rigs of such huge dimensions is to tear them down and rebuild them on the new site. It generally requires a week to tear down and another week to rebuild, but a high-powered crew has been known to demolish and re-erect a derrick on land in 40 hours. It would have been next to impossible to do this in water.

Answering long distance fire is new to the Kinleys. They have tamed a hundred oil and gas well fires in American fields, while Myron also has subdued fires in Mexico, the Argentine, Colombia and Romania. The Venezuela expedition was Floyd's first trip to a foreign field.

Myron Kinley first came into international fame following his successful six months' battle with the world's most famous oil well fire—that of the Standard Oil well in Moreni, Romania—which burned for 18 months, killing nine men and injuring scores of others before Kinley took charge. Traveling with full equipment by land, sea and air from his office in Houston to Romania, Kinley made the longest fire run on record—7,000 miles.

Something of the problem confronting Kinley in extinguishing the man-made volcano in Romania may be imagined if you can visualize a crater 260 feet in diameter at the surface in which a blaze 60 feet wide sends a steady, roaring flame 30 feet over the top of the crater. Developing a temperature of 3,000 degrees Fahrenheit, the fire consumed 250,000,000 cubic feet of gas a day, a supply sufficient to meet the entire domestic needs of Detroit, Michigan, for ten days.

Recalling that job recently, Kinley said: "That fire was the meanest I ever worked on. The well caught fire on May 22, 1929, and burned until November 4, 1931. Tunnels, dug to tap the gas flow from beneath the surface, had caved in and gas seeped through the ground in a wide area and spread the blaze. But it wouldn't have been so bad if we hadn't been delayed so much by government red tape. Old World superstitions about fooling with the phenomenon of nature added to the difficulty. We had to show this and that committee that we could put out fire with explosives. Fear and ignorance played their part. Danger, ingenuity, perseverence and the help of the Lord, according to the Romanian papers, were combined in extinguishing the blaze. They should have included the king, too, for it was not until the arguments were ended by his decree that we finally were able to get to work.

"After shooting the walls of the crater with innumerable charges which smothered the outer blaze with mud and dirt, we succeeded in installing a 30-foot metal stack in a manner that drew the flames to a central point. Several times after the fire had been snuffed out, it reignited from the hot ground and pieces of molten metal we could not remove. When the fire finally was definitely out, we connected the gas flow to the lines of a gasoline plant, and it is still functioning."

But what causes these dread fires? As the well is drilled, casing pipe is inserted to protect the hole from water seepage and cave-ins. When the oil or gas sand is reached, the drilling tools are withdrawn and control valves placed on top of the casing and connected with storage tanks. This is done just before drilling into oil or gas sand because, as a rule, oil or gas do not immediately flow when sand is is struck.

It is the well shooter's job to tap this sand. Oil sand is like a sponge, and may be from 3 to 150 feet thick. From 5 to 300 quarts of nitroglycerin are lowered down the casing to the well's bottom and set off. The explosion breaks up the oil sand, so that it releases the oil much as a soaked sponge releases water when pressed. Gas pressure pushes the oil to the surface and, as the oil comes up, the valves are adjusted and the well becomes a producer.

However, there are times when wells come in prematurely, without the need of explosives and before the tools are out of the shaft or the valves installed. It is not unusual for drilling tools, weighing tons, to be blown through the top of a 120-foot derrick by the gas, which often reaches a pressure of 3,000 pounds to the square inch.

This, of course, means the well is out of control, and there is always the threat of fire which may instantly reach a temperature of from 300 to 3,000 degrees Fahrenheit, burning the derrick like a paper bag in a furnace and reducing the steel and iron equipment to a glowing mass of metal.

Oil well fires can be caused in a number of ways. Sometimes heavy tools, while being drawn out or, in some instances, blown from the well, create sparks as they bang against the casing pipe. Lightning may strike a well. But the exact cause is seldom known. Most who have been close enough to see the actual cause, have been killed.

A trained expert with special equipment is required to put out these wild torches. Kinley's usual method is to set off a charge of gelatinized nitroglycerin at the base of the blaze. It may be days before the shot can be fired at some fires. Red hot metal and debris first must be pulled out, away from the well. If not removed, this hot metal can easily reignite the gas.

Kinley's method, like the fire, is spectacular; but he is decidedly not a stunt man. He goes about his work with the careful strategy of a general in the midst of war. His work is war—a patient battle with nature gone wild.

He has developed a system which includes a special fire truck, unique equipment he designed, based on practical experience and needs, for he is mechanically inclined and has invented many practical devices in the oil fields. When he needs something that can do the job better he says he "just makes it."

He employs a five-man crew to clear away the debris. Two wear heavy asbestos suits, helmets, gloves and shoes, and work up close to the fire, rushing in and out of the terrific heat attaching grappling hooks to the hot metals. The hooks are connected by steel cables to a powerful high speed tractor, manned by a third member of the crew. Two more assistants, standing behind a movable shield, play a double stream of water over the ground near the mouth of the well and over the men working in the asbestos suits. Occasionally bad valves have to be yanked out "by the roots." No two fires are the same.

Finally comes the task of carrying the "gelatin" to the edge of the flame. Kinley prepares his own shot at his nitro wagon stationed a little away from the well. He can estimate the size of the shot needed, which may range from five to 40 quarts, packed in a metal container of a special design with double walls with air space between, and wrapped with a layer of heavy asbestos. Every precaution is taken to protect the shot from the heat.

Attached to the container is a strand of wire, used in firing the charge from the switch.

A final check on the equipment, and Kinley climbs into his asbestos suit, signals the hose crew, and starts toward the roaring flame in a leisurely walk, carefully picking his way over the muddy ground. Tucked under his arm is enough explosive to blow him to smithereens should he miss footing or the trailing wire snag and jerk the container from his grasp.

As though discussing some ordinary job, Kinley modestly admits: "I have had narrow escapes. One never knows in this business. A wind might whip the flames around and then it's all over."

At the mouth of the well Kinley places the shot within a foot or two of the blaze and quickly retires to the switch 100 yards back. Down goes the plunger. A dull red glow appears near the fire. As sight is quicker than sound, the yellow flame disappears in the air a fraction of a second before the explosion is heard. However, the roar of the gas continues, for, when the force of the shot is dissipated the gas resumes its upward flow. But there is no fire. Kinley's work is not completed until he has connected the well with pipelines or storage tanks, putting it in production.

All conceivable equipment is carried in the fire truck. A special pump for spraying the men and cooling the ground is mounted on the front of the motor. Other equipment consists of special nozzles and hose; several sets of asbestos suits, shoes and gloves; hardboiled helmets with heat-resisting glass windows; gas masks, inhalators, stretchers, first-aid supplies, a complete set of specially designed non-sparking and heat-resisting tools, and oil-soaked cotton for the men to plug in their ears as a protection against the roar, vibration and explosion.

Because of the spectacle value of a burning oil well and the interest in Kinley's success, he recently gave a public demonstration at the International Petroleum Exposition at Tulsa. Natural gas was piped to an 80-foot wooden derrick in front of the grandstand.

To increase the pressure sufficient to produce a 60-foot blaze, gate valves on the open flow gas wells 60 miles away were opened. The normal gas flow on the main line is 25 pounds, reduced at the domestic meter to 4 ounces, or one-quarter pound. Opening the valves increased the main line pressure to 100 pounds, at which pressure it was delivered to the exhibition. The demonstration, lasting a little more than an hour, consumed 1,155,000 cubic feet of gas, or enough to supply the needs of ten homes for a year; the cost was about $1,000.

Prior to the adoption of Kinley's method of fighting fires, the most successful method was to smother the blaze with jets of steam and streams of mud. This system is still used on some blazes.

"What was the biggest single shot you ever used?" Kinley was asked.

"Eighty quarts," he replied. "That was on the big Tulsa Oil Company fire at Overton, Texas. The next biggest was about forty-five quarts on the Sinclair Oil Company fire at Gladewater."

"Which was the hardest to handle?"

"They were both plenty tough. The gas pressure was so strong on the Overton blaze that the flames stood nearly 200 feet high. Clearing away the hot metal from that was a real job. But that Romanian job was the meanest to work on."

"How did you conceive the idea of shooting out fires by explosives?"

"I didn't. It was a theory of my father's, K. T. Kinley. Floyd and I only improved on it. Dad was an oil field worker in California. He noticed that gas fires had a mixing chamber, a three to fifteen-foot space between the bottom of the blaze and the mouth of the well, in which gas and air mixed. He figured that an explosion, set off close to that chamber, would break the gas flow long enough for the blaze to disappear before the gas could resume its upward direction. Sort of 'snuff it out,' as he termed it.

"His problem was to place the shot, and the only way he knew how to do it was to throw it, the jar of landing setting off the blast. The danger of a premature explosion discouraged well owners from letting him try it. But eventually a well he was working on caught fire. Steam and mud had no effect and, because of the danger to other wells ready to come in close by, immediate action was demanded and Dad was allowed to try his idea.

"With a heavy charge of nitroglycerin in a crudely constructed bomb, he approached as near as possible to the blaze. A man with a hose started to keep a stream of water on him, but thought better of it, quit and ran. To have as much getaway as possible, Dad tossed the bomb high in the air and fled. The shot landed square on the well and exploded. The fire was out!"

The elder Kinley, retired from active oil field work several years ago and lives quietly at his home in Ojai, near Ventura, California.

Myron Kinley was born in Santa Barbara, California, in 1898 and at sixteen started assisting his father, taking up his profession as an oil well shooter, a technical and dangerous work but vital. Five foot 10 inches, and weighing nearly 200 pounds, he is shy and resents any intimation bordering on the show-off.

As a hobby he collects old guns and weapons he has picked up in the wild regions where he has worked. Between firefighting jobs he manages his own company in Houston and looks after his personal oil production holdings.

Floyd Kinley, born in Bakersfield, California, in 1904, is six years younger than Myron. He studied the profession of oil well shooting under his brother. An inch or two taller, he looks slender despite his 160 pounds. Slightly deaf from concussion around hundreds of explosions, he assists his brother on all fires. His only hobby—as he puts it—is worrying. He resides with his family on his oil lease seven miles northwest of Tulsa.

Also among the half dozen daredevil firefighters is H. L. Patton of Houston, Texas, who is credited with having subdued more than 100 fires and wild wells in the last few years. A quiet spoken man of about 40, Patton claims he likes his dangerous job, and has fought fires and wrestled with wild gassers all over the country. He subdued a 45,000-barrel wild well in the big East Texas field, capped an outlaw in Wyoming when the temperature was 45 degrees below zero, and has entered craters after derricks and all riggings had been swallowed.

One of Patton's last spectacular jobs was on a burning well within the city limits of Corpus Christi, Texas. The roaring fire threatened other wells and parts of the city. Two men were burned to death and two others hurt.

Through such infernos Patton only once sustained serious injury. Fire broke out behind him after he crawled into the derrick floor of a wild well on the Texas coast in 1935. Out of sight of his helpers, who were unable to turn water on him, he was forced to fight blindly through the flames. He was badly burned but ready for another fire within a few months.

"I sort of like a good fire," he says.

Another famous and stout-hearted oil well tamer is John W. Gordon, a Cherokee Indian who lives on a placid farm at Choteau, Oklahoma.

During the early days of the Oklahoma and Texas fields when he was a roustabout and connection man—one who works with a special crew connecting wells to pipelines and storage tanks—two big wells blew in wild. Each ran about 25,000 b.p.d., with 60,000,000 feet of gas, spraying homes with oil and endangering the lives of hundreds of people. Gordon volunteered to tame them. He organized a crew consisting of two boys and subdued the smaller well within three days, and the larger, the Mary Sudick, in eleven days.

When the big Morgan Stout well later went out of control and menaced the east part of Oklahoma City and the State Capitol itself, Gordon was again summoned and succeeded in conquering the giant after a breath-taking battle. Gordon subdued many other wells, but he has learned from long experience that oil wells are like lions—the wild ones look mean but it's the tame ones that get you.

Not long ago while doing a small job on a tame Kansas well he was suddenly knocked down by a chain that broke. A piece of the chain hit him on the leg, and complications resulted that kept him in bed for several months.

"My advice," he says "is to watch the wild ones, but be even more careful of the tame ones."

Others who have risked their lives in dangerous infernos are Ford Alexander, of Whittier, California, who has had many narrow escapes in the Coast oil fields, and W. A. (Tex) Thornton.

Drilling Magazine, November 1939

"FIREFIGHTER"

George Goodlet

Broad must have been the smile on the sooty, smoke-grimed face of K. T. "Dad" Kinley following the successful shooting of the costly fire that was ravaging K.T.O. No. 2, 30,000-barrel well atop Long Beach, California's Signal Hill in 1913: for it was the first time that explosives had been successfully used to extinguish a major oil well fire.

That shot echoed around the entire oil world, creating a new business that has long since become big business. The M. M. Kinley Company of Houston, headed by the son of Dad Kinley, keeps crew and equipment ready to leave for any point on the globe on short notice. Thus far, no oil well fire has been too big or too complex to tackle . . . and get the job done.

Kinley is now at work on what he says has been his most difficult assignment. His job is to bring under control the Missouri Pacific well, near Greta, Texas, in Victoria County.

Having been drilled between the railroad and a highway, several hundred feet of each road was destroyed when the well blew out and cratered June 19, 1936. The railroad company took it over when it was seen that it was completely out of control and threatening the original owners with bankruptcy.

When Kinley took over the job on February 25, 1939, the crater was over 600 feet in diameter, 72 feet deep and filled to ground level with water. It took weeks to pump the water down to a level that would enable them to work . . . then the well ignited again. Four times the water was lowered, and each time something ignited the escaping gas.

Several theories were forwarded as to the cause of this repeated combustion.

One theory was that the gas, not being moisture-laden as before, underwent a chemical change and ignited upon becoming mixed with the air. Another was that static electricity was being created by the mass of high lines, telegraph wires, and steel rails in the vicinity as the water level was pulled dawn. But Mr. O. V. Borden, the office manager of the Kinley Company, gave this as the theory that was finally accepted (until a later study reveals the actual cause):

"We knew that the 'doodle-bug hole' (the inner crater— measuring about 6 feet across and 20 feet deep) was filled with a tangled mass of guy wires, derrick legs, and other pieces of iron and steel, so we figured that gas pressure moving these interwoven metal odds and ends back and forth must have been producing an occasional spark. Such a spark could easily ignite an escaping gas bubble, and if the bubble was large enough to burn until reaching the surface of the remaining water it might easily set the well off again."

The fire hazard has been almost eliminated at the time of this writing, as the "doodle-bug hole" has been cleaned of all debris, and a 10-inch milling string has been placed over the mouth of the well. This is run up through the temporary rotary table and piped out over the lip of the crater through a 16-inch discharge line, sending several hundred barrels of salt water an hour into the two ditches that the railroad company has dug for a distance of two miles on each side of its right-of-way.

On Friday, September 18th, when only 18 inches from the depth that they must reach before capping the well, they ran into an underground spring flowing a stream of water five inches in diameter. Interlocking steel pilings are being used in an effort to cofferdam that side of the hole. When the cofferdam is in place, the completion of the job is expected within a few days; but in this business they have learned to be prepared for almost anything.

Before taking over this latest job, Kinley's toughest assignment was the extinguishing of what is still considered the world's largest oil well fire. Burning for 2½ years, causing the loss of eleven lives and over one million dollars damage, the Romagno-Americano Well No. 160, Moreni Field, Romania, sent for Kinley after several unsuccessful attempts had been made to cap it. It was capped and put on production May 23, 1929, after 189 days.

In spite of the many unpredictible dangers confronting oil well firefighters, the Kinley Company has had only three major accidents in the 38 years that it has been operating. It is a tribute to the careful study and extensive planning that is put into the solving of each problem, as well as the care that is taken to prevent its crews from becoming exposed to any danger that is not necessary. It was just that principle that perhaps saved the lives of three crew members, but cost the life of Floyd Kinley, M. M. Kinley's brother.

This tragedy occurred near Goliad, Texas, March 12, 1938. Floyd Kinley and three helpers were attempting to break out the Kelly of a well under pressure, and after getting the job almost completed, he sent the others out of the way intending to complete the job himself. It blew out prematurely, throwing him back against the derrick and crushing his skull.

Many and odd are the problems that sometimes face the firefighters. Special equipment must sometimes be manufactured on the spot, in order to cope with the situation. Once a derrick was hoisted complete onto a well immediately after the shooting of the fire in order to facilitate getting it back under control. This well belonged to the Standard Oil Company of New Jersey and was located in the center of Lake Maracaibo in Venezuela, necessitating the use of a huge crane mounted on a barge.

As each job presents a different problem, the Kinley Company makes only one suggestion as to what to do until their crew arrives on the scene—get everything that is movable out of the reach of the fire. Many jobs have been so simple to handle that the only charge that was made was for the cost of the trip and any equipment that might have been needed. This has built much goodwill for the firefighters.

A new insurance policy covering drilling operations against fire is now being worked out in which the Kinley Company will figure prominently. Roughly, it will correspond to the Metropolitan Salvage Corps now being employed by insurance companies in many larger cities. The policy automatically will entitle the holder to the services of the Kinley Company in the event of fire.

"THE FIGURE IN THE FLAMES"

Ernst Behrendt

Oil men who visit Central America frequently hear the story of one Ramon Gomez, a former bull gang worker who now lives with his family in a village nestled in the mountains of Guatemala. Some time ago, he and his neighbors were forced to flee from their homes when a nearby volcano erupted. The explosion blew the top of the volcano sky-high, ashes covered the fields, lava set the village afire, and at night the blazing crater could be seen many miles away. When the eruptions had finally died down and the flames burned themselves out, the Gomez family and others returned to what had been their homes. Since there wasn't much left they gathered to discuss the next step—whether to move or rebuild, and, if the latter, what to do if the volcano erupted again. It was then that Gomez, remembering his oil field days, offered the classic comment:

"Next time, call Kinley."

The reason why oil men remember Gomez' remark is that Gomez knew what he was talking about. He knew Kinley. He had worked with Kinley. He had seen the feats that only Kinley could perform. And Gomez—like everyone else who has watched this astonding man—simply could not believe that any fire, from spark to holocaust, could prevail against the one mortal who has never lost a fight against the flames.

This person—who is he? California-born 59-year-old Myron Kinley is very possibly the bravest, most skillful, most experienced and most successful firefighter the world has ever seen. His specialty is fighting oil well fires, but at times he may well have wondered how a blazing volcano could be snuffed out. After all, he has had dealings with burning wells whose heat and ferocity were of volcanic proportions.

Take the "Hell of Qatar." Qatar is a small sheikdom in Arabia; hell was what it looked like in 1951 after a well blew out and caught fire. The well was surrounded by hills; the hills bounced the heat right back into the well area. Hundreds of feet from the fire, the thermometer registered 260° F; closer to the well, the ground was covered with glowing metal. There was no source of water within 22 miles.

Myron Kinley killed the fire.

How he did it, why he did it, and how he has managed to contribute so mightily toward greater safety in the American oil industry is a story that goes back to the year 1913.

At that time, Karl T. Kinley, Myron's father, was a well shooter in Bakersfield, California. One day, Karl was called in to kill a burning well in the Taft field. According to one version, his job was to shoot off a stuck valve in the well; according to another, he was supposed to set off a charge of dynamite which would smother the well under a blanket of dirt. At any rate, Karl T. exploded the dynamite.

No valve came off. No blanket smothered the fire. But the fire was killed just the same. The blast had extinguished it.

Why this was possible was at first a mystery to everybody concerned. Later, Karl T. provided an answer. He explained that the space between the well head and the lowest point of the house-high, swirling blaze could be considered a kind of "open-air mixing chamber." This space is only a few feet high, but it is vitally important because it is here that gas and air get together to form a combustible mixture. An explosion will destroy the "mixing chamber," if only for a second or two; but a second or two will be enough to separate the fire from the oil and gas surging upward from the well beneath, whereupon the blaze will be snuffed out like a candle.

Never mind the theory. The main thing was that it worked.

Now, you can compare a blazing well with a candle, just as you can call a Siberian tiger an overgrown kitten. The trick is to learn how to tame the larger edition.

Myron Kinley began his professional career taming wild wells. Like his father, he cowed and beat them with explosives. He learned still more about explosives in the artillery, where he served during World War I. Afterward, he went into the firefighting business with his younger brother Floyd as his assistant.

But at that time the supply of Kinley was still greater than the demand. Somehow the oil companies seemed convinced that outsiders should not be called in to take care of a well fire. One reason may have been that the number of well fires was steadily decreasing.

This was, of course, quite a change compared to the early days, when "gushers" and black, billowing clouds of smoke had become associated with the oil fields—at least in the mind of an impressionable public that was being treated to sensational movies and headlines. But the oil men had been learning. They knew quite a bit about blowout preventers, firefighting, and safety measures in general. By the time Myron Kinley went into business, the record was very much improved. (It was not, however, nearly so good as it is now. In a recent year there were just 23 blowouts among some 47,000 wells drilled in the United States, and only one out of every four of these actually caught fire—an average of less than one fire every two months.)

There was another reason why Kinley's business was slow in getting started—his method was not the only one. There was, for instance, the "capping" technique, which called for a hollow cone to be lowered over the well head (if you could get near it); still another method was to blowout the blaze with blasts of steam. In 1924, in the Cromwell field of Oklahoma, Kinley had his chance to match his theories against the others.

Two well fires had broken out simultaneously. A battery of 12 steam boilers was brought into position against one of them. Myron Kinley tackled the other. Kinley was working alone. He had no helpers.

Both fires were put out. The difference was that it took the 12 steam boilers ten days to finish the job. Kinley killed his fire in ten hours.

The Cromwell field established Kinley's reputation. It proved that his method was superior.

Just what is the Kinley method?

The public is aware only of some of its more spectacular aspects. Most people have an image of Kinley crouched behind a shield, advancing into an inferno and holding a stick of dynamite while assistants spray him with water to keep him from being roasted alive. At the strategic moment he hurls the dynamite into the flames and races back—if he can make it—to safety. Seconds later the dynamite explodes, and the fire is snuffed out.

This is the drama that is portrayed as the onlookers watch with bated breath to see whether fire or human flesh will prevail, whether the lone figure behind the shield can return alive—once again. But there is far more that they do not see.

Kinley's method is many things. It is experience and boundless courage. It is ingenuity and flexibility. It is, above all, an abysmal hatred of fire. To him, fire is a personal enemy, a vicious living thing that has to be crushed so that it cannot destroy the oil and the land and the people. They have called Kinley a modern St. George, riding forth—albeit in an airplane—to destroy his personal dragon, and there may be more than a superficial similarity between the knight and the oil man. Mention fire to Kinley and you'll see a strange change come over him; his gentle baby-blue eyes suddenly acquire a steely look; his kindly, massive features become rigid and determined. Killing fires is his job, but more than that, it is his mission. Kinley's hatred of fire has much of the quality of a believer's abhorrence of

Beelzebub. You feel that the flames are in contention for his very soul. One thing is certain—if by some grave misfortune Kinley should ever find himself in the Hot Place, he'll have had plenty of experience.

There is, of course, more than a mission and a philosophy behind the Kinley method. There is a technique as well. The basic idea is simple; it is the same he was using back in 1920. To snuff out a well fire you must kill it with a blast of dynamite or nitroglycerin. But the details vary. Kinley never approaches a well with a preconceived notion as to what to do about it; he has to see it first. The moment he arrives on the scene he starts sizing up the fire the way a general would size up the strength of an enemy's army. Then he outlines a plan. Then he prepares for the assault. Then he attacks.

The job may take days or weeks, but during that time Kinley doesn't waste a minute. As soon as he's through he'll rush back to headquarters, or to his home in California, or to a plane which is waiting to take him to another burning well. The next stop may be in Africa, France, Venezuela or Iran.

In his first few years as an independent firefighter Kinley used to lug a great deal of equipment around with him. This included gas masks and inhalators, first-aid kits, heat-resistant tools, and a special fire truck with special nozzles and hoses, not to mention four or five helpers attired in asbestos suits and wearing helmets with fire-proof glass windows. But today Kinley travels light. All he takes along is some extra clothes.

For one thing, there aren't too many planes that will accommodate a special fire truck and all the other equipment; for another, he can always recruit all the manpower he needs wherever he goes. Furthermore, he can commandeer tools, he can improvise them, and as to an asbestos suit for himself, he has long ago discarded that kind of armor as being far too cumbersome. He prefers massive jets of water sprayed on him by his assistants.

It is not uncommon for Kinley to be roused by a telephone call asking him to accept a firefighting job 6,000 or 8,000 miles away. He usually arrives on the spot within two or three days, a feat which is joyously celebrated by the men in the field and by the local citizens. Kinley's name is just as popular in Saudi Arabia as it is in New Guinea, Mexico, Pakistan or Italy. In fact, it was an oil well fire in a foreign country that made him famous abroad and at home.

This was the much publicized "eternal fire" of Moreni No. 160 in Romania. No. 160 was down to 4,800 feet when it blew wild on May 28, 1929. The drill pipe and the tools were blown high into the derrick. The jet of gas, estimated at several million cubic feet a day, caught fire. Four men were killed.

Moreni No. 160 burned for 890 days. First, Romanian government crews (according to Romanian law, the government had to take over in an emergency like this) tried to drill a lateral tunnel to tap the casing 70 feet below the surface. Gas seeped into the tunnel, and an explosion killed ten more men. A second tunnel was tried; poisonous gases drove the workers back. A third tunnel became useless as a result of explosions and seepage. More men lost their lives.

Moreni No. 160 had been burning for a year when Kinley went to Romania, offering his services and submitting detailed plans. At the mention of the word "explosives," government officials turned him down; "explosives" is a word that detonates unpleasantly in the councils of many a Balkan government. Kinley went home.

Moreni No. 160 kept burning. The well had long since started to crater; by now the crater was 70 feet deep and 250 feet in diameter, with numerous little fires springing up out of hundreds of little cracks. A second crater started forming inside the first.

The "eternal fire" was becoming a political issue. Charges of inefficiency and incompetence were hurled against the government. The government fell.

Moreni No. 160 had been burning for two years when at last Kinley was asked to try his hand. There were a few stringent conditions attached (the new government was almost as allergic to "explosives" as the old one), and Kinley had to promise to cap the well.

One of the worst problems was the presence of those hundreds of little fires from seepages in the crater. Kinley attacked them one by one, closing the cracks with cement, proceeding to the next fire, and so on, until he was strategically close to the main blaze. All the time he was careful to remove every scrap of glowing metal that might reignite the fire after it had been extinguished. As it turned out, the blaze was extinguished several times, but it always sprang back to life.

Rain and snow helped. The rain started a landslide in the crater. The slide smothered the fire. Although the fire flared up again, Kinley now knew what he had to do: he exploded dynamite to set off more landslides. Slowly the crater started filling. Finally there was only one blaze left. A mere 50 pounds of nitroglycerin took care of that.

Elapsed time from the beginning of the fire to Kinley's arrival: a little over 26 months. Elapsed time from Kinley's arrival to the end of the fire: a little under three months. He needed another three months to cap the well and turn it into a producer.

Moreni No. 160 once more demonstrated Kinley's basic technique, which was, and still is, to remove everything that could start a new blaze, then get close to the fire itself and explode a few dozen or a few hundred pounds of dynamite or gelatin nitroglycerin. To remove everything is the hardest part. Tractors—their drivers protected by asbestos-lined shields—latch on to the remains of the derrick to drag them out of the way. Bulldozers sweep the site. The men working on these jobs must be just as courageous and devoted as Kinley himself. There is always the danger that they will either be nearly drowned by the heavy jets of water sprayed on them or roasted alive by the burning well.

Water is vital both for the protection of the men and to keep the explosive from going off prematurely. In the "Hell of Qatar," where there was no water nearby, Kinley diverted part of a river and led a waterline through a dammed-up canyon 22 miles to the heart of the inferno; he even requisitioned the contents of a swimming pool. In spite of extensive spraying it was still so hot that the usual fire shields were not good enough. Kinley rigged up a portable asbestos-lined shelter. One end of the shelter rested on a bulldozer so that the contraption could be pushed around. Protected by the shelter, the men behind it could safely remove the debris. Finally, the bulldozer-plus-shelter pushed a 400-gallon tank through which water was circulated, and which contained a 40-gallon drum of explosives, right to where it was needed. There was a deafening explosion, then a smaller explosion, and, still later, the completion of a delicate capping job—and the "Hell of Qatar" was a thing of the past.

One of Kinley's toughest jobs was the taming of Wild Greta in Refugio County, Texas; the Greta well had been on the rampage for 3½ years when Kinley was called in. It took him eight months to conquer Greta; half the time was spent pumping water from a 300-foot crater, which had reached a depth of 80 feet.

Kinley now averages a dozen calls a year, many of them from foreign countries. So far he has won more than 350 battles with fires and blowouts, but he has paid a price. His brother Floyd was killed in 1938 by a blowout that hurled him off a platform. In 1931, while Myron was cutting away the drawworks of a burning well in Gregg County, Texas, a beam fell across him breaking his ankle. A ranger pulled him to safety and brought him to a hospital where the ankle was set. Two hours later Kinley reappeared on the scene, directing operations from horseback. Another eight days and the fire was dead. Then he returned to the hospital to have his ankle rebroken and reset.

He was severely injured in 1936 (he still can't use his right leg properly—his car is rigged for left-leg driving) and in 1945 he was burned when a Venezuelan blowout caught fire; this accident cost him several weeks in a hospital. The deafening roar of well fires has permanently impaired his hearing.

It would seem that Myron Kinley is almost oblivious to the wounds he has received in his war against his personal enemy. He has never been defeated, and he goes on forging new weapons. He has fashioned a fabulous firefighting tool—an enormous 45-foot hook made of pipes and mounted on a tractor, with water circulating from one end to the other; moving toward the blaze, the tool keeps the explosive protected in its cool claws. Kinley has even borrowed old-fashioned ships' funnels and helicopters to change the direction of the wind near a blazing well. One of his best-known improvisations brought into action a 75-mm cannon which he borrowed to shoot off a Christmas tree from a burning offshore rig.

There is a rumor that a few years ago Myron Kinley briefly considered retirement. The fact is that he was thinking seriously about it when the telephone rang and someone inquired how he would like to tackle a fire on the other side of the Atlantic. Kinley hesitated not a moment. Yes, sir, he said, he'd like it fine. He has since tackled many more fires, including the raging wildcat near Iran's holy city of Qum. Shortly after a headline said "Qum Resists Taming," Kinley had tamed it.

Today Kinley is known throughout the world. Thousands have watched him; to millions he has become a legend. Myron Kinley, son of an oil man and an oil man himself, has become far more than an ambassador of American skill and resourcefulness. Today he is a living symbol. People see him as the man who stalks a burning well, a stick of dynamite in one hand and a crutch in the other. He is the man who never gives up. He is the man who, given a chance, might even tangle with a blazing volcano. Ramon Gomez might be right after all. You can't help feeling that the volcano might come out second best.

"TAMING THE WILD ONES"

Myron Kinley was lolling beside the swimming pool of his home, one mild California afternoon in 1951, when he was called to the telephone. The voice on the long-distance wire was urgent. An oil well being drilled in Iran had blown wild; it was now a flaming torch on the desert. Could Kinley shut it in?

Within an hour, armed with a passport and a small valise, Kinley was boarding a plane at the Los Angeles airport. Eighty hours and 8,000 miles from home, he was flying over the wild well for a first look. Without sleep he jumped into the job. In 23 days of grueling work in harsh heat, he put out the fire and capped the runaway, one of the biggest wild oil wells in history.

To Kinley—a gentle, 54-year-old grandfather who is the dean of oil well firefighters—such a wild well summons is routine. Since 1920 he has tamed more than 300 runaway wells in eleven countries, including the United States.

Out of almost 45,000 wells drilled in the United States each year, only 20 or 25 go completely wild. To oilmen, even these few are nightmares, for several reasons: They waste oil and gas. They dissipate underground pressures that are needed to produce oil. And, most important, they can be costly in life and property.

A wild well is nature on the loose. Sudden release of pressure brings forth a jet of gas that sometimes towers many hundreds of feet and hurls strings of drill pipe and massive tools upward like toys. The roar can be deafening a quarter of a mile away. If there is oil or water with the gas, a brisk wind can spray it over the countryside. One wild well in four catches fire. The flames create a billowing shaft of black by day, of fierce yellow and orange at night. No one knows how hot such towers of fire become inside, but they melt steel drilling rigs like candles. Kinley's thermometer once recorded 240° F, 100 feet from a fire, before the mercury sailed out the top. Kinley sometimes works within a few yards of the blaze. Oilmen are awed by his resistance to heat and fatigue.

Myron Macy Kinley—he is Myron, Mac, or M. M. to his friends—has had an inclination toward such a hazardous existence since his early years. He was born in Santa Barbara, California, in 1898. At the end of the eighth grade he quit school to help his father in the field. Karl T. Kinley was an oil well shooter, a man who set off explosives deep in a well to loosen a tight producing formation.

Young Myron grew up with an intimate knowledge of dynamite and nitroglycerin. He picked up further feel for explosives in the artillery during World War I. Then he put his hand to blacksmithing for a while. Finally he got a job as a wellshooter in Tulsa. The firm didn't fare well. Myron one day found that he owned all the tools, in lieu of back pay. Thus began the M. M. Kinley Company, maker of specialized oil field tools, now in Houston, Texas. (Myron Kinley owns a number of patents on oil field tools now in use.)

Myron Kinley's father had made an accidental discovery long before he retired to run a gold mine in California. In 1913, a crew was trying to curb a flaming well with steam. The elder Kinley was called on to blast away some loose fittings at the well head. The explosion blew out the flame just as a breath blows out a candle. When Myron Kinley went into oil well firefighting as a regular profession in 1920, with his brother Floyd as assistant, he took his father's discovery and made it a science. But he had to struggle for almost a decade before he could prove his technique to the industry at large. His big chance came with the most stubborn blowout of all time—Moreni No. 160, in Romania.

No. 160 was being drilled by a Romanian affiliate of Standard Oil Company (New Jersey). It was down to 4,798 feet, and proceeding routinely, when it blew wild on May 28, 1929. Its gas pressure of 4,000 pounds per square inch blew drill pipe and tools high into the derrick. The huge jet of gas—several million cubic feet a day—caught fire. The well burned for 890 days.

Romanian law provided that the government take control in such a disaster. Government crews tried by various means to curb No. 160, principally by drilling lateral tunnels to the well. Ten men were killed by explosions in one tunnel.

The Moreni blowout was big news everywhere. To Kinley, it was a magnet. He made a trip to Bucharest at his own expense, the government wasn't interested. Kinley came home.

After two years, government officials gave up, and Kinley signed a contract with the producing company. For the first time, he agreed not only to snuff out the fire but also to cap the well. With an assistant, he began work on August 3, 1931.

Kinley was able to shoot out the fire several times with massive charges of nitroglycerin, but it persistently reignited. He was plagued, too, by the worst thing that can happen to a wild well. Gas escaping from below the surface ate a huge crater around the well head. Fires sprang up within the crater as the gas found new outlets. But, with the aid of an earth slide and several more shots, Kinley finally subdued the flames on November 4—three months after he had started. It took three more months of tough work to cap the blowout with a valve that could hold the pressure. Not only was No. 160 tamed; it made an excellent gas producer.

No. 160 crystallized Kinley's technique. Today he can step off a plane, size up the quirks of a wild well, and take charge with the authority of a first sergeant. First he calls for a gang of helpers who have his own disdain for danger. Then he orgainzes the equipment he will need: tractors and bulldozers; pipelines, to provide hundreds of thousands of gallons of water, and pumps; hammers and tools of bronze that won't spark when struck against steel; portable shields of corrugated iron to protect himself and his men against fire, and sheds of the same material that can be skidded close to the blowout for better protection. What equipment isn't available, Kinley designs to order.

The preparations take time, sometimes several days. Then Kinley is ready to act. Tractors latch on to remains of derrick and drilling tools and haul them out of the way. Bulldozers sweep away debris and level the site. If the well is afire, men working near it are sprayed constantly by massive streams of water. Kinley stands in the heat and confusion, directing his crew with arm signals amid noise that prevents shouted commands.

Then comes the big test. Between 50 and 500 pounds of gelatin nitroglycerin must be exploded near enough to the well head to blowout the flame. Kinley's preference for this perilous task is a tool of his own invention—a 45-foot hook made of pipes and mounted on a heavy tractor. The tractor inches toward the flame, the explosive in its claw. Water pours through the pipes to cool both the hook and its cargo, which could be exploded by the heat alone. (Before he designed this hook, Kinley and his aids used to carry the explosives to the flame by hand.)

Finally the charge is placed. The tractor withdraws. Kinley and his men race from the well head. A hand plunger sets off the blast. The roar is followed by a wave of dusty air that smothers the flame. If luck holds, the pillar of gas and oil doesn't reignite.

Fire is the most dramatic aspect of a wild well. But, after the fire is out, the runaway still must be capped like a blowout that doesn't catch fire. The firefighters, working only a few inches from the jet of gas, saw off the jagged well casing by hand. (A man who breathes too much of the gas can be dragged out and revived in fresh air; that's just normal risk.) Then, while a crane lowers a huge valve, the crew forces the valve into place against pressure that could blow it skyward like a kite. The valve is bolted into place. If gas and the sand it carries don't scour away the valve seat before it can be closed, the wild well is tamed.

Oilmen will tell you that it's far more than Kinley's cool nerve which makes him dean of his perilous trade. They see his special gift as a kind of disciplined imagination which gives him an extraordinary ability to improvise, to size up a wild one and write a prescription for it on the spot. Often he'll take a look and then start scribbling plans for special tools on the back of an envelope.

He is always trying new devices. Once he borrowed an old ship funnel to use as a tower to lead off a stream of gas while he worked below. On a recent job he borrowed a 75-mm cannon to shoot off a damaged well head which was deflecting flames so that he could not get close enough to work on it.

You'd never take Kinley for the world's champion firefighter. He looks like a department-store Santa Claus without the beard. His baby-blue eyes twinkle behind a ruddy outdoors complexion that extends up to where his hair used to be. His 5 feet 8 inches weigh 222 pounds, partly muscle and partly the product of good eating around the world.

Kinley has trained himself to be tireless. Early this year he fought two wild wells on a drilling platform in deep water of the Gulf of Mexico. An amphibian plane, waiting near the scene, picked him up as soon as he had the runaways capped, and flew him to a Louisiana airfield where another plane was waiting to carry him to a wild well in New Mexico. He tackled the new job without a break for rest.

Even in an industry of specialists, Kinley is a super-specialist. For three decades, he has never had more than two or three competitors at a time. Accidents keep the ranks of oil well firefighters thin. His brother was killed in a wild-well accident years ago.

He himself has not escaped unharmed. His hearing is impaired, as a result of his having worked at close quarters to the terrific roar of wild wells. In 1931 he broke a leg on a job; a Texas Ranger pulled him to safety, whereupon Kinley went to town, had a cast put on the leg, and returned to squelch a fire that already had killed nine men. An injury to his knee in 1936 left his right leg permanently immobile; he has rigged his car for left-leg driving. From his neck down, he is covered with scars of wounds and burns.

Kinley made a feeble effort a few years ago to retire, but he didn't quite make it. The old firehorse still answers the alarm, which is never far away. He isn't happy without a telephone at his elbow; he has four listings in the Houston telephone directory, even though he now considers California home.

Owners of wild wells always want the fireman in a hurry so Kinley is ready to answer a call within a few minutes. He travels light. Three suits of khakis over woolen underwear are his uniform; they absorb water and shield him against heat. Gas masks are a hindrance. Tools can be made at the scene.

Kinley thinks vaguely of quitting sometime and is training his assistants to take over. But so far he can't keep away from the fireworks.

But Kinley isn't entirely without nerves.

A few weeks ago he was driving with an acquaintance down a rural Texas highway. They passed a team of men working atop those skeleton towers that support cross-country electric high-lines.

"Look at those crazy guys, working up there with all that juice," Kinley observed. "I wouldn't have that job for anything. That's plain dangerous."

Petroleum Week, Vol. 3, No. 13, Sept. 20, 1956

"HIS SPECIALTY: TAMING WILD WELLS"

Myron M. Kinley has walked into danger and skirted death for nearly 30 years. But he's lost none of his zest for fighting oil well fires and blowouts throughout the world.

Kinley has been specializing in foreign jobs the past few years. He's also found occasional time to do battle with blazing wells or blowouts in the U.S., such as Union Oil Company's gas well that blew out of control off the cost of Louisiana in June.

When Iran's rank wildcat at Qum blew wild in late August, a hurry-up call went out for Kinley. The international fireman flew to the site immediately. Within two weeks he had succeeded in stopping the wild flow.

In the past two years, Kinley has taken on such hazardous jobs in New Guinea, Pakistan, Africa (twice), France, Italy, Sicily, Canada, Venezuela, and Mexico, among other places. The veteran firefighter also was in Saudi Arabia in late July to extinguish a raging fire at Arabian American Oil Company's No. Fadhili well.

Kinley went into the oil firefighting business about 1920, after working several years with his father, Karl—first man to snuff an oil well fire with explosives.

Karl Kinley had been a machinst and later a driller and well shooter in Bakersfield, California, before he moved his family to Tulsa. Quite by accident, he hit on his new technique for putting out oil well fires in 1913.

Kinley had been called to shoot off a stuck valve on a blazing well in the Taft field. He rigged up a charge of dynamite to blow off the valve. The charge wasn't heavy enough to do the job. But it did put out the fire.

His son, Myron, joined him on many of his later firefighting jobs, picking up the first experience that would later make him the unchallenged king in this field.

Shortly after World War I, Karl Kinley returned to California. Myron stayed in Tulsa to organize the Standard Torpedo Company and to go into the firefighting business with his brother, Floyd.

Kinley fought for recognition in his specialty during the early 20s. But his successes soon silenced the skeptics.

Two fires broke out a short time apart in the Cromwell (Oklahoma) field in 1924. One burned ten days before it was extinguished with steam from 12 boilers. Kinley killed the other with dynamite.

Kinley's performance was all the more impressive because he did it single-handed.

Kinley's efforts went far to overcome the insistence of most oil companies on fighting their own fires. The professional firefighter was not yet accepted. One trade publication writer, as late as 1931, wondered about this strange insistence and concluded, in head-shaking fashion, that oil men liked to fight fires just for the hell of it.

Then came the great Moreni fire in Romania—history's most publicized oil well fire. It had burned so long it was known as Romania's "permanent" fire. But Kinley liked it.

The Moreni gas well was in the heart of the oldest producing area in Romania. On May 22, 1929, it blew out, spitting drill pipe over the landscape like broken teeth. Four men were killed then, and another ten were to die before the well was finally harnessed.

The first effort to tame the well involved digging a tunnel, to tap the casing 70 feet below ground. Gas seeped in and exploded. A second tunnel was tried, but poisonous gas drove the workers out. A third tunnel was tried, deeper, and lined with concrete. Explosions and water seepage ended this effort. A directional well also failed. The death toll was mounting.

By this time, the escaping gas had dug a crater 67 feet deep and 250 feet in diameter.

A year after the fire had started Kinley went to Romania with detailed plans on how to put out the fire. When he mentioned explosives, however, the government shied away.

But other efforts failed. The fire became a political issue and the government fell. The new regime called Kinley back.

Hundreds of small fires, touched off by seepages, encircled the main well. Molten debris from the original rig and the numerous devices used to fight the blaze littered the crater. Kinley diverted some of the gas through the old No. 1 tunnel. Then he used water and cement to attack each small blaze, slowly edging toward the central well, removing debris as he went.

Rains came, then snow. A landslide smothered the main fire. But it flared up again, only to be smothered by another landslide and flare again. Kinley began forcing landslides with explosives. The crater began filling up and a final explosive shot snuffed out the main blaze. He brought in a 30-foot stack, maneuvered it over the gas jet with tractors, and cemented it.

The job was done, and the well was put on production. It had taken Kinley 189 days to bring the Moreni fire to its knees.

In May, 1936, Kinley took on another tough job, perhaps his

toughest—the Greta fire, in Refugio County, Texas.

Two relief wells and various other methods had failed when Kinley volunteered to do the job at no charge—the only time he has made such an arrangement in his life. The well had been blowing wild for nearly three and a half years when Kinley stepped into the picture. It took him eight months more.

When he arrived at the scene, Kinley found the wild well had dug a crater 300 feet in diameter and about 80 feet deep. This crater bubbled to ground level with water that had to be pumped out before work could begin. This took several months.

Kinley then brought in a wooden rig and a steam engine to drill a directional well. With all the escaping gas in the area, Kinley had to make sure the equipment wouldn't start a fire. Yet the well ignited itself four times thereafter, though no one could determine why. The well finally was closed permanently after Kinley ignited 600 quarts of explosive at the base of the directional well. The explosion collapsed the casing of the wild well, permitting cement to be set.

In the early days, Kinley battled a well fire with explosives and special equipment they carried to the scene. Now he takes along a few extra layers of clothing—nothing more.

In his early years as a professional firefighter, Kinley used a special fire truck, nozzles and hose, gas masks, inhalators, first-aid supplies, nonsparking and heat-resistant tools, and a crew that wore asbestos suits and helmets with heat-resistant glass windows.

The time factor has forced him to travel via the airways, and to use whatever material the locality can provide or that his ingenuity can devise. He usually has no difficulty in obtaining gelatinzed nitro or dynamite.

The explosive—usually placed in asbestos-lined oil drums—is placed in position over the well mouth by use of Athey booms— which have extensions on the end for holding either charges or special tools, to pull equipment or clear wreckage near the fire.

If the equipment isn't available, or can't be built on the spot, Kinley has it brought in by the fastest available means. Once, on a job in Africa, Kinley found that he needed a blowout preventor, high-drill, and other equipment. The equipment cost $18,000—the air freight was $23,000.

When Kinley works close to a fire, he has hose water poured on him constantly. A metal shield also is rigged up to protect him from the flames. Kinley says asbestos clothing is too bulky, limiting movements.

Each of the more than 350 well fires or blowouts Kinley has tackled has posed unique problems. Knowhow, born of experience, has met most of the challenges.

When Kinley arrives at the scene of a wild or burning well, he makes a careful, deliberate study of the situation. Then, in general, he subdues the well by assuring access to the site, tying into an abundant water supply, clearing away hot debris, snuffing the blaze with explosives, and capping the flow. (This capsule summary, of course, drastically understates the hazards and problems involved.)

Though he's been battered and burned, the 60-year-old Kinley gives no thought to quitting. "Retire, hell!" he says. "What would I do then?"

Kinley suffered a broken ankle and bruises when fighting an oil well fire in Gregg County, Texas, in 1931. The fire had killed nine men and burned or injured others. Kinley was cutting away the drawworks when a beam fell across him. After having his ankle set in a local hospital, he returned to the fire within two hours, directing operations from horseback, or limping about on crutches. The fire was put out in eight days.

In 1936, he was preparing to shoot stuck drill pipe at a well in Matagorda County, Texas. A steel shell, which hadn't been properly cleaned of explosives, blew up when a welder's torch was applied. Kinley received injuries the length of his right side.

Kinley also was burned severly in 1945, when a Venezuela blowout caught fire. (It also was a blowout that killed his brother, Floyd, in 1938. Floyd was capping a well in Goliad County, Texas, when it blew him off the platform.)

These and other mishaps only seem to confirm that Kinley has a complete disdain for longevity. Yet he is the first to caution those who would follow in his path. (Strangely enough, the Kinley headquarters in Houston and Tulsa receive so many bids for jobs as oil firefighters that a form letter has been devised as a reply.)

"The only quality a man needs to become a firefighter is to like to do that sort of thing," Kinley says. "It's not the kind of business you just jump into. You need to have plenty of oilfield experience before getting into this kind of work in the first place. After you do this firefighting work for awhile it becomes a job, just like any other kind of work."

Kinley adds that some modern aids have made firefighting easier now than it was years ago. For instance, he explains, "in the past eight years we have developed a water-cooled hook that we can use for removing equipment from in, or near, a fire." On the other hand, today's deeper wells pose new problems, particularly pressure.

One quality Kinley insists his coworkers have is dependability. Once, many years ago, one of his workers said he didn't want to go out on a job. He wasn't fired. He simply knew he couldn't come back.

"OIL WELL FIRES BRING FLAME AND FORTUNE"

CINDY RUGELEY

GRAHAM— Standing in the driving rain next to a blazing oil well while looking for a light for his cigarette is not a strange scene in Coots Matthews' world.

Matthews' career as an oilfield firefighter has taken him all over the world. This week it brought him to Bunger, near Graham in North Texas, where a burning well has been shooting a 150-foot-tall column of flame since early Friday.

E. O. Matthews is the "Coots" half of the Houston oil firefighting firm of Coots and Boots. He and two crew members have been in Bunger since Friday.

"This one isn't too bad," Matthews said Tuesday. "On a scale of one to ten, with ten being the worst, I'd give it about a two.

"This is not a big fire. What makes it bad is that it is burning oil. If it were burning gas, it would not be so hot. Also, when gas is out, it doesn't make a mess.

"Actually, this may seem strange, but it's better when these things blowout for them to burn because it doesn't do so much damage to things around it," Matthews said.

If an oil well blows out and doesn't burn, it spews oil for yards around it, killing trees and grass and sometimes polluting nearby water sources.

The "Boots" half of the firm—Asger "Boots" Hansen didn't make the trip. He is tied up this week with another fire near Jackson, Mississippi, that the firm has been working on since June 22.

"That one's a poisonous gas well. We need to keep it lit until we can cap it, or it will probably poison everybody in Mississippi." Matthews said.

All in a day's work.

The company name of Coots and Boots is usually not the first one to come to the public's mind when oilfield firefighters are mentioned. That distinction belongs to Red Adair, also of Houston ("He gets the publicity . . . and we get the business," Matthews said).

However, Coots and Boots also is an internationally known oil-field firefighting firm, and the two owners used to work for Adair.

The Bunger fire was the 19th that Coots and Boots have fought this year. "We're a little behind schedule," Matthews said. "If drilling is down, there are fewer fires."

During the oil boom years in the early part of this decade, the company averaged between 55 and 60 well fires a year. Coots and Boots answer fire calls from throughout the world, with about 25 percent of their business in foreign nations.

Matthews and Hansen learned their craft, as did Adair, from Myron Kinley, a man Matthews describes as the pioneer of oilfield firefighting.

"He taught all of us how to do this," Matthews said. "This is not the kind of job you go to school to learn."

When Kinley retired in 1959, Adair took over his business, and Matthews and Hansen went to work for him. In 1978, they formed their own company.

In 1969, Adair, Matthews and Hansen were technical advisers for *Hellfighters*, a movie about oilfield firefighters starring John Wayne.

"The strange thing about that movie is that we outlived the people that starred in it. I guess firefighting is safer than acting," Matthews said.

Tuesday, Matthews and his crew, with the help of bulldozers and a winch truck, pulled the remains of the rig from the burning well. To do so, Boots and Coots workers walked within 30 yards of the flames to hook cables onto the debris.

The debris had to be removed or it could reignite the fire.

As the men worked, jets of water were sprayed on the blaze to cool it down. "We are wet and wearing two layers of clothes; it's not so bad," Matthews said.

Sometime early Thursday or Friday, they will use explosives to try and blowout the fire. Then the well will be capped—shut off.

"This is dangerous work we do," Matthews said. "It's dangerous enough that Lloyd's of London charges us $250 per day per man for insurance. They charge more than that for offshore."

Matthews said the only serious injury to any of his crew was to himself several years ago. "I lost about an inch and a half of my leg. A rig fell on my leg."

Matthews is 62 and Hansen is 59. They have been training workers who will take over the company when they retire.

"I'm almost ready to retire now," Matthews said.

As the sun began to set on the fire Tuesday, Matthews and his crew packed up to return to a hotel. "We don't work nights," he said.

At the same time, another oilfield worker walked by. "You got a match?" Matthews asked. "Oh, you don't smoke either."

Reprinted by permission of the *Forth Worth Star-Telegram*

"KINLEY FIGHTS OIL WELL FIRES"

Weldon Hill

"It's just another job, like cooking or digging a ditch."

That is the opinion Myron Macy Kinley has of his job. And his job is extinguishing oil well fires and controlling wild blowouts.

Mr. Kinley first embarked on his hazardous job back in 1913. At that time he was working with his father in California shooting wells for oil production with nitroglycerine.

He later moved to Oklahoma and formed his own company. Since that time, Mr. Kinley has travelled to remote places on the globe, putting out oil well fires and controlling gassers.

Controlling Gulf Refining Company's No. E-2 Buras Levee Board, at West Bay, Plaquemines parish, coastal Louisiana, was his 129th job.

At first Mr. Kinley just put out the fire and let the owner control the gas or oil flow. However, today his largest business is controlling wild gas wells.

"Fires are not as frequent now as they were some years ago," He said. "However, deeper drilling has caused unusually high gas pressures in wells in Texas and Louisiana, resulting in blowouts."

With his father, K. T. Kinley, Mr. Kinley and others first used nilroglycerine to extinguish an oil well fire back in 1913. It was his first taste of this treacherous job and it started a young man on a career of one hazard after another.

Mr. Kinley doesn' t consider his job the most dangerous profession in the world. Records show that more people are killed crossing the street than there are fighting oil well fires.

The only time Mr. Kinley gets excited is right after he receives a call on a wild well. He just doesn't seem to be able to get to the wild well quick enough. However, once on the job, he goes about his work with steel nerves.

Mr. Kinley has made three trips to South America. Once he put out a flaming oil well in Columbia and the other two times the wells extinguished themselves before he arrived on the scene. It seems that calling Mr. Kinley to a job has some effect on the well, just like the pain leaves you before you sit down in a dentist's chair.

The job that gave Mr. Kinley international publicity as a wild-well fighter was controlling a well in Romania. The well had been on fire for two and one-half years, resulting in the death of 14 men and causing more than $1,000,000 damage before Mr. Kinley was called on the job in 1931. Mr. Kinley extinguished the fire and capped the wild gasser. The experience gained in capping this gas well gave him his start in expertly capping wild wells.

The next job which gave him wide recognition was the famed Greta crater in Refugio county, Texas. This well, drilled on a railroad right-of-way, blew out of control and destroyed parts on the highway and railroad when it cratered. Mr. Kinley and his crew worked for eight months before completing the job.

Fate, however, has not always smiled upon Mr. Kinley. Two or three years ago his brother, Floyd Kinley, also widely known as a wild-well fighter, lost his life while attempting to control a gasser in Goliad.

In 1936, Mr. Kinley was shooting stuck drill pipe in a well in Matagorda county, Texas, when a shot went off unexpectedly and almost cost him his life. He suffered an injured knee and leg and today he has to work around wild wells on crutches.

Every well he works on presents a different problem. Devices and methods used in controlling one wild well are not suited in controlling another. His first task after arriving at the scene of a wild well is to study the blowout or fire from every angle. He then starts out on one theory to control the well. If this theory fails he starts over and this procedure is continued until the well is tamed.

Strangely, the only thing that irks Mr. Kinley when he is working around a wild well is people who keep asking him when the well is going to be brought under control. Actually, Mr. Kinley doesn't know when a well is going to be controlled until almost the minute the well is capped.

While working on the Greta wild well a native persisted in asking him when the well was going to be harnessed.

"Listen, I have ordered an especially constructed cork stopper," Mr. Kinley told his questioner, "and as soon as it arrives, I am personally going to stab it in the pipe."

Taming an oil well fire has as many angles to it as a diamond. Most every oil well fire is handled differently. On a routine fire Mr. Kinley and his men get behind a galvanized iron shield constructed with handles so as to move the shield in front of them as they approach the blazing well.

The men behind the shield are dressed in any woolen clothes with tin helmets and an asbestos covering over their face and neck. Water is played upon the men as they approach the well.

After getting into position the men then clear away the crumbled derrick and rig and remove all top connections so as to allow the flame to shoot straight into the air. Burning oil wells shooting flames upward in one centrally located place are easier to extinguish. The shot is then placed into position and set off. The shot usually extinguishes the flame.

Capping a wild gas or oil well also has many angles with every well presenting a different problem. In most cases the wild well fighters work freely around the blowout. In an ordinary case the men try to stab a Christmas tree in the pipe, if pipe has been set, and then close the connections, allowing the well to bleed off gas and water.

Mr. Kinley handles his own work. He has his own crew which is ready at any call. These men know their business.

The average loss of an oil well fire is hard to determine. If the fire burns for any length of time the derrick and rig are destroyed. Equipment used in drilling a deep test on the Louisiana and Texas gulf coast usually cost from $75,000 to $100,000. The loss of oil or gas by burning depends upon how long the fire burns.

Blowouts naturally are less expensive than fires as the derrick and rig are not destroyed. Rigs and derricks usually are covered by insurance and the loss of oil is hard to determine. An oil well blowout and fire can run into a pretty good pile of chips.

Mr. Kinley's charges for putting out a fire and controlling a well vary according to the type of job.

Oil companies and drilling contractors are always taking precautionary measures against blowouts.

The Saturday Evening Post, May 2, 1959

"HE FIGHTS THE WILDEST FIRES"

Stanley Frank

The burning oil well had been a screeching, 500-foot blowtorch for weeks, consuming as much as $250,000 of petroleum a day while the drilling crew stood by helpless to cut off the subterranean gas jet feeding the fire. Now a 60-year-old man, limping heavily on a crippled leg, approached the inferno behind an iron shield. In his partially paralyzed right arm he carried a 100-pound charge of nitroglycerin wrapped in asbestos to prevent a premature explosion by the intense heat. Protected only by water sprayed on him from distant hoses, he crept within eight feet of the blaze, placed the nitro, then took cover. The charge was detonated and instantaneously the pillar of flames vanished as though it had been snuffed out by a supernatural hand. Myron Kinley had tamed another wild well.

Kinley has thus flirted with sudden death more than 450 times since 1921 while practicing his trade as the most unusual—and highest paid—fireman in the world. His global beat has taken him to every continent to fight oil and gas well fires that annually destroy untold millions of dollars' worth of equipment and raw material. There once were dozens of free-lance specialists in the field, but today Kinley is the man almost invariably summoned for major emergencies. Practically all competitors have been killed, maimed, or driven out of the business by his reputation.

"I've never met Kinley, but I always carry his Houston phone number in my wallet," says E. V. Watts, manager of exploitation for the Socony Mobil Oil Company. "I never know when someone will call from Libya or Turkey and yell, 'All hell has busted loose here! Send Kinley on the next plane.' He's the one indispensable man in the entire industry."

A millionaire with six grandchildren is an improbable type to be risking his neck in daredevil heroics, and Kinley's appearance hardly helps to make stories of his resourcefulness more credible. His 220-pound body has been broken, burned and blasted in so many accidents that he moves like a ponderous old man racked by arthritis. His hearing has been impaired by the roar and vibration of fires and, like many people who are hard of hearing, he speaks in a soft, hesitant voice. In a group of oil executives he looks like a night watchman who wandered into the place by mistake, an impression heightened by the rough work clothes he habitually wears.

"An amazing transformation comes over Kinley when he goes into action," reports Carl L. Reistle Jr., executive vice-president of the Humble Oil and Refining Company. "He barks orders like a marine sergeant and shames 'roughnecks' into following him by his disregard for danger. He dominates a situation so completely he seems to be twelve feet tall. "I still remember the first job I saw Kinley tackle. It was an oil well blowout near Galveston more than twenty years ago. Underground gas was escaping so fast through a leak in a big surface valve that the well was on the verge of catching fire momentarily. Kinley's younger brother had just been killed in a blowout, and Myron himself was recuperating from an explosion that had killed a man standing next to him. He was on crutches with his leg in a cast, but he hobbled up to the valve, swung his good leg over it to brace himself, then went to work.

"The guy literally was sitting on a volcano that could have been touched off by a spark igniting the gas. Kinley, handicapped by the cast, would have been fried to a crisp in five seconds, but he calmly examined the valve until he found and tightened the loose connection. It was the damnedest demonstration of professional skill and poise I've ever seen."

Kinley's long firefighting career has been confined exclusively to oil and gas wells. When a major brush fire around Los Angeles last December threatened to raze a palatial home he owns in Bel Air, Kinley was in Houston. He made no effort to protect the property personally. "I'll just be in the way out there," he said. "I don't know how to lick that kind of a fire." At the first sound of an alarm in his specialty, though, he plunges into harness like the proverbial fire horse.

Last April Kinley was having lunch in Houston at 12:30 p.m. on a Saturday when he was notified that a well had flared up in Ahwaz, Iran. At three o'clock he was on a plane bound for New York. Sixty hours and 8,000 miles later he arrived on the scene and worked 18 consecutive hours preparing for a successful frontal attack on the well.

Nothing interferes with Kinley's response to the siren call of a fire—not even a honeymoon. On November 12, 1958, he celebrated his sixtieth birthday and second marriage. (His first wife died two years ago.) The bride was the former Jessie Dearing, manager of the Little Nick Oil Company, of Chickasha, Oklahoma, whom he met while subduing a blowout that almost ruined the company. After the ceremony the newlyweds drove south through Texas and wound up at Freer where, as the groom knew, a well had blown out. Kinley put it back into operation, then headed east to see the sights of New Orleans.

The Vieux Carre was not on his itinerary, however. The big attraction for him was five burning offshore wells that his assistant, Paul (Red) Adair, was battling in the Gulf of Mexico. Kinley never got a chance to inspect this disaster because an urgent message to phone the Atlantic Refining Company in Caracas, Venezuela, was waiting for him at the hotel. A well had been on fire for two weeks. Could he come immediately? He could and did.

"I bet Jessie was the only girl ever sent home from a honeymoon on account of a fire," Kinley comments in relating the incident. It was the one facetious remark he made during the three days I spent with him.

Kinley talked of retiring in 1956 after completing a series of long, difficult jobs in New Guinea, Iran, and Saudi Arabia with practically no breathing spells in between. "I'm not a spring chicken anymore," he told friends. "My tail is starting to drag. I better quit before it gets caught in the wringer."

Everyone agreed it was a splendid idea. He could live comfortably, without touching a dime of his capital, on the income from his plant in Houston, which manufactures drilling equipment. He could get reacquainted with his family, do some fishing or just loll beside his pool in Bel Air. But everyone, including Kinley, knew the talk was hot air. Sure enough, an alarm rang on the opposite side of the globe, and Kinley took off on a 40-day tour of duty.

The trip began with a washout for a British company that engaged Kinley to contend with a stubborn oil fire in Pakistan. He took one look at the destruction and advised the client to "kill" the well by pouring concrete into it. The well had "cratered"—a term we'll explain presently—so badly that the cost of fighting the fire would have been prohibitive. Upon arriving in Calcutta, Kinley was informed that a French firm wanted to see him in Paris regarding a fire in the Cameroons, Africa. En route to Paris, he was detained overnight in quarantine at Cairo for inoculations he had had no time to get in India. From Paris he went to the Cameroons, saw he needed equipment available only in the United States and flew back to Houston to have it made to order.

Back home word of another assignment awaited him—a blowout in Nigeria, next door to the Cameroons. So he went to Paris by way of Calgary, where he delivered a lecture on fire prevention, stopped off in Nigeria to handle the blowout and reached the Cameroons a day before the special equipment arrived. The air-freight charges were $23,000. Kinley put out the fire and landed in Houston 40 days after leaving for Pakistan.

During this time he flew approximately 46,000 miles, slept in real beds a dozen nights—and collected $90,000 in fees. His total earnings usually are estimated at $100,000 a year, a figure that evokes raucous horse laughs in informed circles. People in the industry say Kinley has been averaging at least $200,000 a year since the exploitation of the Middle East's rich oil fields after World War II, with only a small portion coming from his equipment business.

Kinley refuses to divulge his fees, but executives who have engaged his services say that his flat charge for going anywhere in the Eastern Hemisphere is $30,000 plus expenses. If he is required to spend more than a month on an assignment, which is not unusual, a surcharge is added. The minimum for South America and remote regions of Canada is $2,500 for a quick stint lasting two days, and the bill for a major fire runs into five figures. Kinley averages 20 calls a year, four of them in foreign countries.

"Now and then people kick when I turn in my bills," he admits. "They always pay up, though, because they may need me again. I honestly believe my fees are reasonable when you consider the money at stake. A short while ago a fire down here in Texas was costing an outfit sixty thousand bucks a day for several weeks. I buttoned it up in six days. What would you have charged under those circumstances?"

"I keep telling Myron he should raise his fees," Carl Reistle declares. "He just shrugs and says, 'The government already gets most of my dough, so why bother? Besides, an independent operator takes such a bad beating on a fire I don't want to make things tougher for him.' Maybe I'm a sucker for saying this, but Kinley would be a bargain if he charged three times as much as he does."

The total damage of one big oil well fire can be so fantastic that educated guesses by engineers run into billions of dollars. One thing is certain: A wild well is the costliest of all industrial disasters. The visible destruction, extensive as it is, represents a minute fraction of the loss. A blowout, an eruption of natural gas which always precedes a fire, sends 10,000 to 15,000 feet of steel tubing hurtling through the air like strands of spaghetti. The fire reduces a 135-foot rig costing $800,000 to a mass of wreckage in twenty minutes. All offshore rig with living accommodations for the crew can cost as much as $2,500,000.

Even the vast quantities of crude oil and natural gas consumed by a fire are negligible in the over-all picture. In 1956 a well at Qum, Iran, burned for 40 days, destroying 3,500,000 barrels of oil worth $3.25 a barrel, before Kinley extinguished it. Although the gas is less valuable, it adds up to important money. At Ahwaz, Iran, last year, before Kinley went to work, 4,000,000,000 cubic feet of gas was lost. In the United States the gas would have brought $840,000.

But the most devastating effect of a fire occurs far below the surface, where the dissipation of the pressure that produces oil can reduce the yield of an entire field by as much, as 50 percent. Most people labor under the delusion that oil is found by drilling a well until an underground pool of the stuff is struck. Your gasoline bills would be trivial if that were all there was to it.

Oil is obtained from rock formations containing tiny globules of crude petroleum which literally are squeezed out by gas under extremely high pressures. It is essential to control the release of the gas, for if it escapes too fast the resultant loss of pressure will directly affect the surrounding area. An oil field can be compared to an enormous bottle of soda pop. The bottle will fizz for a long time if a pinhole is punctured in the cap, but it will go flat very quickly when the cap is ripped off and the carbonation is permitted to escape freely. During drilling, the pressure of the gas is controlled by a continuous flow of chemically treated mud pumped into the well. When the drill suddenly pierces an unexpected high-pressure pocket of gas, however, the mud and pieces of rock are forced back up the pipe in a violent spurt, or blowout. There is no oxygen for combustion inside the well, but the jet of gas can be ignited at the surface by a spark from a stone striking the casing. Such flashes have set off fires that lasted more than three years and bankrupted hundreds of companies. When that happens, other operators in the field chip in to battle the fire and check the depletion of the pressure vital to their own properties.

Fires always have plagued the oil industry, which, incidentally, is celebrating its centennial this year. Six weeks after the first well in America was dug under the supervision of Edwin L. Drake at Titusville, Pennsylvania, on August 27, 1895, it went up in flames. Smothering the blaze with dirt was a simple matter, for the well was only 69½ feet deep and the gas and oil were coming up at relatively low pressures. As drillers probed deeper into the earth, live steam was used to blanket fires, but the tremendous pressures encountered below 10,000 feet made that method ineffective. Although millions of dollars have been spent on research, the industry has been unable to improve on the procedure Kinley has employed for nearly forty years.

Laymen who never have seen a burning oil well have reason for wondering why it causes so much trouble. Unlike a conflagration raging over a wide area, the flames shoot out of a pipe only a few inches in diameter. It seems a simple matter to choke the blaze at that point until you realize the gas and oil stoking the fire are inaccessible, thousands of feet under the ground.

The solution was discovered inadvertently by Kinley's father, Karl, and Ford Alexander at Taft, California, in 1913. They were unable to remove a big valve from a burning well head and finally decided to blast it off with dynamite. The valve and the fire disappeared simultateously in the explosion.

"The fire started again in thirty seconds, but nobody knew why it went out in the first place," Myron Kinley recalls. He carries in his wallet a snapshot taken of his father and Alexander that day. "The incident was passed off as a freak until Alexander killed a fire with dynamite at Elk Creek, California, four years later. Most guys went on fighting fires with steam, though, because they thought working with explosives was suicide."

Actually the use of explosives is as sound as the principle behind it. As every schoolboy knows, there can be no combustion without oxygen. When an explosive charge is set off beside a burning well, the blast displaces the oxygen mixing with the gas in the slender column of fire. The break lasts only a split second, but it is sufficient to interrupt the combustion, just as a candle is snuffed out by touching the wick with a moistened fingertip.

Before accepting an assignment, Kinley demands full authority to handle it without interference. "A big wheel watching thousands of barrels of oil going up in smoke every day is liable to holler bloody murder when I tell him a job may take three or four weeks, " he explains. "People who've never seen a fire expect hocus-pocus miracles. I'm not going to let anybody put pressures on me when I am risking my life. One mistake can kill you."

Kinley's first requirement is an unlimited supply of water for dousing the area around the well head—and for his protection. At Qatar, on the Persian Gulf, a 22-mile pipeline had to be laid across the desert before he was ready to start. Kinley once worked in an asbestos outfit, but he discarded it because it was too bulky. He now wears work pants over two suits of woolen underwear. The water which is sprayed continuously on him relieves the heat, which sometimes hits 250 degrees within 100 feet of the fire.

The next step is to root up all the vegetation within a wide radius and haul away the molten drilling rig and other debris. This is necessary to prevent a wind-borne ember from rekindling the gas which still will be spewing from the well after the blaze is extinguished.

When a producing well catches fire, the mop-up is complicated by half a dozen tongues of flame spurting from the "Christmas tree," a series of valves and oil lines bolted to the casing. The Christmas tree must be removed because the trick in licking the fire is to confine it to one jet. Wrenching the big Hydra-headed gadget loose is a laborious task, especially in an offshore operation.

Several years ago, Kinley borrowed four Army marksmen and their bazookas to try to knock off a Christmas tree in the Gulf of Mexico. They scored 32 direct hits, but were unable to dislodge it. Kinley finally had to do the job himself the hard way. He was hoisted aboard the drilling platform from a boat and tied a huge hook to the tree. The hook was attached to a crane that ripped off the valves.

When a land fire is not controlled fairly quickly, preparations for the explosion are often delayed for months by the "cratering" of the well. The pressure of the escaping gas cracks the ground around the casing, creating outlets for scores of small fires which must be put out before the main blaze can be tackled. After the charge is detonated, there is the ticklish business of capping the blowout with a new set of valves. This takes Kinley within arm's length of the gas, which can be ignited in an instant by a spark of static electricity.

Kinley established his international reputation in 1931 by conquering a fire that had been raging for 890 days in Moreni, Romania. The Standard Oil Company of New Jersey was drilling Well 160 in the rich Moreni field when it flared up on May 22, 1929, killing four men. A year later Kinley asked Standard Oil for a chance to have a go at the fire, but major companies in those days were pretty stuffy about hiring free lances, and he was brushed off. Kinley went to Romania at his own expense and, after inspecting the site, announced that he could put out the fire in 40 hours. "It would have been a cinch for Myron," says Fred Jackson, a petroleum consultant in Houston who was a field supervisor at Moreni. "The well had not cratered, and the flames were coming out in a single jet, a perfect setup for him. By that time, though, the fire was a political issue in Romania, and the government had taken over the installation as a national-defense measure."

Premier Iuliu Maniu put his nephew, a mining engineer, in charge of the fire. Four lateral tunnels were dug in a attempt to reduce the pressure of the gas, but the plan was abandoned after ten men were killed in an explosion. The disaster was a factor in the fall of the Maniu cabinet, and the government threw the ball back to Standard Oil. In the summer of 1931 Kinley was recovering from a broken leg and decided to attend an international Rotary convention in Vienna.

"The convention was just my excuse for going to Europe," he confides. "I was itching to take a whack at Moreni."

Standard Oil no longer was in a position to turn down any help it could get. By that time the fire had formed a crater 200 feet wide and 70 feet deep; some experts advised sealing up the well with concrete to stop the ruinous drain of pressure in the entire field. On August 3, 1931, Kinley was put in command of the fire with the understanding that he would receive no fee if he failed to cap the well. A narrow-gauge railroad was built into the crater, but Romanian authorities were so chary of more casualties that they permitted only Grady Chupp, an American driller, and a native mechanic to work in the pit with Kinley.

The chief obstacle confronting Kinley was hundreds of fires in the fissures of the crater. It was futile to attack the 500-foot torch from Well 160 until he doused those potential matches that could have igtnited the gas roaring up the drill pipe at a pressure of 4,000 pounds per square inch. A landslide started by a violent rainstorm smothered a number of the small fires. This gave Kinley an idea. A man-made landslide would bury all the fires, but the drill pipe had to be left accessible if the well was to be put into operation again. Kinley designed a concrete hood with an opening in the top, lowered it over the well, then touched off an avalanche with dynamite. After the dust had settled, the only flames in the area belched from the hood.

Well 160 had been burning for 26 months when Kinley arrived. Three months and one day later, on November 4, 1931, an explosive charge blotted out the great fire. Kinley capped the well with three more months of arduous work. According to Fred Jackson's figures, Standard Oil lost 1,000,000,000 barrels of oil and 180,000,000,000 cubic feet of gas in the fire, but the well was saved and eventually showed a profit.

Kinley says his toughest job was the Wild Greta well in Refugio County, Texas, in 1936. "Maybe I feel that way," he adds laconically, "because I had an awful lot of money riding on it." He did indeed. Wild Greta made him a millionaire.

The well had been seething for 3½ years when the Missouri-Pacific Railroad, which took over the property on its right of way after the original owner went broke fighting the fire, gave the green light to Kinley. Again a crater was the big headache. A section of railroad tracks and a stretch of a state highway had caved into a hole 300 feet wide and 80 feet deep, filled with water gushing from the well. Kinley spent eight months on the job, four of them pumping out the water.

"I had the same sort of deal as at Moreni," he relates. "I had to kill the fire and cap the well to get paid, but the gamble was worth taking. The railroad agreed to give me twenty-five thousand dollars in cash and a lease on twenty acres in the oil field. I sold the lease to a drilling syndicate for a 25 percent interest in the royalties. Later we hit a real big well that's still producing." he paused reflectively. "It was a nice touch for a guy who quit school in the eighth grade."

Kinley said farewell to formal education at Bakersfield, California, in 1912. After a year in a blacksmith's shop, he joined his father to learn the rudiments of well shooting, an old method for stimulating the flow of oil by dropping dynamite down the drill pipe. Kinley acquired more experience with explosives as an artilleryman in the Argonne and Saint Mihiel offensives of World War I, and then joined a well shooting company in Tulsa, Oklahoma. When the firm failed a year later, he took an old car in lieu of back wages and knocked around the oil fields working at anything he could get.

Firefighting was a sideline that Kinley had practiced on a few small jobs until he got his first big chance at Cromwell, Oklahoma, in 1924. Two wells caught fire at the same time. One was put out in ten days by a veteran crew. Kinley and his 17-year-old brother, Floyd, wrapped up the other fire in 18 hours.

On at least four occasions Kinley missed death by margins measured in inches. His leg was factured in a blowout that killed six men at Gladewater, Texas, in 1931. He broke his heel jumping off a drilling platform to escape two-ton steel "blocks" falling from the top of a derrick in Hidalgo County, Texas. His entire right side was riddled with shrapnel, and his right arm and right leg just about paralyzed in an accidental explosion of a dynamite shell that killed a man standing next to him at Bay City, Texas, in 1937.

His closest call came in Venezuela in 1945 when a blowout caught fire while he was working 20 feet from it. He started to run as soon as he heard the great whoosh of the ignited gas, but, handicapped by his bad leg, he was almost steamed alive in his wet clothes by the frightful heat. He was in the hospital for six weeks recovering from excruciating blisters that covered him from his neck to his feet.

It is customary to describe Kinley as an utterly fearless man, but this is an inaccurate appraisal. "I get a knot in the pit of my belly every time I go into a tight spot," he confesses.

"I don't know whether that's being scared or careful. The secret of my job is knowing what you can't get away with."

Kinley's stepsons by his first marriage, Jack and Dan, once worked with him during school vacations. Significantly, he made them quit 20 years ago.

"After my brother Floyd was killed in a blowout down in Texas, I thought it was stupid for more than one member of the family to be risking his life at the same time," Kinley says. "Besides, the boys take after their mother. They run to brains. All you need in my line are muscles and experience."

Both boys were graduated from the Harvard Graduate School of Business Administration after completing their undergraduate work elsewhere. Jack, who holds a degree in mechanical engineering, manages the tool plant in Houston, and Dan is with an advertising agency in New York. A daughter, Mrs. Joyce Knoble, is married to a Los Angeles real-estate man.

In 1946 Kinley took on as his assistant, 24-year-old Paul Adair, a former driller who had been with a bomb disposal squad in the Pacific during World War II. Although Adair is a highly competent man, the boss still is the first one down the pole when a four-alarm call comes.

What keeps the battered old man going so furiously?

"What do you think?" Jack Kinley answered. "Dad will tell you fires are routine to him," and he's tired of the whole business, but that's just a cover-up for the terrific satisfaction he gets from knowing he's the one man in the world who can bail a big company out of a jam."

Although safety devices and better-trained crews have reduced the incidence of wild wells, fire still is a constant hazard. The oil industry keeps voluminous statistics, including the average daily consumption of gasoline in Old Overcoat, Idaho, but no one knows how many wells go up in flames every year.

"Figures aren't kept because every fire means someone in the crew goofed," Paul Swain, editor of Oil and Gas Journal, explains. "Proportionately, very few new wells catch fire. Last year approximately fifty-seven thousand were drilled throughout the free world and, at a guess, about one hundred acted up. The majority were put out quickly, but at least thirty were serious blazes. The loss on each one is so great, though, that the percentages give a misleading picture. Kinley still is the industry's best protection when something goes wrong. I shudder to think what will happen after he retires."

This emergency may not occur for some time. "I've got to keep working to provide for my family," Kinley told me with a straight face. "I haven't been able to get a life-insurance policy for the last forty years."

When I left Kinley in Houston in January, he was talking of taking a leisurely drive to Los Angeles to visit his daughter. Two days later I called Swain for some technical information. After giving it to me, he said casually, "Do you know where your man Kinley is now? Up near the Arctic Circle, working on a fire in the middle of nowhere in the Yukon. It should be a nice change from the heat of Saudi Arabia. The temperature is 60 degrees below zero."

"LONDON DAY"

London, England, 1952—Yesterday morning I joined several thousand of the Anglo-Iranian Oil Company's stockholders for two hours watching five films arranged for their pleasure and edification.

It had occurred to the company that its stockholders might care to see films it has made to illustrate enterprise in Persia. I am told 13,000 responded to the invitation, and several cinemas were taken over yesterday to accommodate them.

All five films have been appearing and will continue to appear spasmodically at commercial cinemas. The one called Rig 20, which won a first prize at the Venice Film Festival this year, would adorn any programme.

In 15 minutes it tells the story of the fire which broke out in May, 1951, at oil well No. 20 at Naft Safid. It was the first time in fifty years of drilling in Persia that such a thing had happened.

America would enjoy this too, for her biggest firefighting expert is summoned and arrives by air in 80 hours. His battle, first with flames and then with gas—the discharge each hour equalled the total gas consumption of this country in 24 hours—makes an epic.

The whole episode was filmed, with no small risk, by the company's own cameraman.

These films and yesterday's response to their showing stimulate rather wistful reflection. Had they been widely shown a year ago they might well have shifted the trend of public opinion here, if not the course of events in Persia.

Verity Films, 1952

"RIG 20"

A DRAMATIC AND UNIQUE RECORD OF A GROUP OF MEN FIGHTING
AND FINALLY OVERCOMING ONE OF THE MOST SPECTACULAR FIRES
IN THE HISTORY OF THE QUEST FOR OIL.

Oil, the life-blood of the 20th century mechanical world, is docile enough with the men who understand its qualities and know its vagaries, but when anything goes wrong it goes wrong in a spectacular way. Rig 20 shows the vicious savagery of an oil well fire and tells the story of the courage and endurance of the men who fought it.

For 50 years the Anglo-Iranian Oil Company had drilled in Persia, and never once had there been a fire. On the first day of May, 1951, at 5 a.m., that record was broken when a sheet of flame nearly a quarter of a mile high leaped from an oil well being drilled at Naft Safid in the Hill country 108 miles northeast of Abadan.

Girders and steel pipes of what had been known as "Rig 20" twisted and melted like candles in the sun.

It happened when drillers were trying to "fish" out a stuck drill pipe. Like the contents of a gigantic soda water syphon, oil lies below a cap of highly flammable gas in the cracks and pores of its reservoir rock. Both oil and gas are often under high pressure, which a slurry of mud inside the drill-pipe controls until the oil is ready to be released.

On this day, however, a "blowout" occurred and the escaping gas caught fire. The Company sent at once for Myron Kinley, the world's most experienced oil firefighter. At 3:30 p.m. on the same day he left his American home, and eighty hours later, after traveling some 7,500 miles, he began work.

The flames gave off heat equivalent to an estimated 400,000,000 thermal units—enough to heat two-thirds of the homes in England. Bulldozers had to be screened with sheets of corrugated iron, and Kinley designed a large mobile shelter for himself and the men who would work on the well. Unprotected in the air temperature of 250° F, they would have died in a few minutes. Millions of gallons of water therefore had to be played on them, their shelter, and all surrounding equipment, throughout the fight. To enable this to be done, 6-inch water pipes were manhandled over 22 miles of hill country to carry water from the nearest river.

Every unit of the company's fire service that could be spared was hurried to the spot, and as the approach track was unusable a new road had to be driven over four miles of rocky mountain.

Under a curtain of water from high-powered monitors and within their mobile canopy, the first party reached the blaze. Fallen debris deflected the flames dangerously in horizontal tongues, and a sudden change of wind would have engulfed the workers. Kinley blasted the wreckage clear with a heavy charge of gelignite which was carried forward in 50-pound parcels by volunteers. If any of them had stumbled, "Rig 20" might well have claimed some lives.

As the charge exploded it released more than half a mile of 4½ inch drill pipe lodged in the hole, which rose like a twisting string in the air. Behind it a single column of flame signified that man had won the first round of the battle.

Days later when the earth and wreckage had sufficiently cooled, a second charge was fired to snuff out the flame like a candle, leaving only the escaping gas.

Two giant valves were flown out, one from Britain and one from the U.S.A., to cap the well. Every man had to have his ears sealed with wax before he could approach the shrieking jet, and many were deaf for days afterwards. But after six hours, during which any false move might have caused a spark to reignite the gas, the operation was complete. "Rig 20" was silent, after six weeks of battle.

THE SCREAMING ROAR BECAME A WHINE; THE WHINE BECAME A WHISPER; THE WHISPER BECAME SILENCE. FOR THE FIRST TIME IN MANY WEEKS, MEN COULD SPEAK AND HEAR WHERE ONCE HAD BEEN NAFT SAFID, "RIG 20."

The story was recorded by Martyn Wilson, the Company's cameraman who was at Abadan, only 100 miles away when the fire occurred. He spent six weeks at Naft Safid filming every phase of the battle.

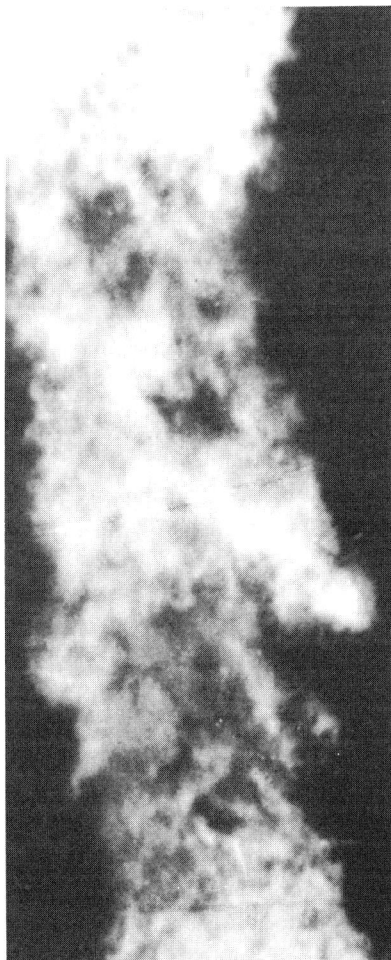

APPENDIXES

MYRON KINLEY'S WORLD WAR I DIARY

Arrived in Liverpool, England, July 8, 1918. Walked to Knotty Ark and stayed night, leaving 6 o'clock in the morning for Romsey, arriving in Romsey July 9, 1918, at 4 o'clock.

Stayed in Romsey for 2 days. While there visit Romsey Abbey and River Tiel. Grub and bunks were bad all through England.

Left Romsey July 10, 1918, at 4 o'clock and marched 6 miles to dock at Southampton, arriving in the afternoon about 4 o'clock. Stayed around dock until 6:30, boarded a fast pleasure boat and left at 8 o'clock packed like sardines. While leaving harbor seen several steamers which had been torpedoed but not disabled.

Came across channel in convoy, arriving in Le Havre about 3 o'clock in the morning. Had coffee and hard bread—only meal we had since leaving Romsey. Landed about 6 o'clock in the morning and marched to an English rest camp—No. 1—where we starved to death. Stayed in camp for 3 days, leaving on the 3rd day at 1 o'clock, marching to depot, were packed in box cars and issued rations for 3 days. Left Le Havre at 5:30 o'clock in afternoon, July 14, 1918, arriving in La Contini July 17, 1918, and had our first real meal since leaving the ship.

July 19, 1918, I transferred into 59th Art C.A.C. and company left July 21, 1918, for 1, 2, and 21 division.

Left La Contini August 13, 1918 with full equipment and arrived in Village Sue Marne August 15. Had to unload guns at Wassy August 16. Left Wassy for Village Sue Marne August 16. Cleaned up Village which had not been clean since built. Were billeted in barnes. Went past Joinville the first night, traveling on guns.

Arrived at Pwinelle woods just in back of 3 line trucks August 31 at 5 o'clock. A711. Camouflage trucks and started to lay platforms.

Saturday slept night step in truck and 5 gas alarms were sent back. Sunday heard first German shells pass over head. Was shelling a battery in rear of us. Started to lay platform on old French position but changed No. 4 and 1 gun and made new position. No. 2 and 3 guns used old position.

We were put in dugouts that had been used by French and were packed like rats, a gun crew to a dugout. While in dugouts one night the Germans shelled road all night, sending over 300 shells during my two hours gas guard. No one hurt in battalion. Our kitchen was moved 2 miles to the rear and grub was pulled up in a wagon by a detail every meal.

Barrage started September 12, 1918, at 1 o'clock and quit next morning at 9 o'clock. The small guns were out of range at 6 o'clock. 6" Howitzers were moved up 4 kilometers. Next morning saw first German prisoners pass by. Mostly old men, a few boys. Went up to Maney and seen first real shell. First, the Germans long range guns were trying to put 75 out of action that were in and around the town.

September 15, 1918, left position to go ahead and went 3 kilometers and order was changed, so came back. Long-range guns were firing on Metz.

September 16, 1918, left woods and went to Belleville and convoy stopped for 2 days. French railroad artillery were firing on Germans. At night the Germans shelled the town. Took first cooty bath in Moselle River. September 17, 1918, left and orders were to go to Argonne woods, arriving at the woods September 20, riding guns. B-section were sent ahead to dig position and unload ammunition, but were not fast enough so had to dig our own. Regiment was billeted at Camp Dubeville near Florent. A-section used French dugouts which were 2 years old and loozy and rats as big as cats. Water was bad.

September 26, a.m. open fire on Varinnin which was full of machine gun nests.

September 27 started out souvenir hunting and ran into front line just as a barrage was sent up from our guns and French guns so had to hurry back, arriving just as crews were called out. It happened that every A-section man was out hunting souvenirs, so B-section were sent after, but were not needed, orders came not to fire. Saw a mine laid by Germans about 50' deep and 100' across in no man's land, also first dead American. 116 infantry lost about 65 men trying to go by machine gun nest so made slow progress, woods being thick and no tanks to break the German lines.

October 5 started to move back by orders—were changed to go ahead riding in truck. Traveled all night, got stuck and *October 6* arrived at Vanvey about 8 o'clock a.m. Started to lay position which was known as Death Valley. About 1 o'clock were shelled but no harm done. Started firing with only 2 guns in position out of batallion at 7 o'clock. Our guns started firing 1 hour later. Fired all night and up until 8 o'clock a.m. and went to bed in a hole. Got up at 4 o'clock and cleaned gun, going to bed after supper.

Next morning started to move, getting ready at 12 o'clock and ready at 6, B-section riding guns, A-section in trucks.

Arriving at Epôneville at 7 next morning in trucks. Both of our guns were 5 men shy. German got range with shrapnel of infantry coming up and gun stuck so had no trouble hitting someone: One man died from crew, and 8 lost by infantry, about 40 wounded.

Guns arrived about 9 o'clock and position was on edge of Chepy Woods in plain view of enemy from airplane. Laid platform in good time and gun laid ready to fire about 4 o'clock and at 6 o'clock found out we could not get on target so had to move rear beam and use chalks and fired that night.

Next day had to lay platform over again ready to fire that night. Only 2 guns ready. Fired very near every night. While firing one night they came close getting some of us putting a shell just in front of gun, splashed mud all over us but no one hurt.

Slept in an old Quarry but most of battery slept in gunman barracks. Were shelled night and day with gas and high explosive shells. No one hurt in Position. October, 1918 order to move and had to lay over for one day, a hard place to get guns out so moved next night and were shelled by a long-range gun which could not be found by our aviator and caused a lot of trouble, no one hurt. Went through Romagne October, 1918, and were lucky, the Germans ceased firing a few minutes before and let us get by. They shelled the town and put a shell through an ambulance coming back with wounded, killing driver and all. Our position was in back of a hill about 2 kilometers in back of front lines 75. Went all around as one could get on top of hill and see shell bursting over in the lines and could see patrols in no man's land through glasses. Slept on side of hill in holes. A large German cantonment over hill and good beds in them so we slept pretty good. We fire on, no damage done, one horse killed in French battery in rear of us.

O.P. got data on Huns moving a gun and were ordered to fire at 12 o'clock on target putting it out of commission in first few shots. 12 teams of horses helped us to move gun.

Open fire in barrage at 11 o'clock firing till 3 o'clock and barrage started were shelled back by shrapnel but not long. No one hurt. One man killed Romagne night before. Only one killed outright from batallion.

Armistice signed November 11, 1918. Hostility closed at 11 o'clock a.m. Transfer to truck section as second driver on truck that driver was killed in Romagne and order back to Dubeville first loading up with material for B at B. Stayed in Dubeville and order out November 18 drive to Romagne for gun material. Loaded up and drove to Vassy to loading platform and returned to Dubeville with Kitchen. Left November 21 for Vignory, arriving the same day at 10 o'clock p.m. and billeted in cheese factory, ordered back to Vassy two days later with guns. Turned in truck in Ordinance at Dijon. Coming back to Vignory and left for Brest December, 1918, arriving December, 1918.

LIST OF IMPORTANT FIRES

One day, as Myron and I were discussing specifics for this book, he gave me a list of the most important dates of his life relative to his work as a firefighter. There were twenty-two dates on that list, beginning with the first oil well fire put out with explosives after the use of steam had failed to extinguish it. That was the day in 1913 when Myron's dad finally had a chance to test his theory about how fires in burning wells could be put out by the use of explosives. The last two are the first wells Myron killed that had tremendous bottom hole pressures. Both were Texas wells.

Here is the complete list of those dates:

1. First Fire (Steam) 1913
2. Elk Hill Fire (Steam) 1920
3. Back to Oklahoma (Steam, explosives) 1922
4. Bald Hill Fire 1923
5. Deep Rock Fire (Cromwell, Oklahoma) 1923
6. Wilcox Well (Cromwell, Oklahoma) 1924
7. Carter Fire (Little River Field near Crow, Lousiana) 1929
8. Moreni No. 160 (first trip to Romania) 1929
9. Sinclair Fire, Stamper No. 3 (Oklahoma City) 1929
10. Sinclair Fire, Cole No. 1 and first hook
    (Gladewater, Texas) 1931
11. Moreni No. 160 (second trip to Romania) 1931
12. Barco Trip - Gulf (Maricoba) 1933
13. Pure Oil Company Fire 1936
14. Largo Petroleum Corp. (near Lake Maracaibo) 1936
15. Greta Crater (Refugio, Texas) 1939
16. Dammam No. 12 (first trip to Middle East,
    fire extinguished itself) 1939
17. Naft Safid (second trip to Middle East) 1951
18. Pure Oil Company Platform
    (near Morgan City, Louisiana) 1952
19. Alborz #5 (third trip to Middle East) 1956
20. Ahwaz #6 (fourth trip to Middle East) 1958
21. Stanolind Well (Houston)-5,000# pressure . . . . .n.d.
22. Sun Well (Palacios, Texas)-6,000# pressure . . . . .n.d.

EXCERPTS FROM CHAPTERS 7 AND 8 OF *THE HISTORY OF PETROLEUM ENGINEERING.*

The diameter of a shot hole after shooting with nitroglycerin or gelatin was a problem that aroused the curiosity of every man who worked around such wells and is one that is important if the well is to be plugged back. Myron M. Kinley invented a caliper in 1935 for determining the size of shot holes, but its design would not permit using it in a hole full of fluid. It was redesigned to operate on an electric cable and was used first in 1940; and on the whole, the results were not unexpected. In the beginning it was run on an experimental basis—or, one might say, to satisfy curiosity—but with greater interest in better cement jobs, the caliper became a valuable tool. If cavities existed, there was less chance of a good cement job in such intervals; and improved mud and drilling practices could reduce and perhaps eliminate many of the irregularities, thereby increasing the probability of a good cement job. The volume of the hole could be calculated, and the quantity of cement run to fill to the desired level.

The man to build a caliper commercially and use it in the oil fields was Myron Kinley, the oil well firefighter of world fame. His invention was disclosed by Beckstrom in 1935 and covered by two patents in 1937 and 1941. The original instrument had four expanding arms. It had a length of 9 feet, all the lower 6 feet of which consisted of a 5-inch pipe in which the four arms were locked as the tool went down the hole. The upper part contained the recording instruments in a liquid-proof case. When released, each arm operated a ratchet which raised and lowered a recording stylus. The stylus in turn traced a curve showing the diameter of the hole. There were, therefore, four curves showing the continuous measurement of two diameters of the hole, at right angles. Later, this complicated recording was replaced by electrical methods of recording at the surface. Figure 33 shows a type of caliper built by Kinley in the early 1940's. The first tools were equipped with a tip or rod at the lower part. This rod would release the arms of the instrument when hitting bottom. However, it would not operate reliably when the bottom was filled with soft mud. In present measurements, the arms can be released mechanically or electrically.

Kinley worked successfully in many areas (Oklahoma, New Mexico, Kansas) in the 1930's; but because he was himself engaged in other activities, he experienced considerable diffculty in managing the sales end of this business. He therefore entered into an agreement on a royalty basis with the Halliburton Oil Well Cementing Company on August 1, 1940. Later, on January 1, 1947, he sold his patents outright to the same firm. The caliper service was offered to the industry commercially by the Halliburton Oil Well Cementing Company about January 1, 1947.

Working independently—and knowing little or nothing of Kinley's activity—Bossler, in the oil fields of Pennsylvania, built a caliper which—like the first edition by Kinley—was crude but very effective. Good descriptions of it were made public in 1930. Illustrations showed that the data were transmitted electrically to the surface.

At first, calipering was used for controlling shooting and making it more efficient. Soon, however, it appeared that the knowledge of the "cavities and constrictions" of an oil well were of interest for other purposes. Bossler pointed out that in secondary-recovery work it is important to set packers at a place where the diameter is regular, not in front of caves. Salnikov reports that in 1936 The Carter Oil Company had difficulties in the South Burbank Field in Oklahoma, in trying to exploit it by pressure maintenance, because of high gas-oil ratios. They made an attempt to shut off upper gas zones by means of specially designed underset formation packers. There was a need of a tool to assist in selecting the proper spots in the open hole, below the casing shoe, where packer rubbers could effectively seal off gas. As a result, a caliper log by Kinley was run in a well preliminary to setting the packers. It worked successfully. This was in the latter part of 1936. Other uses followed; e.g., the surveying of the contours of a well after an acidizing operation, the controlling of heaving shales, the computing of the amount of cement necessary for casing cementing. Finally, the caliper log is helpful in production testing and for a more complete interpretation of the electrical log.

Since the early 1940s activity in calipering work has increased greatly. Caliper logs are run routinely in a considerable proportion of oil wells. The fact is that the knowledge of the diameter of the well is useful for many purposes, as already mentioned—cementing, testing, heaving-shale control, acidizing, electrical-log interpretation. Many excellent papers have been published on the subject. Most electrical-logging companies perform caliper logging on a contracting basis.

APPENDIX D

"CALIPER WELL LOGGING"

WILLIAM H. FARRAND

Important data on hole bore derived from study of caliper runs by William H. Farrand, Superintendent Drilling and Production, Pacific Coast Division, The Texas Company.

It has long been the belief of everyone connected with the drilling of oil wells that the actual diameter of the hole made by a bit is seldom the same as the gauge of the bit. Fishing tools only a fraction of an inch under hole gauge would pass the fish, indicating oversize hole. This belief has been substantiated by the use of open hole calipers, which have been run in a number of wells during the last few months and which have disclosed conditions that were somewhat unexpected as well as informative. Utilization of the data supplied by caliper logs has been varied but it is natural that the full scope of the adaptability of the equipment has not been realized in the short time it has been available.

The use of calipers to determine the size of hole actually made by the bit was conceived several years ago by Myron M. Kinley, known throughout the world for his firefighting technique and performance, who developed a mechanical type of caliper. Then, in cooperation with Halliburton Oil Well Cementing Company, joint experimental and development work was done and the present calipers, which combine mechanical and electrical principles, were perfected. These calipers are run into the well on a wire line in a closed position and when they reach the bottom of the hole or the lowest point of the distance through which a caliper survey is to be made, four arms that contact the wall of the hole are released. The calipers are then withdrawn at a rate up to approximately 100 feet per minute and automatically record the variations in diameter of the hole on a chart at the surface.

The arms are independent of each other and as each rides over the irregularities of the wall of the hole it indicates by electrical means its varying distances from the center line of the calipers during its upward travel. The movement of the individual arms is measured by electrical resistance and the sum of the resistances of the four arms is automatically divided by four by an instrument at the surface. The average thus resulting is recorded by the instrument in inches to give a continuous reading of the mean diameter of the hole, as shown in accompanying illustrations. Although the shape of the hole is not given, the cross-sectional area is indicated by the mean

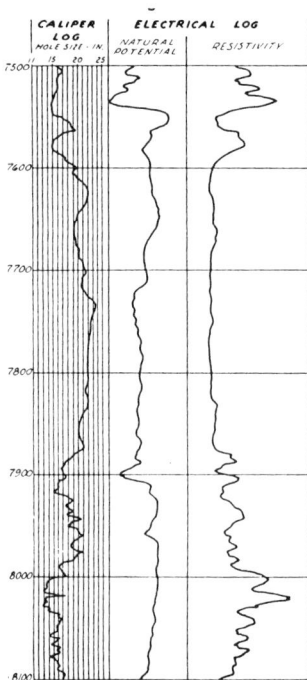

FIG. I

diameter, which thus shows tight spots as well as enlargements . The maximum diameter measured by calipers now in use is 36 inches

As the arms move individually, errors that would otherwise arise from elliptically shaped holes, from measurements taken in holes at an angle from the vertical, or from other irregularities such as key seats may not always be picked up by the calipers but such conditions will probably be rare and the size of hole indicated by the calipers will be very close to actual. Moreover, the slight errors due to irregularities of the wall between contact points of the four arms will probably be compensating.

Contrary to the expectations of many, logs both in California and in other areas where the calipers have been run show that in general the hole is larger in shale than it is in sand. There are naturally different kinds of shale and different kinds of sand so any relative difference in hole size in shale and sand cannot be expected. The extent to which a hole is enlarged beyond the gauge of the bit will naturally vary with the drilling technique (see Figure 1).

When the caliper log has been taken before cementing, it has usually been found that the volume of slurry that would otherwise have been placed behind the casing was inadequate. In one field where the practice had been to use 700 sacks of cement for a certain string, nearly 2000 sacks were necessary to fill to the point desired (see Figure 2).

Another use of this instrument is to determine whether the hole needs reaming before running pipe. As holes become smaller in diameter there is less clearance around the casing. Long reaming jobs have resulted as drilling foremen were reluctant to run pipe with greatly reduced clearance. The hole caliper run overcame this difficulty and if the log of the run was satisfactory no reaming was done. At the most, "spot" reaming of tight hole was sometimes indicated. This lead to much less unnecessary reaming and to the practice of not carrying full sized reamers or stabilizers while drilling. A consid-

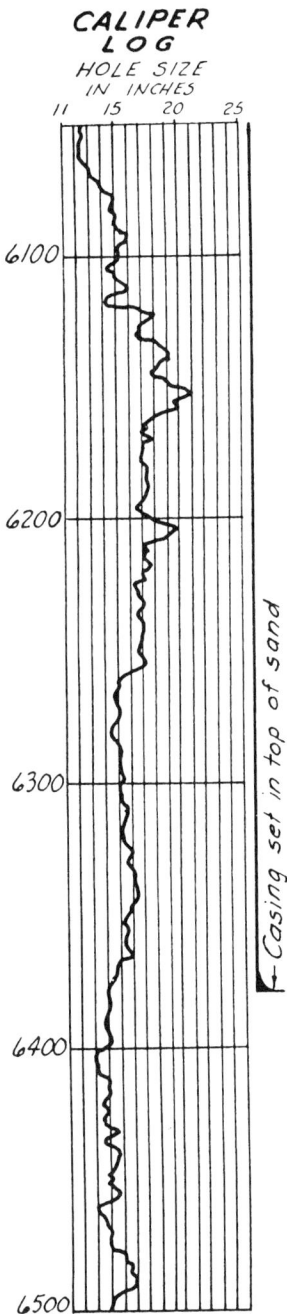

**CALIPER
LOG**

HOLE SIZE
IN INCHES

| 11 | 15 | 20 | 25 |

← Casing set in top of sand

FIG. 2

erable saving in time and material resulted from this application.

If multiple jobs are to be employed, the caliper again indicates how much or how little cement is necessary to effect the shut-off at points up the hole. In this use it is quite likely that a squeeze job can be saved by an actual determination of the hole diameter at the places where upper hole jobs are to be used by multiple stage cementing the shut-off string or for future perforating opposite upper productive sand bodies.

After the hole has gone a little too deep and a bottom hole plug is necessary, again a caliper survey shows how much cement is needed to raise the plug to the desired height, and a recement job may be saved by this process.

A caliper log indicates the places the casing stabilizers or guides should be attached to pipe before it is run.

The guides are obviously useless if the spring ribs cannot contact the sides of the hole and thus center the pipe to permit a good collar of cement to surround shoe and lower section of the string.

The same information will indicate where the hole scratchers should be placed to clean the walls for the cement job. Many stabilizers and scratchers have been placed opposite shale bodies when caliper surveys show the hole usually to be enlarged.

Another application is the determination of the cement point by the use of this log, in combination with an electric log of the formations. It is customary in oil field development to set the casing in shale above the sand from which production is expected. The hole caliper logs indicate that this may not be the best procedure, and the shales are usually the places in which oversized bore

HOLE SIZE
in inches

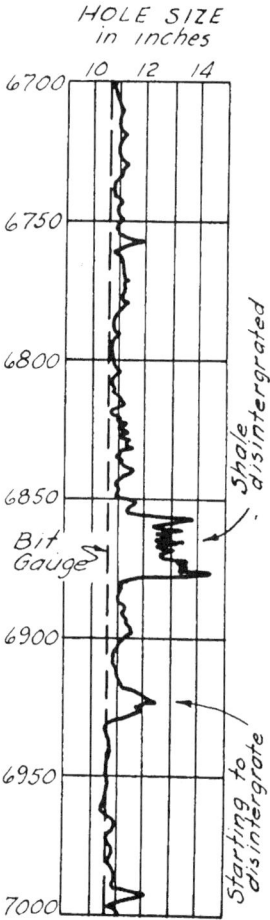

FIG. 3

develops. This explains why sometimes a shoe set in a good shale body is found to have a faulty shutoff. The cement failed to scour the wall at this point and water enters from the overlying sands, with the resulting squeeze job.

Later failure of the shutoff may develop for this same reason. A progressive disintegration of the shale due to the presence of water in the hole may allow water to enter around the cement, which during the shoe test successfully shut off the unwanted fluid (see Figure 3).

Correlations by the use of the caliper log are also possible. As the shales in the holes tend to develop oversized bore, and the sands remain nearer to hole diameter size, the logs when studied give another bit of necessary information the engineers need to make their correlations more correct. Sandy shales vary and, although they offer similar characteristics in adjacent holes, they are not quite the clear evidence offered by the all sand and shale sections. It has been noted, however, that sections of holes will show the same general character that is found in other holes, and the correlations are thereby affirmed.

Many formation test misruns could have been saved by use of the caliper. The expansion of the rubber on a formation tester is limited and if the hole is oversized at the selected point above a sand to be tested the packer cannot hold and the test is a misrun.

One company ran a caliper after some failures of the tester to hold over a sand in a wildcat well. This caliper run showed oversize hole at the points selected and indicated where the tester could be set successfully. The formation tester was again run—this time it held and the sand was tested.

A more specialized use of the hole caliper is to determine the hole volume for gravel packing. The volume shown by the caliper run may be accepted as a check on the completeness of the job. Formerly the size of the wall scraped or underreamed hole was used,

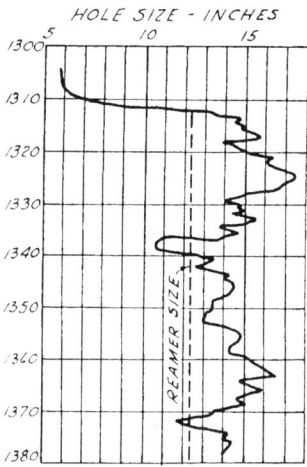

HOLE SIZE - INCHES

FIG. 4

and possibly too little gravel was thus placed behind the liner with the result that some sand trouble developed when the well was placed on production.

Now a run of the caliper should be made after the hole has been wall scraped below the shutoff string (see Figure 4). If the job of scraping is to gauge the liner may be run and a reverse circulation gravel pack job is performed. If the hole is not to gauge—and this is by no means a rare occurrence—the hole is rescraped, another caliper run made, and the job accomplished.

Incidentally, this has been a good test of the caliper accuracy. Many jobs have checked the hole volumes as shown by the caliper run with considerable accuracy, sometimes to within a cubic foot. If the volume of gravel calculated by this method does not check the volume while performing the job within reasonable limits the liner should be pulled out and the job re-done. This infrequent check on the well caliper has led to its accuracy being accepted without question. The one or two occasions when the liner was pulled because of the discrepancy between calculated volume of gravel and the amount put away while doing the gravel pack job have only demonstrated its accuracy. On these occasions considerable cuttings were found in the hole and after removing them the job went off as calculated. This has been eliminated by more thorough circulation after the hole has been scraped to bottom.

AID TO FISHING

Inability to "get over" a fish has long plagued the drilling departments. The hole caliper logs show why this is often the case.

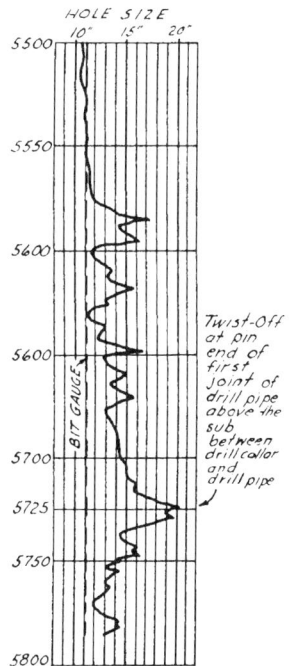

HOLE SIZE

Twist-Off at pin end of first joint of drill pipe above the sub between drill collar and drill pipe

FIG. 5

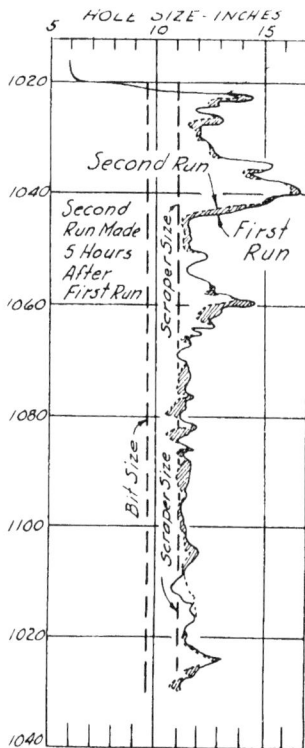

FIG. 6

Shale tends to disintegrate while the drilling proceeds and the shale sections of the hole become enlarged. Hence when a twistoff occurs, the hole is composed of sections of large and small diameter. The smaller diameter sections prevent the fishing tool from getting over the fish, particularly if the fish is in one of the enlarged sections of the hole.

A perfect example of this is shown Figure 5 where the twistoff occurred at a depth of 5725 feet leaving the top of the twisted-off drill pipe and drill collar in the largest portion of the hole. Considerable trouble was en-countered in trying to locate the top of the fish although the drill pipe measurements were accurate.

It is very interesting to note that the twistoff occurred in the lower part of the single above the drill collar opposite the enlarged hole. In this particular case only two of the six drill collars were recovered. The caliper run proved useful, however, when it was decided to cement the four collars left in the hole and sidetrack them. Nearly double the volume of cement was necessary to fill the hole to the required height for this operation, thereby saving the placing of a second plug.

This oversized hole is probably the cause of much drill pipe grief as the irregular and enlarged hole leads to excessive gyrations and much bending of the drill pipe.

Also note in Figure 5 how the hole from 5500 to 5560 feet, together with the sandy shell at 5630 to 5635 feet, prevented the socket when run with drill collars from getting over the fish. With the drill collars removed and a bent 5-inch single a hold was secured. Figure 6 shows how mud cake forms on the walls of the hole after drilling and before running the liner. Notice that in 5 hours the wall cake had formed opposite the sands. Also, the enlarged hole under the water string shoe is typical of must runs.

Figure 7 is another example of washout under the shoe. This time a surface string is shown.

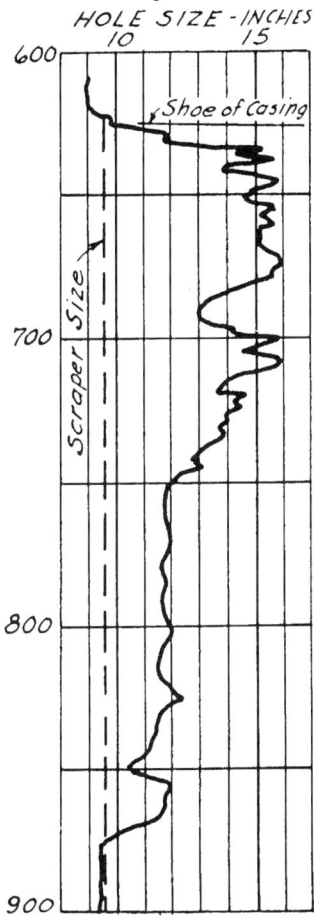

FIG. 7

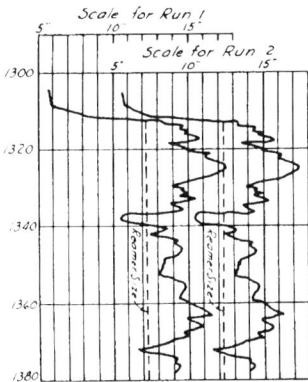

FIG. 8

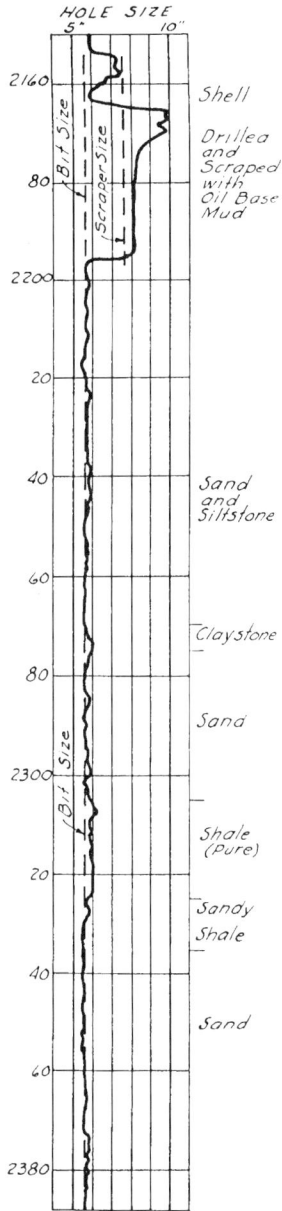

FIG. 9

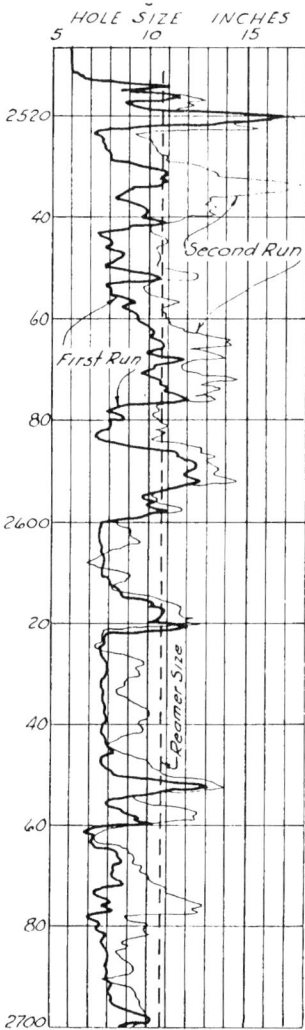

FIG. 10

Figure 8 shows two runs with the caliper in a hole drilled with oil base drilling fluid. This hole stood 13 hours between runs yet no measurable cake had formed.

Figure 9 shows a hole drilled with oil base drilling fluid. It is interesting that much of the hole is nearly to gauge although drilled in various sediments that themselves lead to enlargement with water base mud.

Wall scraping must be carefully done or the instrument blades will not perform their job. Two runs on one well, Figure 10, illustrate how they had failed to scrape the hole to full gauge and a third run was required.

Figure 11 shows two runs in a hole with ninety-four days between runs. The increase in hole diameter is attributed to the water loss in the mud. That is, the water loss of the mud dissolves the shale. This action goes on until such a thick cake is formed that no more water from the mud can reach the formation. Then the action reverses and the cake builds up, filling the hole opposite these cavities. This, of course, is one cause of stuck drill pipe when coming out of the hole.

Figure 12 is a part of the same run illustrating the action mentioned above. Here the cave has filled with mud cake and a potential stuck drill pipe job is present.

CONCLUSION

The oil industry has much to learn about the bore of the holes from which they draw their crude. More study should be made of this information by the technical branch of the industry as much new

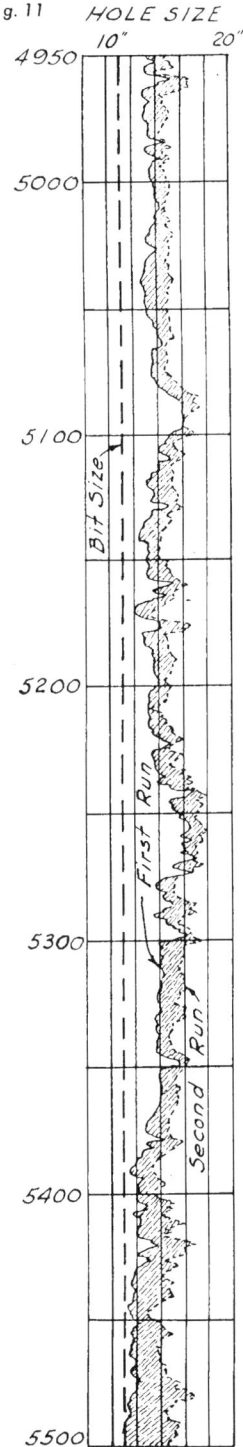

data can be obtained and many savings made by use of the caliper.

Other applications are being tried and their results will become known as the method demonstrates its usefulness. Quite likely improved initial production from wells drilled in developed territories will result from the study of the caliper runs.

A new study of circulating fluid is also indicated from the scant data now available.

The use of the caliper has added much accurate information to what was one of the unknowns in the oil industry.

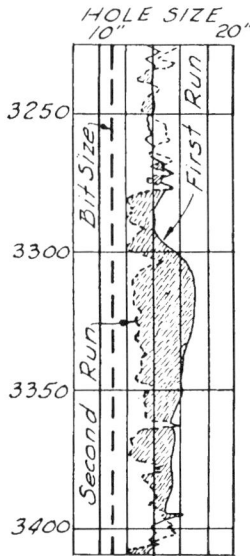

FIG. 12

FIG. 11

COLE #1
GLADEWATER, TEXAS, MAY 1931

BLAZE AT WELL DEFYING FOES

Gladewater, Texas, May 5, 1931—The flaming Sinclair Company No. 1 Cole oil well today again brushed aside human ingenuity which has struggled for a week to extinguish the blaze and another postponement in plans for shooting the well with nitroglycerin was necessary. The well had raged since the explosion a week ago today which cost the lives of nine men.

M. M. and Floyd Kinley, oil well firefighting experts from Tulsa, were keenly disappointed when weary workmen strove in vain throughout the night to dislodge the "kelly joint" from the casing-head in the hole. S. C. Phillips, one of the Sinclair men directing the fight, said it had been learned that there was a second loose joint that would have to be taken out after the main kelly joint had been removed.

A ring of men labored tirelessly in the edges of the flames trying to unscrew the great piece of pipe with a "goose-neck" that spouted a withering stream of burning oil. Floyd Kinley first had gone into the flame and hooked a cable to the hot metal.

It was possible that a charge of nitroglycerin would be placed in an effort to dislodge the pipe, which alone stands in the way of the effort to choke off the flames with the greater nitro blast.

Rain fell in heavy showers Monday night and early today, the water helping some in the fight, Phillips said, since it served as an auxiliary to men with blistered faces who stand hour after hour playing stream of water from hose over fellow workmen who must stay near the flame.

WILD OIL WELL STILL DEFIES FIREFIGHTERS
Tulsa Daily World, Wednesday, May 6, 1931

Gladewater, Texas, May 5—-Fire broke out in the woods north of the blazing Sinclair No. 1 Cole late tonight, just as crews were completing preparations to shoot the well with nitroglycerin. Workmen were withdrawn from the well to fight the fire in the woods.

All operations at the well were suspended as workmen left the tanks of chemicals and the runways which had been built for sliding the heavy nitroglycerin charge to the burning gusher. Henry Bogess, Sinclair official, said the woods fire would delay blowing of the well until tomorrow morning at least.

It had been decided at noon today to blow the kelly joint from the well with nitroglycerin. It had been impossible to unscrew it and its presence kept the Kinleys from dropping the nitroglycerin down the well to snuff out the fire.

Gladewater, Texas, May 5—Placed with their backs to the wall because a stubborn piece of pipe—known in oil fields as the "kelly joint"—refused to be dislodged by human hands, M. M. and Floyd Kinley, Tulsa oil firefighters, tonight planned to set off a charge of 70 quarts of nitroglycerin at the mouth of the wildly burning Sinclair No. 1 Cole oil well. The well caught fire a week ago today, fatally burning nine men.

The Kinleys primarily hoped to get the pipe joint out of the way for a scientific effort to snuff out the week-old blaze but they were hopeful at the same time the charge would do double duty by cutting away the roaring blaze as well.

An improved runway was in place, the explosive had been placed in an iron drum and awaited only a shipment of chemicals from Dallas before Floyd Kinley could touch an electric button which would ignite the fuse out over the fiery geyser.

All plans had been made to shoot the well at daylight today but after workmen spent hours trying to get the pipe out of the caldron, the attempt had to be postponed. They had worked all night, circling the roaring flame propelling a cable attached to the pipe, which revolved it. It was believed seven revolutions would disconnect it but 14 did not accomplish the task. It was then the firefighters decided to resort to explosives.

CAPPING TOOL MAY SHUT IN WILD WELL

Milwaukee, May 5—A capping tool which may curb the fury of the wild well at Gladewater, Texas, was shipped from Milwaukee tonight. Tomorrow it will be flown from Chicago to Dallas over N.A.T. and then to Gladewater in a chartered plane.

The apparatus is described as consisting of metal that will not spark when it makes contact over the well. It is manufactured by a Milwaukee firm.

DISASTROUS OIL FIRE CONQUERED BY NITRO BLAST

Gladewater, Texas, May 6, 1931—The Sinclair No. 1 Cole, giant geyser of flame that had defied efforts to control it for eight days after killing nine workmen when it caught fire, was snuffed out by the touch of a man's finger.

Floyd Kinley of Tulsa, younger of the pair of firefighting brothers who came here to battle the well, pressed a switch that detonated 200 pounds of nitroglycerin jelly shortly after 6 p.m. The explosion was heard in Longview, 20 miles away. The great torch of fire was blown out like a candle. Fifty yards away, 18 men were crouched behind a big steel storage tank filled with water. The explosion hurled a steel beam from the well barely missing the workmen. Still farther away stood a motion picture cameraman, taking pictures of the explosion for a news reel. He didn't get his picture; the blast shattered all the lenses in his camera. Snuffing of the well left the scene in darkness and the attempt to cap it was delayed until day-break. Ranger Sergeant M. T. (Lone Wolf) Gonzaullas, with a band of impromptu helpers, kept guard around the big gusher. Only workmen were allowed in the neighborhood and every man in the vicinity was searched for matches, lanterns, flashlights—anything that might possibly set the well off again. The ranger ordered his men to fire their guns under no circumstances whatever lest the shot itself might start another fire. Gas from the well hung heavily about the neighborhood, needing only a spark to kill another working crew.

Oil from the big gusher still spouted 50 feet into the air. How much of it had spouted away or gone up in smoke since the well blew in out of control ten days ago, nobody knew, but it was thought the waste amounted to something like $200,000.

Of the nine men who lost their lives, the body of one has never been recovered. He was Bill Harroun, brother of the Sinclair official in charge.

Kinley used four 50-pound sacks of nitroglycerin for his shot. They were skidded to the well inside a steel drum. For each of the packs there was a detonating cap and the whole charge was set off at once by an electric wire.

The troublesome kelly joint, which had delayed the shooting, was blown off the well this morning by an earlier charge. When efforts to cap the well are renewed tomorrow, a wooden derrick 100 yards away will be skidded into place. To prevent another fatal spark, brass tools made to order in Milwaukee, will be used. They arrived by air mail in Dallas today, the transportation charge being $400.

FIRE AT TEXAS WELL PUT OUT BY NITRO SHOT
Oklahoman, June 7, 1931

Gladewater, Texas, May 6—The Sinclair No. 1 Cole was extinguished by a shot of nitroglycerin shortly after 6 o'clock Wednesday night.

The nitroglycerin brought to an end the disastrous flame which killed nine men and destroyed an estimated 1,500 barrels of oil hourly since it caught fire just a few hours more than eight days ago.

The Kinley brothers from Oklahoma, Floyd and M. M., well known fighters of oil field fires, had been working at the well since shortly after the blaze started. M. M. Kinley had kept on the job, despite an injury several days ago that caused one of his legs to be placed in a cast. He helped direct the work while walking on crutches, or reclining in a chair.

The strong explosive jarred the countryside for miles around. Workmen immediately began to skid a new derrick over the well. The job was expected to be completed before morning. Then will come the fight to shut off the oil flow. If everything goes well, workers expected to get the well in leash sometime Thursday morning. After the derrick is in place, workers were to erect a christmas tree over the well.

The blast hurled flames high in the air as a grand finale to one of the most stubborn and disastrous oil fires ever experienced in the southwest. The charge was placed at the base of the casing block.

The successful "shot" was the second the well had received Wednesday. Early Wednesday, 70 quarts of the high explosive were loosed at the well, but without extinguishing the fire. The flames receded upward for an instant, then climbed back down the black geyser to within a man's height from the ground.

The Gladewater fire was the latest of a series of oil fires in the highly productive east Texas field which have claimed almost a score of lives.

Almost 300,000 barrels of oil, it was estimated, went up in huge billows of smoke that for nearly 200 hours overcast the countryside.

BLAST STIFLES OIL WELL FIRE

Gladewater, Texas, May 7, 1931— The lofty pillar of smoke that for eight days had marked the site of the Sinclair No. l Cole, visible as far as Longview, 20 miles distant, was gone today. The blazing gusher was extinguished last night by a 200-pound nitroglycerin charge.

But the well was still running wild today—the eleventh day since it blew in out of control. Sinclair employees prepared for a new attempt to cap it. A week ago Tuesday, such an attempt touched off the fire that took the lives of nine men.

Floyd Kinley, younger of the firefighting brothers from Tulsa, snuffed out the blaze Tuesday night. Aided by a youngster named Huxley Bunch, who substituted for M. M. Kinley when the latter had his leg broken, Floyd placed four 50-pound packs of the explosive in a steel drum beside the well and touched off the charge by electricity. It was fired a few minutes after 6 o'clock last night.

The blast was heard twenty miles away in Longview. A great umbrella-shaped yellow blaze was blown upward for 200 feet, the most dazzling display since the well first caught fire. The next instant there was darkness intensified by memory of the glare that had come from the well before. A newsreel photographer had come to take a movie of the explosion, but it shattered the lenses in his camera.

Sergeant M. T. (Lone Wolf) Gonzaullas, of the Texas rangers headed a squad of men who kept guard about the well last night. Gas hung all about the scene, needing only a spark to kill another crew of workmen. No one was allowed to carry matches within a mile of the well and automobiles were parked far away.

Today the crew prepared to slide a new derrick over the well, still spouting oil 50 feet into the air from the crater left by the explosion. Workmen carried specially made brass tools to prevent another fatal spark in this new attempt to cap the runaway gusher.

MYRON KINLEY'S DIARY OF RIG 20, NAFT SAFID, 1951

Left N. Y. City, Wednesday 8 o'clock a.m. TWA for Gander, Newfoundland, Paris, Zurich, Rome, Cairo and Basrah. Met there by company plane flying to Abadan. Cleared through Customs leaving for fire at Naft Safid and arriving there at 12 noon on Friday.

After going over the ground and finding the well located in a pocket with high mountains surrounding it, and finding it a very difficult location to work in, plans were made to tackle the location from the pipe rack side. A waterline was started to a dam site upstream. Water cooled hook was started. Also shed to work under. Cats were brought in to have shield built on.

Saturday—Still building up equipment and laying waterline.

Sunday—Waterline complete. Dam site ready to receive water. Still building cat and hook equipment. Also wind changed. A very good chance to work from down hill side. More room to move around the equipment.

Monday—Building up equipment and getting water supply rig up. Hook and shield ready to mount.

Tuesday—Fire change for the better. Gas flow consolidated in cellar. Water pit being filled. Tractor almost ready. Building up shed and hook.

Wednesday—Waiting water supply. Pulled over diesel oil tank.

Thursday—Played water on fire—cooled it down. Much more able to walk around without shield when water goes in flame. Preparation made to start working at midnight pulling out pipe that was on rack.

Friday—started working. Removed about half casing. Fire increasing in cellar. Working under shed.

Saturday—finished moving out casing and casing rack. Could see rotary table and junk in hole. Late start on account of getting fire pump in place and chain brake on shed. A good day's work though.

Sunday—Made an attempt to try and pull off rotary table but did not do any good; decided to try and shoot it off with artillery tomorrow or next day.

Monday—giving up cat and getting ready to shoot off connection. Also fixing waterline. Ready in morning.

Tuesday—Welding box to put shot in. All ready to go in morning. Had to burn out derrick leg.

Wednesday—Leveled up runway. Put shot in and shot off rotary table and Cameron valve. Fire going straight up. Drill pipe came out when connections were removed. Got a shell flame going 300 feet in air. Getting shed repaired; also, building new one. Making preparation to work from a different side. Will have to dig pond for water. A new 6" water system ready to go tomorrow. Supply should be O.K. when we get water in fire. Left on train for Teheran.

Thursday—Arrived after 24-hour train trip at Teheran. Very tired. 45 Tunnels in one range of mountains. Anna at station to meet me. A good night's rest.

Friday—Met Anna had dinner at her apartment. She is fixing it up nicely. Seems to be very happy. Went to bed early.

Saturday—Invited out to a barbecue in afternoon. Enjoyed it very much at the Howes. That night a party of four went to Park Hotel for supper and dance. Arrived back about 2 a.m. Sunday.

Sunday—Rested at guest house. Anna and I visited museum. Very interesting and nice. We met the Librarian who was French and Anna was very interested in being able to know there was a place to go.

Monday—Left Teheran by Iranian Airway. Arriving back in camp about 1 o'clock. Waterlines are finished to pump shed. Will probably get ready to start working around well tomorrow sometime.

Tuesday—Put in 4" waterline. Made a noticable change in column of flame.

Wednesday—Started to clean out cellar but ran out of water. Decided to shoot fire out as it is impossible to work cleaning out cellar. 8" valve shows leak. Traveling block down in sub-cellar.

Thursday—Getting ready to shoot out fire. Tested shed and it collapsed. Repairing it. Took temperature at different locations around. 240-220-160-175-140.

Friday—Preparation made to shoot out fire but from site picked it was too hot so moved to cellar open side. Dummy run made ready to put in shot tomorrow.

Saturday—Shot loaded but unable to place it on account of jack-knifing between Cat and Athey wagon. Had to bring it out. 500 pound shot loaded. Fire at valve very small. Gas has been leaking there for several days.

Sunday—Shot fire out —500 pounds 60 percent gelatinite and started in afternoon to clean out but drag line had to have water cooled exhaust put on. Also wind changed in afternoon.

Monday—Started cleaning out cellar and dug larger place around connections. Made fair progress with Dragline.

Tuesday—Digging in cellar with Dragline.

Wednesday—Digging in cellar. Made fair progress. Went to M.J.S. Spent day there and they started assembling head. Valve arrived from U.K. Air.

Thursday—Digging at cellar trying to break up concrete and clean out. Not much luck so far. Dragline operator dam poor.

Friday—Digging cellar with paving breaker. Making some headway. Am leaving today to see about connections. Turned digging job over to Barker. Went to M.J.S. to see about connections and valve assembly. O.K. Stayed there until Wed. Sat. - Sun. - Mon. - Tues. - Wed.—Still diggin' in cellar.

Thursday—Taking off connection and getting ready to get a ⅝" casing clear. Dragging out back side of cellar.

Friday—Cutting off 11⅝ casing. Putting in dead man and fixing flange in crane. Slow.

Saturday—Rigging up to put on flange.

Sunday—Put flange on 8⅝ casing. No trouble. Well making large volume of gas. Cementing a block around base of flange. Earthquake very severe as the bed shook and fan rack hanging from ceiling shook, too.

Monday—Put on valve. Had trouble owing to pin too tight. Took about 4 hours to put valve on. Bolted it down and flanged up connection. Closed in. Everything O.K. Pumped at about 2400 pounds.

APPENDIX G

FIELD NEWS ARTICLES ON AHWAZ NO. 6, 1958

MYRON KINLEY TACKLES THE FIRE

May 4, 1958—The active phase of the firefighting began at 3:15 on Thursday morning, when Kinley reached into the flames of Ahwaz Well No. 6 with a 20-metre steel arm and pulled out a large, twisted beam. This was the first fragment of the crumpled well to be removed from the fire.

Before the sun was up a small stack of wreckage had been neatly pulled out of the way of the salvage machinery. Many times when Kinley's tractor backed out of the flames there were disappointments, as the hook emerged empty from the flames, smoke and steam; Kinley had moved in close for a clear view, and then decided to unweave the next piece from a different angle.

Just after dawn, on May 1st, Kinley backed out of the fire to say that he had cleared a path for the salt-water nozzle. This spout, mounted on a steel sled, was quickly assembled on a long pipe and pushed forward by pipeline crews. Then Kinley caught the spout with his hook and carried it into the fire, where it now sits, shooting salt water from well No. 5 into the flames and greying the billowing black smoke with cooling steam. The water supply continues to be adequate, even though three fire hoses consume $7\frac{1}{2}$ tons of water each minute.

A stream of run-off water is carrying a thin film of unburnt oil to the safety reservoir half a kilometre away.

During the first two nights the more important pieces of burnt steel recovered were a spare rotary table, two swivels, two skids and several sections of pipe racks. On the third night, when Myron Kinley probed into the centre of Ahwaz well fire, he found a large assembly of heavy equipment still connected together. He was only able to pull it partly out, even after having another tractor team up with his. But last night, the labour of pulling twisted steel out of the fire was more successful. Several major pieces were recovered from the heart of the flame. These included the crown block and the travelling block, which are the pulleys weighing 1,000 kilos each, a large section of derrick, several heavy pieces of pipe rack, and three spare tanks.

The base of the fire became about six metres narrower during removal of the wreckage, presumably when a piece of steel that may have been deflecting the shooting column of oil was shifted.

Work continues until rising morning temperatures hamper the workers. Then a daytime crew of welders, fitters, and mechanics take over the equipment to make repairs, modifications, and manufacture new equipment to be used in later stages of the fight to control the well.

A new object on the skyline cheered the workers when they came to the well side at midnight, last night; this was the derrick of the relief well, which was pulled erect yesterday afternoon. It is now almost ready to begin drilling the well that will be used to extinguish the burning well by cutting off the oil, if it should be impossible to extinguish the fire on the surface.

DYNAMITE ATTACK WILL BEGIN—FIRE CREW ORDERED TO RETREAT FOUR TIMES LAST NIGHT

May 7, 1958—Myron Kinley was forced to postpone the expected dynamiting, this morning, by a large tangle of drill pipe which prevents his placing the explosive close enough to the well head until it is removed.

The dynamite expert, a Scotsman borrowed from Geophysical Services Incorporation Ltd., contractor to the Consortium, was busy yesterday preparing his firing lines, even as Kinley was supervising the final touches on the water-filled container in which the explosive will rest safely inside the fire until he detonates it from a safe distance.

Yesterday, for the first time, wreckage was being cleared from the Ahwaz well fire in the daytime, in order that Kinley could dynamite the blaze this morning.

He was delayed Sunday and Monday nights, because repairing and reinforcing of the carrier of a special new wrecking boom, which cracked as Kinley was wheeling it to the fire, had not been completed. On the end of this boom is a particularly heavy tool, shaped like a rake, with which Kinley clears a path through the debris to slide a dynamite charge into the well head.

The first dynamite charge will not be the one that extinguishes the fire; instead it will blow off some heavy steel that is suspended above the jet of oil and spraying a part of it in all directions, hiding the source of the oil, the well head, in flames. If the explosion removes this obstruction, the fire will be concentrated in one straight, tall shaft and Kinley will be able more quickly to clear the area of hot metal and extinguish the blaze.

Last night, several large pieces of wrecked drilling equipment were pulled flaming from the oil-soaked centre of the well.

Four times Kinley ordered the fire crew to leave their equipment and retreat a safe distance, as he hooked into heavy sections that might have bent the well head and sprayed blazing oil at them. Then he, his assistant, and his driver walked away and signalled a pair of tractors to tow his machine with its load out of the fire.

Rigging of the relief well was finished by Monday morning; the progress has been good and 130 metres (420 feet) drilled by this morning.

THE 20 TON DRAW WORKS WAS PULLED OUT OF THE FIRE—WELL RESPONDS WITH ANGRY ROAR TO KINLEY'S HOOK

May 13, 1958—The largest single piece of equipment in burning Ahwaz well No. 6, the 20-ton draw works, was pulled out of the fire last night by three tractors.

Next to be removed was the heavy foundation on which the draw works rested, followed by other pieces of burned equipment.

The only major pieces remaining now are the engines and pumps.

Stories are told in the villages of Khuzistan of a large dragon, living in the Bakhtiari mountains, who breathes fire when man angers him.

Such a thing is the runaway oil well, Ahwaz No. 6. Every night at midnight, when the firemen begin their painfully slow, waterless walk to the foot of the fire, following the fire tractor with its water hose on their shoulders, the well seems to waken, and its roars become explosive, as though it would like to frighten the challengers away.

Then when Kinley moves in, his long steel crane dipping and weaving like a sword too big for its warrior, the roaring seems to grow angry; when he dips the hook into the flames, they boom and crack.

It is all illusion, of course. The noise rises and falls continually, day and night. But it isn't noticed as much until men approach close enough to be hurt, should something go wrong, and then the fire seems to become a vengeful, living thing.

That's how it happened on Sunday night. Kinley's tractor waddled to the well head, which is now completely cleared of drill pipe.

He lowered the hook onto a heavy piece of the substructure of the well, and a surge of pressure sounded as though he had opened a hydrant of noise. He pulled—and two tons of burned steel tore loose from the pile of scrap, to be dragged out of the working area and dumped by Kinley, and again to be pulled further aside by waiting cleanup crews.

Before the night was through, he had pulled out two blowout preventer valves and some large pieces of the substructure, leaving the draw works, power plant and pumps, more substructure, and another blowout preventer valve still to be removed.

Always the noise was on hand, rising and falling in waves—and overriding other sounds so completely that the firefighting seems almost like a silent motion picture shown in a noisy room. A dozen roaring, squeaking tractors move at once, but not a sound can be heard from them. Under the firemen's shed at the base of the fire, a man's mouth opens wide in a shout and his lips form words, but not a shred of his voice is audible. Kinley rips several tons of steel out of its mounting, and all seems to be in silence.

Just over a small rocky ridge from No. 6, the relief well, Ahwaz 6R, drills ahead, just in case it should be impossible to tame the fire from the surface. Electric lights glow in its derrick, but are unnecessary; the jumping, yellow fire provides plenty of working light. They had reached a depth of 1185 feet by this morning.

Today, May 13th, is the 25th day since the well blew out.

WELL NO. 6 IS STILL BURNING

May 20, 1958—The flame was extinguished for 51 minutes on Monday.

The Ahwaz well is still burning in spite of two large charges of dynamite. A larger dynamite container is being prepared for tomorrow.

The first blast, fired last Monday, was primarily intended to clear the well head for capping. It not only did that job well but extinguished the fire. Then the blaze roared back after 51 minutes.

It was successful even so. The 450-pound charge left the bottom blowout preventer valve standing with its flange in good shape to receive the shutoff valve.

The second was fired this morning, 350 pounds of dynamite ten feet in the air beside the shaft of spurting oil and gas to prevent damage to the well head. It went off with a sharp report throwing up a large quantity of dust which formed into a hollow column around the pillar of flame but failed to cut the fire.

The relief well is now being prepared for the first stage of the slant drilling which will aim it at the bottom of No. 6. The hole is presently 2910 feet deep.

AHWAZ FIRE OUT BRIEFLY

May 25, 1958—Kinley blew fire out at 8.07 a.m. but fire flares again in ten minutes.

The Ahwaz oil well fire was blown out at 08.07 this morning but reignited only ten minutes later. An 800-pound dynamite bomb fired from the ground was used.

Myron Kinley telegraphed to the United States for his other assistant, Red Adair, to join him and Boots Hansen after the well refused for the second time to remain extinguished. Today's blast was the fourth, and it was the second to blowout the fire. It remained out for 51 minutes the first time.

Firing of today's shot had been postponed three days because of a bad south wind that stubbornly refused to change direction until this morning, when Kinley decided to blast in spite of it.

Meanwhile the relief well was drilled to 3030 feet during the day. Drilling was halted one time to allow a special instrument which measures the direction and angle of the well to be lowered to the bottom of the hole.

THE FIFTH BLAST OF WELL NO.6

May 27, 1958—Myron Kinley decided this morning to completely blast off the well head of Ahwaz No. 6, after a 750-pound bomb blew out the fire again for eight minutes, and removed the remaining blowout preventer valve.

Still bolted to the top of the well is a mud cross; a large steel fitting with a two inch port on the side, which is spraying gas and oil at right angles to the near-vertical main column. This side spray is comparatively tiny, compared to the mainstream, but Kinley thinks it is the reason that the flame will not remain extinguished. He believes that this small fire, which is now the only fire touching the ground, heats the surrounding earth enough to relight itself after the explosion, and reignites the main flow of oil.

The only way to remove that mud cross is to blow off the flange which holds it to the outer casing pipe of the well.

To do that the emergency construction crew is building, by the wellsite, a low, horseshoe shaped dynamite tank which will fit below the flange and drive the explosive force in and up from three sides, breaking off the flange. If they can complete it in time, the next bomb will be fired tomorrow morning.

The relief well is now down to 3102 feet and headed at a good angle.

May 28th—Construction workers welded through the night to prepare the shaped bomb, but were unable to complete it in time for a blast this morning. Kinley spent the time filling the crater left by the last bomb.